FINDING CYN...

Second Tenant of the Kersey Cottage

By

CAROL SUE RAVENEL

To Hank —
Following our dreams!
Traveling on,
Carol Sue
June 6, 2004

ISBN: 1-4107-9592-6 (e-book)
ISBN: 1-4107-9591-8 (Paperback)

This book is printed on acid free paper.

1stBooks - rev. 10/30/03

King

ACKNOWLEDGEMENT

Patti and *THE KERSEY COTTAGE* had much more to share than just one book, so after much research on the FBI and German U-Boats, I created *FINDING CYN*...to continue the story and introduce Neal.

My sincere gratitude goes to those who read *THE KERSEY COTTAGE* and encouraged me to write this next story. For your patience, love, and support, I thank you all, especially my husband, Jim. And I thank God for the talent that has afforded me the opportunity to create.

CHAPTER ONE

As the L-1011 taxied down the runway, Neal Park, seated in his usual row twelve window seat, watched as the black tarmac passed beneath the wings. He held tightly to the small, grey, canvas carry-on bag at his side, and closed his eyes. Trying hard to imagine the events of over fifty years ago that prompted this flight today to Europe and the hopeful delivery of the bag's contents, he drifted off into slumber.

****

LUBECK, GERMANY 1939.
"Guten Tag, Frauleins," the tall, blond youth said as he approached the bench where Cynthia and Margaret were sitting.

"No sprechen sie Deutsch," Cynthia replied as he stopped in front of them and took off his cap.

"Oh, excuse me, I speak English," he laughed. "Good afternoon, ladies. Are you enjoying your visit here at the Ostsee Resort?"

Cynthia Stiles and Margaret Overstreet, friends since childhood, had been touring the grounds of the Ostsee Resort where they were staying with their families. Residents of Sudbury, East Anglia, in England, the two families always spent holiday time together, and this year they chose to visit a resort north of Lubeck, near the northern coast of Germany. It was a cool May day as Cynthia and Margaret left parents and siblings to explore the thick beech and oak woods, and the clear, blue streams surrounding the old stone buildings. They decided to stop beside one of the streams for a short rest before continuing their walk.

The handsome boy looked to be about twenty, and Cynthia, who was seventeen and the most outspoken of the two girls, responded to his query with lively enthusiasm. "Yes, we're having a most delightful time and have even found some wildflowers to add to our collection.

1

Well, to my collection, Margaret is more interested in books," Cynthia said, as she gave Margaret a smirky smile. "Are you visiting here as well?"

Standing up straight as a rod, Gerhardt Prien smiled and said, "I have just delivered a truckload of fresh vegetables to the cook. You should have a fine dinner tonight."

Coyly smiling, Cynthia asked, "And just why should it be so fine?"

"Because they come from my family's farm just north of here near Ponitz am See at Schmiedekamp. We raise the best in Germany."

Margaret, sensing a bit of sparring going on, joined in. "You seem to be very sure they are the best. How will we know? Are they to be so different from the delicious meals we have been enjoying all week?"

"Ladies, in all the area surrounding Lubeck, our farms are known for certain chemicals in the earth that produce sweeter corn and carrots, firmer, greener cabbage, and the best onions for the sauerbraten." Gerhardt smacked his fingers with his lips to show the described essence.

His assertive and confident demeanor intrigued Cynthia and she stood up to get a closer look at this tall man of assurance. As she did, she realized how very tall he was…at least six feet three she would think. Even on tip toe, she would only come to his shoulder. In a school girl tone she blurted out, "Well, I don't care how fresh your vegetables are. I don't even like vegetables."

"Oh, but you surely eat some, miss. Your fair complexion belies the lack of vegetables in your diet," Gerhardt remarked, as he looked with favor at her light brown hair and her clear, blue eyes.

By now Cynthia was starting to blush and Margaret was getting impatient with this cat and mouse escapade of flirting. "Let's go, Cynthia. Our families are probably waiting for us to go out on the tour boat in the lake," Margaret said, as she took Cynthia's arm and started to guide her toward the lodge.

"Ladies, might I ask for your company at the dance tonight at the lodge?"

Margaret pulled harder on Cynthia's sleeve, but found resistance. "Stop, Margaret. I just might want to go to the dance." She pulled away from Margaret's grasp. "Sir, do they do the polka there?"

"Ya, fraulein...excuse me...ma'am," he stuttered as a broad smile crossed his face. "And excuse me for being so rude. I did not introduce myself. My name is Gerhardt Prien. And, may I respectfully ask yours?"

"Come on, Cynthia. Our parents may not like this one bit,"
Margaret said with determination in her voice.

"Margaret, if you are in such a hurry, just go on without me. I want to talk to Gerhardt and hear more about these miracle vegetables of his," she said as she laughed.

"I'm Cynthia Stiles, and Miss Impatient here is Margaret Overstreet. We really are best of friends, but she does try to move me about now and again."

"I'll see you back at the lodge, Cynthia. Do hope your mum and dad won't be too upset when they hear you're out here alone with a German."

1939 was stirring with visions of the winds of war, yet the United Kingdom and Germany were still very much aligned in many ways.

****

The evening air was moist from a late afternoon shower and the fragrance of Edelweiss drifted over the night like a mist of heavenly

3

vapor. Sounds of the orchestra playing lively dance music could be heard on the path as Cynthia and Margaret followed their families into the lodge. Gerhardt had arrived about ten minutes earlier and as he stood watching the partygoers, he thought…"Ich will mein Tanzbein schwingen." (I want to shake my dancing legs.) The truth be known, he really wanted to be closer to Cynthia…to hold her near and drink in her fair beauty. Already he had found a curious and warm attraction to Cynthia's mischievous smile and her infectious laugh. From Margaret's remarks today, he knew he would have a rising barrier to overcome with the changing political scene in Europe. As a German citizen, he had certain duties and responsibilities, but in his heart he had no desire to be a part of Hitler's Nazi confrontations between nations, confrontations now inevitable. He dreamed of finding happiness with a loving wife, many children, and a prosperous life as a farmer. Little did he know that his and the dreams of others like him would soon explode into a change of life yet to be seen by the entire world. A demon to reckon with was growing among them and they would be helpless to rebel or react.

Margaret chose a purple dress with little yellow daisies embroidered on the neckline and sleeves. Her blonde curls were tied at her neck with a silk ribbon and she had carefully colored her cheeks with a bit of rouge. Cynthia, not to be overshadowed, and desirous of impressing the tall German boy, wore a pale blue cotton blouse and a ruffled skirt. "This should twirl about as I do that polka dance!" Her wavy hair hung free and the blue of the dress shone in her reflective eyes.

"Margaret, don't let your negative attitude toward the Germans interfere with us having a good time tonight," Cynthia urged as they approached the heavily carved doors at the lodge entrance.

"Well, I just don't want us to get too friendly with someone who could cause us any problem in the future." Margaret hesitated, just then the huge door swung open.

4

As he held the door and gave a small bow, Gerhardt smiled and said, "Guten, er, Good evening, ladies. Come join the dancing."

Tables in the lodge's main dining room were covered with red check cloths, and each table had a bouquet of different colored flowers. Waitresses served large steins of a local beer, holding as many as eight or ten full steins, much like the waitresses at Oktoberfest in Munich. The ten piece band was playing a fast polka as the group entered the dining room and Gerhardt, gently taking Cynthia's arm, said, "Now I teach you to dance our polka."

Without regard for her parents or friends, she eagerly followed him onto the dance floor and tried to pick up the beat as he showed her how to take the steps. "One, two-two, one, two-two, give a little hop each time, Cynthia," he said, watching her feet and enjoying her happy smile as she tried to keep up with the fast pace of the music and the other dancers, many of whom were moving around the periphery of the highly polished oak floor. Within a few minutes she had begun to feel confident, and Gerhardt sensing this, turned her arm and twirled her around, her ruffled skirt raising just enough to reveal pretty legs and a lace petticoat.

"Oh, I am having the best time, Gerhardt," she exclaimed as he led her to the table where the Stiles and Overstreets were sitting. "I have always loved to dance, but this is such a different kind of dancing. It seems the dancers are celebrating or playing a game...everything is so fast and happy."

"So glad you are enjoying it," he responded as they approached the table. "Please pardon my manners for taking Cynthia away from your group before you were seated, but she seemed so anxious to do the polka that I could not resist the moment," he offered to her family and friends. Though normally reserved, Cynthia's father smiled and accepted Gerhardt's apology. Margaret sat still in her chair, staring at her stein, debating with herself as to whether she should be bold and ask Gerhardt to teach her as well.

Before Margaret could reach a decision, Gerhardt reached for her hand and asked, "May I have the next dance to teach you the polka, Margaret?" Startled, but pleased, she stood up and held his hand as he led her to a spot near the band. She was quick to feel the pace and soon they were twirling all around the dance floor. Cynthia noticed Margaret's evident dancing prowess and felt a twinge of jealousy as the laughing couple began another dance, the loud band striking up a lively tune. She was also aware that they were carrying on what seemed to be a serious conversation. Little did she know that it was all about Cynthia.

It appeared to Margaret that Gerhardt had a mental list prepared to quiz her on Cynthia…"What did she do in her spare time? Did she have a sweetheart? What were her plans after she finished high school? Had she made any mention of him? Did Margaret think he would find difficulty if he wanted to visit Cynthia, meaning her family's feelings toward Germans?"

"Gerhardt, I can't answer all these questions. We hardly know you, and though I am sure you are a good person, please be warned that Mr. Stiles is very protective of his daughter," Margaret stated, a stern tone in her voice. "I suggested to Cynthia that we take a holiday in Paris, just the two of us, and he was livid when we asked him. Yes, we are young, but we are not children. I guess he is right though, given the news we read everyday about war coming."

"Thank you, Margaret, perhaps I was out of order to even ask you, but I want to know her better before you leave to go back to England."

The polka was over, and catching her breath, Margaret told him she understood and would try to help him if she could. She let him know that they would only be at the Ostee Resort for a few more days. "Thank you, Gerhardt, for teaching me to polka. Now find me a dance partner so you can spend the rest of the evening with Cynthia." Laughing at this bold request, she made her way back to the table and the quizzical glare of Cynthia.

6

Cynthia asked the waitress for directions to the restroom and stood up to excuse herself. "Cynthia, I'll go with you, I want to tell you about a lady I saw on the dance floor," she said, making a reason to join her.

Not a word was spoken as they went down the long hallway. Entering the colorfully tiled room, Cynthia broke into tears. "How could you spend so much time with him. You actually looked like you were his date, not me."

"Oh, Cynthia, please don't think that. He spent our entire dancing time asking me all kinds of questions about you. He is terribly smitten, but I think a bit afraid of your father."

Dabbing a linen handkerchief to her eyes, Cynthia smiled. "Really, how curious. He doesn't seem to be the kind of man who would be intimidated, even by Father," a sad feeling of disappointment coming over her, she continued. "We have such a short time here, I do hope he won't get off on his wrong side."

They returned to the table just as the waiter was bringing their meal, a traditional German evening meal of smoked pork loin, sauerkraut, applesauce, and thick slices of dark bread. Also on the table was a huge bowl of salad with onion rings..."From the Prien gardens," Gerhardt told them. "And the sauerkraut was made with our best cabbage." Proudly he offered, "The applesauce is from our apple orchard's harvest last year. They were the sweetest we have had in many years." His obvious pleasure in sharing information about his family's bounty was of keen interest to Mr. Stiles.

"Gerhardt, tell me, how long has your family been farming in this area?" Mr. Stiles asked, looking through horn-rimmed glasses that seemed to be slipping off his nose.

"Mein vater, "he said, relapsing into German, "inherited the farm from his father, who had inherited it from his father," he laughed, adding, "Actually, it has been in my family for five generations. The Priens have always had a reputation for selling only the finest to our customers. Anything that does not meet our standards is turned under. There have been years of bad weather that made us wonder if this was gut, but we do it anyway."

"And do you aspire to be a farmer just like your father?" asked Mr. Stiles, as he studied the young man's nervous twiddling of his thumbs.

Realizing the stare, Gerhardt quickly placed his hands on his lap and answered. "Ya, I love the land. Our earth is good and we work hard. This makes me happy." Hoping he was saying the right thing, he glanced over at Cynthia who was sipping from a glass of Liebframilch wine. She gave him a slight smile and he continued. "Unfortunately my future plans could change. You know what I mean," he cautiously stated, waiting for a reaction from the man who obviously controlled his immediate plans. "I am a peaceful man," Gerhardt added, "I do not like the war clouds I see on the horizon, but I am first a citizen of Germany and must obey my country's laws."

Mr. Stiles, chewing slowly on a piece of the tender pork, looked Gerhardt directly in the eyes. "I admire your honesty, Gerhardt, but do not take this as encouragement."

"Ya, ya, I understand, sir," Gerhardt said with a tone of sadness in his voice. Accepting this as a challenge, he gave a few minutes thought to a new plan.

Everyone at the party seemed to be enjoying the meal and eagerly looked forward to the Black Forest Torte for dessert. Cynthia asked the waiter if she could have a small dish of custard, thinking the rich torte would not be wise for the diet she was constantly trying to keep. Margaret said she thought that was a good idea and asked for custard. In dining, as in most everything, they mimicked each other's preferences, and had years prior pledged to always stay close friends.

To Gerhardt's surprise, and that of Cynthia and Margaret as well, Mr. Stiles stood up and announced that the "elders will be retiring, leaving the young people to finish the dancing."

"Mr. Stiles," Gerhardt breathlessly asked as Cynthia's father led his wife and friends from the table, "I would like to ask you and your friends to come to our farm tomorrow for a country lunch and a tour of our farm. My parents would be most honored to have you and I think you would find it a pleasant afternoon."

"That is most generous of you, Gerhardt. We had planned to drive to Plon to tour the old Renaissance castle, but I do suppose we could postpone that until the next day. I should very much like to see how your family farms the land, as my firm has interests in unusual methods of production and your 'turning under the bad' is most unusual."

Gerhardt could hardly contain his exuberance. "Ya, gut..." catching himself, he thanked Mr. Stiles and said he would expect them about noon. "Perhaps meine mutter, er, mother, will let us have our meal picnic style under the oak trees by the lake. You will have a good time, I promise."

Cynthia and Margaret lowered their heads to hide their smiles and muffle giggles. The 'old people' left as Gerhardt looked around the room for a friendly face...a friend who would dance with Margaret, leaving him free to have all of Cynthia's time. Across the room he spotted Helmut Schragen, a friend of his from high school. Helmut lived near Ostee Resort and worked part time there as a gardener. Reluctantly the owners allowed him to attend the dances, partly because his family dined there frequently. Additionally, his eagerness to dance made for an extra man on occasions such as this.

"Mochte du tanzen mit eine Dame?" Gerhardt said, asking Helmut if he wanted to dance. He told Helmut about Margaret, and without hesitation, Helmut followed him to their table. After introductions and a new order for wine, Gerhardt asked Cynthia to dance, this time the music was soft and tender…the band was playing "Edelweiss."

He held her close, the pressure of her body against his bringing emotions to the surface that made him aware of his feelings for this beautiful girl. She seemed to be wrapped in a cocoon of euphoria as they turned and stepped gracefully to the strains of the band which now performed more as an orchestra than a polka band. With each movement his heart beat faster. Looking into her eyes, he pulled her closer yet to his face, touching her cheek with a sensuous slide of his fingertips. She lifted her chin, opened her mouth with the intent of saying what was in her heart, when all of a sudden there were loud voices at the dining room door.

CHAPTER TWO

"Wir gehen in die! We're joining up," the loud youths were yelling as they burst through the dining room door. Obviously beyond their allotment of beer, the five noisy boys, arms intertwined, came stomping onto the dance floor. The tallest and loudest of them all continued to let the resort guests know that they had just signed up to join Hitler's cause. He led the others as they headed toward Cynthia and Gerhardt.

"Guten Abend, Gerhardt," he said in a slurred manner. "Who's the pretty Fraulein you have in your arms?" He pushed Gerhardt aside and started to take Cynthia's arm, when he felt a large hand come down hard on his shoulder.

"I don't think you better do that. Get out of here, all of you. You're drunk and disturbing us all," Gerhardt ordered, as he gently took Cynthia to his side. The waiters appeared and began to push them out the door. Still shouting their news, they stumbled down the lodge steps and into the night.

"Gerhardt, I feel most uncomfortable and am quite glad Father did not witness this exhibition of poor manners," she said with perplexing emotion, her pleasure of being with Gerhardt overshadowed by this mention of the war situation. "You don't think you will have to join the German Army, will you?" she asked as despair crept into her thoughts.

"I have no plan to join up, but should there be need for me to serve I will probably follow my uncle, Guenther, who is an Unterseeboot commander." Gerhardt answered with truth, but trepidation of the inference to support the war effort.

Guenther Prien, in his early thirties was one of Admiral Karl Donitz's best U-boat commanders and daily gave Donitz reason to encourage Hitler to invest more in the sea effort than in his Panzer divisions or his prized Luftwaffe. By the end of World War II, he would be the third ranking ace in U-boats, having been credited with sinking 32 1/3 ships, mostly merchant ships at the beginning of the war in the Atlantic. He also scored a great war prize, when one night he sneaked his submarine into Britain's Scapa Flow naval facility and sunk their prized battleship, *Royal Oak*. Then they sneaked out, the entire maneuver undetected. The ship sunk and 783 lives were lost. During holidays at his nephew Gerhardt's family farm, he would thrill and amuse the teenager with stories of life at sea and fun in port.

Though Gerhardt loved to hear his Uncle Guenther's stories, his heart was in the land. But knowing that he would inevitably have to serve his country, he knew Uncle Guenther could help him get a good place in the military.

Gerhardt walked Cynthia back to her family's rooms, stopping at the door to their building. He gathered her into his arms as the songs of night birds filled the air. Looking up, she met his smile as he gently pressed his lips to hers. He was trembling with eagerness but knew this was neither the time nor place to go beyond, yet he could sense her responsive feelings as she clung to him. His breath was moist and warm as his hands stroked her face and neck.

"Gerhardt, I think it must be time for me to go in," she said with a sound of reluctance in her voice. "I have had a wonderful time and now I know how to do the polka." Beginning to recognize the increase in her feelings, she felt it wise to bring an end to what could be passions beyond fulfillment.

Wondering how he could tell her what he felt in his heart, when they had only know each other one day, Gerhardt took her hand to his lips, kissed it gently and laid it aside his cheek. "The future is too clouded for me to tell you now what I would hope for us. We will have to be patient and let this grow. Please allow me the privilege of writing to you, and I will do the same."

"Of course." But she could not stop herself from pondering where these moments of warmth and feeling would lead. "We'll be together tomorrow at your farm and I'll give you my address." She wanted to say something more, but could not compose the words that would capture her emotions. "Oh, I almost forgot Margaret. Do you think Helmut took her back to her room? I didn't see her after those boys burst into the dining room."

"I'm sure he did, Cynthia. As a matter of fact, if you look through those trees ahead you will see them standing at the door." A big smile on his face, he added, "Looks to me like they are getting a little better acquainted."

Margaret and Helmut were in an embrace, the evening light from the lodge door shining down on them. Cynthia returned Gerhardt's mischievous smile.

Only about twenty miles from the resort, Mr. Stiles drove his car cautiously as they left the sea coast road and headed for the farm. The ride to the Prien farm was mostly one lane country roads with beautiful views of farms, small lakes, and trees putting out their green summer leaves. Pastures of cows, sheep, and goats gave evidence of the good cheeses that were in great abundance in the nearby markets. Margaret rode with the Stiles in their car and Cynthia's younger brother rode with the Overstreets. This gave them the chance to discuss the events of last night, though they made a concerted effort to avoid bringing up the situation in the dining room after their families had left.

Passing a long fence of black boards, Mr. Stiles turned the car into a dirt driveway with hedges on either side. In the distance they could see a traditional Schwarzwald farm house with shingled sides and a slate roof. Outbuildings and the barn were made of native stone. Acres of spring planting was bringing forth tender plants that would supply the resort and other Prien customers. A big black dog barked and greeted them as they came to a halt in front of the house where Gerhardt appeared through the door. He was followed by a man and woman, each with a big smile, waving their hands at the visitors. "Willkommen, willkommen," they all shouted as Gerhardt opened doors for the Stiles family and Margaret. He introduced his parents, letting the visitors know that they spoke no English and he would translate for them. The Overstreet car pulled in and the entire group followed the Priens into the house where they were served wine and the offer to freshen up before a tour of the farm and the picnic lunch.

Gerhardt's father led the entourage as they walked for an hour through the barns and fields. Ending up beside a pond, he spread his arms wide and announced that the "Prien farm was the finest in all of Germany".

"Please excuse my father's boasting, but he loves to show off the farm. He does not travel, and only goes into the city for supplies, so you can see that this is his entire world," Gerhardt said, as he apologized. "I am grateful he has kept the legacy growing that I might someday be the master here."

In the distance Mrs. Prien was coming toward them, pushing a cart with the picnic lunch. Gerhardt ran to join her, and as they settled the cart into the side of a tree, both of them started to unpack bowls of salad, sausages made on the farm, fresh baked dark bread and chilled bottles of German wine.

"Now we have big German picnic," Gerhardt said as he spread blankets on the warm grassy area and offered his arm to help the ladies onto the blankets. His father opened the wine, filled glasses and raised his own to make a toast. "To our new friends from England. May we live to see new changes and peace in our countries. You honor us in sharing our bounty and we ask that you return often."

Mr. Stiles, never the one to be outdone, stood up, raised his glass and responded. "And you honor us, Herr Prien, with your generous hospitality. We accept your hope for peace and return your invitation."

Gerhardt and Cynthia, having finished their lunch, walked down one of the paths toward the house. His hand firmly holding hers, Gerhardt spoke and his voice trembled. "Cynthia, this morning I had a call from my uncle, Guenther. He said it is getting close when a decision must be made about my future serving Germany. This is not what I choose to do, but it is best for me to join now, rather than be forced to be a foot soldier for Hitler. Uncle Guenther has arranged for me to get a place in the next class of airmen in the Luftwaffe. He will be able to guide me and perhaps I will be an officer."

Listening to his voice, she ached with an inner pain. This news would definitely drive a wedge into the new friendship of their families. Suddenly, the realization of what he said struck her. "Gerhardt, this means we will for sure be on opposite sides now." Tears came to her eyes, "How can this be happening to us, when we just find out how happy we are together?"

As the tears rolled down her cheeks, he looked into her eyes and then abruptly stared upward. Turning his gaze back to her, his voice was stern. "Cynthia, I told you I must serve my country. I will try to do my best to make sure the coming developments will make our future safe."

"Cynthia," called Mrs. Stiles. "We must go now, please hurry along."

She reached into her pocket and gave Gerhardt the card with her address. Also in the envelope was a small picture of her taken in her mother's garden. "I promised to give you my address. Please let me know where I can write to you, Gerhardt," she said.

He stepped forward and wrapped his arms around her shoulders. Whispering, he tenderly said, "Dearest Cynthia, not only will I tell you where you can write to me, but I will make it my goal to see you again as soon as possible."

She pressed her face to his cheek, he turned, and their lips met with a soul-reaching message. "Gerhardt, I will pray for your safety every night. Look at the stars and as they twinkle, think of me smiling to you."

He kissed the tip of her nose, took her hand in his, and they walked toward the two cars, both of which had running motors and impatient drivers. "Auf Wiedersehen, Danke," the voices shouted.

****

Cynthia and Margaret spent the summer of 1939 each day anxiously waiting for the mail. Gerhardt had sent one letter in July, the first week he was in flight school, and said he would probably not be regular with correspondence because they were in secured quarters, being instructed for duty he could not disclose. Helmut did not write. Margaret could only suppose he had a special girlfriend when they met in Germany and did not want to tell her.

Just one week after Cynthia received Gerhardt's letter, he called her from Lavenham. "Cynthia," he said, speaking loudly, "I am in Lavenham on special short term duty."

"Oh, Gerhardt, it is so wonderful to hear your voice," she answered breathlessly. "Why didn't you let me know you would be in England?"

"I can't discuss this with you, but I do want to see you. I have a twenty-four hour pass tomorrow," he offered. "Could you meet me somewhere near here?"

Her heart pounding, Cynthia knew she wanted desperately to see him, but was fearful of her parent's reaction if they found out. "I'll take the chance," she said to herself, "This may be the last time I will see him for a long time."

"Gerhardt, I can meet you tomorrow about noon in Kersey. It is only fifteen kilometers from Lavenham on the Hadleigh Road." She waited

16

for his response and wondered if Margaret could be trusted to share in her secret.

"Gut," Gerhardt said with enthusiasm. "I can get a car for the day." Taking a deep breath, he asked, "Do you know of a guest house where we could stay?"

Now Cynthia was beginning to have second thoughts. "I'll have to stay with him," she thought, with mixed emotions of fear and excitement. Trying to act as if this was a normal occurrence, she said, "Yes, there is a nice guest house on Mill Lane. It is behind the Old Vicarage. Someone at the Bell Pub can give you directions."

Margaret was giddy with the drama of Cynthia's request for conspiracy.

"Margaret," Cynthia pleaded," I want to do this and I need your help. If Mum or Father question my whereabouts, tell them I met one of our school chums in Stowmarket for the day, but forget their name. Tell them it was a spur of the moment idea."

"Right, I can do that, and I promise on me dear departed grandmother's name not to tell a soul."

The next morning Cynthia packed a small bag and took a taxi to Kersey. She was glad the regular driver was on holiday and his friend from Bures was filling in.

The pink-cheeked lady who owned the guest house led her to room two. "Tis a bright room, dearie, with a nice view of the vicarage and St. Mary's Church," she said as she plumped the pillows and pulled back the lace curtains. "Will you and your husband be wantin' me to bring your breakfast up, or do ya' want to join the other guests in the dining room?"

"Oh, my, uh, husband doesn't eat much breakfast, so we'll probably just have tea, "Cynthia replied, almost choking as she said the word *husband.*

At ten after twelve there was a knock on the door. Almost losing her shoes as she leapt from the chair, Cynthia flew to the door, took a deep breath, and opened it. Gerhardt dropped his bag and swept her into the circle of his arms. "My dearest," he said as his mouth covered hers with unleashed hunger, "I have dreamed of this moment."

Cynthia was shocked at her own eager response and did not deny the spark of passion she felt as he gently moved her body inside the room, closing the door behind them. Waves of excitement were flowing through her and she gave no resistance to his ardor as his hands searched and gently traced the lines of her body.

****

"Your tea's here on the tray," said the lady of the house, as she tapped on the door and placed the tray on a small table nearby. The sun's rays came through the lace curtains, making designs on the bed linens like fancy spider webs. Cynthia could hear Gerhardt humming a German tune as he stepped out of the tub. A white towel wrapped around his waist, the ripples of his muscular chest glistened with water drops. Walking to the bed, he smiled at Cynthia and said, "Dearest, you are not only the most beautiful lady I have ever known, you are also a most responsive lover."

Blushing, Cynthia pulled the sheet up to her chin. She was finding it hard to believe what had happened to her in the past ten hours. "Gerhardt, I did not know love could be so overwhelming and thrilling."

Continuing on the path to ecstasy, they spent the rest of the day in the tiny sunlit room talking about their future. His dreams of life on the farm in Germany seemed to drift further away as she watched the clock tick closer to the time when he must return to the airbase at Lavenham.

She listened with dismay as he told her his next assignment was highly classified and she should not expect to hear from him for several weeks or more. Hesitating, he said, "And then, uh, depending on the approaching war, it could be a very long time." Cynthia dropped her eyes to hide her hurt as he continued. "Meine Lieb, ich liebe dich," his arms encompassed her, their lips met in gentle and tender harmony. Gerhardt released her, picked up his bag and left the room.

Cynthia shared with Margaret as much as she dared, hoping Margaret would feel some obligation to keep the secret. Margaret silently wished it had been she and Helmut.

****

September was approaching and time to enroll in university. Both of the girls decided they would rather take a job in Sudbury and do volunteer work to help the coming war effort. Prime Minister Neville Chamberlain did not make the future look "rosy," when on September 1, 1939 he announced to the British citizens that Germany had occupied Poland.

Noticing a help wanted sign in the window at Winch & Blatch, the only department store in Sudbury, they applied as sales clerks and were immediately hired. Their days were filled with helping customers, restocking inventory, and keeping up with the latest war news. Cynthia hoped that somehow Gerhardt would be able to write to her even though he was in training for that "special duty." Her hopes faded as no letters were posted to her from Germany. In the evening she and Margaret rolled bandages at the town hall and organized items sent to Britain from the Americans...sweaters, caps, and other knitted and much needed pieces of clothing for the coming winter.

Thursday, August 8, 1940 the Battle of Britain began as Hitler's Luftwaffe came across the English Channel from France with sixty dive bombers attacking a convoy. The Germans rained bombs and fire on most of the large cities, including London. This siege continued for eighty-four days. Other cities and villages in England, especially those with any industrial or military-related installations were also targets. The new Prime Minister Winston Churchill told his people, "We shall go on to the end…we shall defend our island, whatever the cost may be…"

"Think of all the money we saved by not going to university," Margaret said to Cynthia as they were eating lunch in the store's employee break room.

"We can save and take a trip back to the Ostee Resort after the war is over," Cynthia said.

"Well, you have a good reason to go back there, I don't," Margaret retorted, a bit of dismay in her voice as she opened the little glass milk bottle her mother had packed with the lunch. The disappointment of not hearing from Helmut was still fresh in her mind. But not so fresh that she did not accept a date from one of the American RAF Eagle pilots. This group was made up of American pilots who, though the United States was not yet in the war, felt it their duty to help defend democracy. Many of these young men, mostly in their early twenties, had very little flight time, but the intense desire to conquer Lord Haw-Haw, as the British called Hitler.

Danny Geiger, a tall, good looking redhead from Nashville, Tennessee, was one of those young pilots who "embellished" on his credentials to be accepted into the RAF. Only twenty, he learned to fly a Piper Cub at Berry Field in Nashville and was now flying from the airfield in Lavenham. The Piper Cub flew at one hundred twenty-five miles an hour, while the Spitfire he now flew for the RAF would go more than three hundred miles an hour. What these "boys" lacked in experience they made up for with drive, determination, and sheer daring.

During a visit to Sudbury, Danny was walking down King Street, looking in the windows and trying to find a cheap souvenir to send to his mother back home. With pay of only sixteen dollars a week, and rent to pay when on leave, his funds were limited. His British buddies usually stayed with family on leave, giving them a better standard of living...and home cooked meals as well. Danny missed his mother's fried chicken and gravy over biscuits, a real southern treat.

"Excuse me, ma'am. Do ya'll have any little 'ol souvenirs from this part of the country?" Danny asked in his Tennessee drawl.

Looking up from behind the counter, Margaret was not sure what this handsome man was asking. She had never heard this accent and curiously looked at him as she tried to respond. "Don't believe I understand what you're asking. Did you want to buy a souvenir?"

"Oh, yes ma'am. That's what I want. Thought I better send somethin' back to my momma in the States, but this here RAF don't pay us too well so I can't spend much," he said, a bashful smile crossing his face. "S'pose ya'll got some kinda little knick knack?"

By now she realized he was a boy from the South and the way he spoke was just like what she was reading in the newest American novel, *Gone With The Wind.* "We do, yes, we do have some nice little china tea pots. You can buy one for about a pound." She showed him several and he chose one with a blue and white English scene painted on the side.

"Thank you, ma'am. I think my momma will like that one right well," Danny said as he reached into his pocket for the money. "She likes to have a cup of tea when she's rockin' on the front porch."

Margaret wrapped the tea pot, gave him change from his five pound note, and handed him the package.

The young airman grinned, took a step backward, and after a deep breath, calmly asked, "Ma'am, this shore ain't proper, but we have a dance tomorrow night at the base and I'd be right happy if you could be my date."

Without hesitation, Margaret smiled coolly and answered. "That sounds like most fun, but I don't even know your name."

"Oh,'scuse me, ma'am. I'm Danny Geiger from Nashville, Tennessee. In the United States that is, uh, the Southern part."

"Very nice to meet you, Mr. Geiger," she responded, thinking to herself that this man seemed so innocent and polite that surely she would be safe to go with him to the dance. "Yes, I'd like to be your date tomorrow night. I finish work at six. Would you pick me up here, or should I meet you at the base?" She knew most of these men had no personal transportation and Lavenham was fifteen kilometers from Sudbury.

He had no way to pick her up, this trip to town had been on an RAF bus. She told him that was fine and she would meet him there at eight o'clock.

The base dance hall, usually the indoor basketball court, was decorated in colored paper streamers and a ten-piece band was playing the dance music so popular with Americans. Jitterbugging was the choice of dance and Margaret found she did it well. Danny kept her glass filled with American Coca Cola and she noticed that he did not add something to his like the other airman did. Awkward as Danny seemed, he was polite to Margaret and made sure she had a good time.

The next few weeks the RAF Eagle Squadrons saw continual duty, now being joined by new American aircraft...P-40 Tomahawks, P-37 Mohawks, and medium bombers, the Hudsons. President Roosevelt had said, "We will give England all help-short of war." The help continued, with America eventually at war. England in the meantime pulled out of a joint project with Germany that was being developed in secret quarters in Lavenham. Gerhardt Prien was among the Germans sent back to Germany where they would proceed with the project.

Just as Britain was championing their cause, American Eagle Danny Geiger, from Nashville, Tennessee, gave his life for his friends. His Spitfire caught German flak as he was heading back across the English Channel and crashed into a field outside New Romney, south of Dover. Margaret got the news from his Wing Commander one morning as she and Cynthia were preparing to put Halloween decorations in the window fronts.

Crisp, cool mornings turned into sunny afternoons and evening fires lessened the damp English chill. Life went on with hope for peace, but daily reminders of the present war.

CHAPTER THREE

"Don't you think it would be a smart idea if we leased a flat and lived on our own?" Margaret asked Cynthia.

Surprised, Cynthia looked at her and answered, "I guess we could do that. My mum wants to rent rooms to workers from the Lavenham air field anyway and I would probably have to give up my room."

Lavenham was approximately ten miles from Sudbury and the workers were assured bus transportation to Sudbury and other villages if they could not find housing in Lavenham. Most of the workers were coming from London and would only want sleeping rooms since they would go back to the city by train on the weekends. A large contingent of Americans, the Mighty Eighth Air Force Wing based in Lavenham, had also stationed many of their men in the area now that America was in the war, and housing was becoming scarce.

"We might have a problem finding a place, with all those Yanks coming over. But maybe Charles Abbott can find us a wee place," Cynthia said, the idea now sounding better to her. Charles Abbott was an estate agent in Sudbury and a friend of her father's.

"Won't it be fun! We can sleep until noon, go out when we want…" Margaret gushed with excitement.

"Margaret, slow down. We still have to work to pay for a flat. And who do you suppose will clean it and do our cooking?" she asked with a sarcastic tone in her voice.

Both girls were living in a mechanical and almost moribund state. Though they did not talk about Gerhardt, Helmut, or Danny, each knew the other harbored sadness and frustration with their losses. "Perhaps living on our own will give us a new outlook on life. I am so tired of bombs and death," Cynthia blurted out as she thumbed through the telephone book for Charles Abbott's number.

"Charles Abbott here," said the strong, male voice on the other end of the line.

"Mr. Abbott, this is Cynthia Stiles. I do believe you know my mum and dad."

"Right, right. You must be that cute little girl who used to skip past my father's office on your way to the pastry shop," he answered, with a laugh in his voice. "How old are you now, Cynthia?"

Pausing to remember those childhood days when her mother gave her twenty pence to buy a bag of fresh scones for tea, she would skip along the broken sidewalk, dragging a stick from the hedgerows, usually hawthorn or wild crabapple. Cynthia said, "I'm almost nineteen."

"My, my, but it doesn't seem just yesterday you were a wee little bairn. Well, what can I be a doin' for you."

Charles Abbott found them a small flat on Quay Lane. It was two rooms with a small bath and was on the fourth floor of a building not too far from Winch and Blatch, the train station, and the nature trails that led to the River Stour. One room had twin beds and the other they used as a parlor. Their families had given odd pieces of furnishings, and by buying a few marked down items at their store, they managed to make it a cheerful place to rest and contemplate the future. Weather permitting, they frequently packed a lunch and a good book and walked to the river. The quietness, interrupted only by birdsong, was becoming part of their personalities.

KEIL, GERMANY 1940
"Congratulations, Fahnrich zue See Prien" offered the commander of the newest command in the German Naval Air Force, as he pinned silver wings on Gerhardt's uniform.

Standing proudly in a line of fifty new midshipmen aboard a U-boat in Kiel Harbor, Gerhardt's heart was racing as he thought of this culmination of almost a year's training for one of Germany's most secret missions. Hitler was beginning to realize that his naval forces could be as good, if not stronger, than the Panzer units and the Luftwaffe in his charge to win the war. Gerhardt's entry into the Luftwaffe, and then the Naval forces school, was a prerequisite for his appointment to a special joint project of the Navy and the Luftwaffe, and only because his Uncle Guenther Prien was so highly favored as a war hero did he feel he was appointed to this extraordinary duty. Starting with U-boat school in Kiel, Gerhardt received tutelage from Uncle Guenther. Guenther drilled him on all the details of U-boat engineering, capacity, ranges, ordnance, and crews.

"A U-boat can go 7.3 knots max when submerged, but will run out of power at 64 miles. Batteries need to be recharged while surfaced for 7 hours." Gerhardt pondered this, evaluating it with risk. *"While on the surface a U-boat can go 18 1/4 knots max, but for economy will usually run at 12 knots. On the surface at this speed, the boat can go 8,700 miles before refueling."* Every evening he studied his notes and tried not to think of the farm and his family back home. His thoughts did, however, drift to Cynthia with a high degree of regularity. He questioned why no mail could go out from this particular base, but realized it was not his place to question. "If only I can do well, then maybe this horrible war will end soon and we can be together," he silently said to Cynthia. And, he wondered how the outcome would affect his relationship with her family.

Gerhardt had endured tight quarters, moldy food, stale air and other inconveniences that accompany life aboard a U-boat. After evening study or watch duty, he would write a letter to Cynthia, storing it in a small, lead-lined, steel box under his bunk. He did not put the letters in envelopes, knowing full well that he could not mail them, but there was therapeutic value in writing. It was his plan to mail them all to her once he received official permission. Upon finishing a letter, he would place it on top of the others, close the box and lock it. The key he kept on a chain around his neck.

The war in the Atlantic was raging on and Germany was in the lead. Guenther Prien, Germany's third ranking U-boat ace, highly honored for his sinking of the British battleship, Royal Oak, was killed with his crew on March 18, 1941. Credited to him was the sinking of 211,393 tons of ship. Gerhardt took this news with deep emotion. His mentoring and encouragement were the main reason Gerhardt studied so hard. He wanted to please his uncle. It was Guenther who suggested Gerhardt for the secret Kleiner Spion project.

****

December 7, 1941 United States Naval forces were bombed by the Japanese at Pearl Harbor. With the Americans in the war Hitler had increased determination to win, and on December 11, 1941 Germany declared war on the United States.

In the last few years before German aggression became visible, they were developing an experimental reconnaissance plane with Great Britain. Trying several methods of launch from rockets to catapult, the British did not foresee success and pulled out of the project after Germany invaded Poland. Hitler believed his favored Luftwaffe could succeed in anything and proceeded with the project which he based in Neustadt, north of Lubeck. Near open water and numerous small naval installations, the development of this plane and the training of its crew would be safe and secure. Airfields at Wismar and Grube offered flight facilities and the U-boat availability in Kiel, thirty miles away, provided the "mother ship" arrangement.

At the beginning of 1942 Admiral Karl Donitz began *Operation Drumbeat,* his U-boats sinking 500 American ships, mostly tankers. Hitler knew America would retaliate with increased patrolling, and the time was most imminent to complete the project in which Gerhardt was assigned. The means to discover information about this patrolling would be the result of the "Kleiner Spion" (little spy), a very small reconnaissance plane that Gerhardt would fly over the Southeast coast of the United States. By now a seasoned Luftwaffe

28

pilot with U-boat training as well, he was the perfect candidate to carry this experiment through. His height of six foot three was at first considered a risk, but the plane's engineers created a bubble on the top which allowed for more headroom. This increase also added more visibility to the pilot.

Kleiner Spion was being built to fit into an expanded conning tower on U-352. Special doors on the tower would allow for departure and re-entry. The U-boat would travel to the coast of North Carolina, about five miles off Ocracoke, and within sight of the Cape Hatteras lighthouse. Surfacing in early morning mist, her conning tower doors would open, Kleiner Spion attached to the catapult, and the catapult would throw the plane into the air. Once airborne, the little plane, painted gray with no visible markings, would fly low over the beaches, heading inland where suspected military installations might be. Equipped with a high-powered German camera, Gerhardt would be expected to take as many photos as possible, while at the same time watching for detection. Returning to the U-boat, which by now would arrive near Cape Lookout, some thirty miles south, Gerhardt is to inflate the plane's pontoons, land on the water, catch a hook from the boat, and ease into the conning tower...the doors shutting snugly behind him. U-352 submerges and heads back across the Atlantic to Kiel. This was the plan.

Practice and drilling on this project consumed long days and left little time for Gerhardt and the crew of U-352 to think of nothing but their day of departure. Hoping for a leave to visit family before their departure date, he was disappointed to learn that all leaves were being canceled during *Operation Drumbeat.* The date to leave was set for May 7.

Kapitanleutant Hellmut Rathke, his back straight and his chin tucked under, saluted the officers and crews on the dock as U-352 slowly pulled away from Neustadt the morning of May 7, 1942 with an intended course set for Southeastern United States. His 46 crewman, all hand-picked with high security clearances, anxiously anticipated this moment...the time when they would embark on one of Admiral

Donitz's most daring projects to date in the Atlantic war. Their goal was to photograph, undetected, as many American installations as possible in preparation for an invasion of the coast.

Gerhardt knew his part in this project was extremely sensitive and vital to its success. Though he did not doubt his expertise as an airman and a Naval officer, his entire purpose, unlike others serving Germany, had never been to participate in war. Saluting to Hitler always gave him a feeling of evil that he could not accept. But to the motherland Germany he would be true and he would carry out his duties as he had been trained.

Steaming across the Atlantic on the surface, which was customary unless in the area of the enemy, U-352 made good speed and by the morning of May 9, 1942 they could see the coast of Virginia in the distance. Wishing that he could send a few torpedoes to the enemy's capitol in Washington, instead of heading further south, Rathke ordered his ship to head south/southwest toward the North Carolina coast, while Gerhardt was wishing he were in Lubeck with Cynthia at his side and was writing this to her. He placed it in the box, picked up his flight helmet, and headed to the conning tower.

It was a little after four in the afternoon, off Cape Lookout, North Carolina, when U-352 picked up sound contact from the 165-foot Coast Guard cutter *Icarus*, on a course from New York to Key West. Rathke ordered a torpedo fired. Something went wrong and an explosion went off two hundred yards off the cutter's bow, leaving the telltale sign of a swirl on the water. The *Icarus* dropped five depth charges over the site, causing tremendous damage and the death of Rathke's first officer. U-352 came barely to the surface as the machine guns of the *Icarus* swept her decks.

As sirens wailed, Rathke realized they were in grave danger and ordered the ship abandoned, leaving it last after his men. U-352 sunk, taking thirteen dead men down with her. Of the thirty-three survivors, several were badly wounded. They were taken aboard the cutter and on to Charleston, South Carolina for interrogation. Before reaching their destination one more crewman died.

One hundred-twenty feet down in the ocean, thirteen men, most caught at their battle stations, gave their lives for Germany. Kleiner Spion was still in the conning tower, her pilot strapped in and ready for catapult.

CHAPTER FOUR

SUDBURY 1942

Life in Sudbury during World War II was disrupted on a daily basis by the departure of young men to military service and the arrival of telegrams to families stating the death or injury of loved ones in service. Everyone was loyal to the King, doing their part either in the military or in volunteer work. Cynthia and Margaret joined the *Queens Messengers*, volunteers who staffed mobile canteens that went to stricken cities and offered food to workers and families who had been bombed out by the Luftwaffe. One British city, Bexleyheath, was hit by over 8,000 bombs between September 1940 and May 1941. The need to help the country was overwhelming. Equipped with stoves, ovens, and means to store and cook, the canteens provided much welcomed soups, stews, bread, and tea to the hungry British citizens. Winch and Blatch management gave Cynthia and Margaret leaves of absence to participate in this service to Britain and the two girls quickly forgot their loneliness as they worked long hours, many times sleeping the night on the canteen floor.

While on temporary duty in Plymouth, Cynthia received a letter from her mother. Included in the letter was a small note from Gerhardt's father. Written in true German formality, he "wished to inform her that Gerhardt had died at the hands of the American enemy while serving Germany and the Nazi cause." Cynthia found the last two words hard to believe and chose to remember Gerhardt's own statement of dislike for Hitler's regime. Mr. Prien invited Cynthia to visit the farm in Lubeck "when Germany has won the war."

"Doesn't that man realize that now we are the enemy, too?" she shouted as she threw down the letter and looked out the canteen door at the rain coming down on the cobbled street.

Startled at her outburst, Margaret asked, "What are you talking about?" She picked up the letter and read the sad news. "Oh, Cynthia, I am so sorry." They were both crying.

"I don't even know what he was doing in the Navy, or where he was when he died. Actually, I know very little about Gerhardt Prien except that he took my heart and I shall miss him ever so much." She went down the two steel steps of the canteen, out onto the wet street where they had been parked for two days, and began to walk. Two blocks away she entered the rubble-cluttered doorway of St. Michael's Anglican Church. Shattered stained-glass windows, burned floors and pews, a damaged organ and choir, all offered little evidence that this was still a church, but someone before her had lit candles on the altar, which miraculously had been spared. Cynthia swept away ashes and wood splinters from a pew still intact and sat down. Looking at the altar, a cross carved on the front, she bowed her head and prayed.

The tears she had tried to hold back came forth and a voice she recognized as her own cried out in agony…"Why, God, why?"

Margaret had quietly followed her to the church. Putting her hand on Cynthia's shoulder, she said, "Now, dear, I know you're hurt, but this is war and we can't do anything about it. Come on back to the canteen. Let's have a cuppa and think about getting home next week."

****

Their orders were to head back to London, drop off the canteen, and go home for a two-week leave. They had been on the road for three months and the long days and tight quarters were beginning to make them both cross.

"It will sure feel good to have a nice long tub bath full of rose oil and then a good night's sleep in me own bed," Margaret chirped as she tried to say something to cheer up Cynthia. "Don't you agree?"

"I suppose so," she responded glumly, no expression in her voice. "I'd just like to go to sleep and wake up when all this is over."

****

June 1945. Victory in Europe and nations begin to heal.

Cynthia and Margaret settled into a routine suited better to widows and the elderly, choosing to stay to themselves. They continued to work at Winch and Blatch, they argued over politics, they dutifully visited their families on Sunday afternoons, and they walked the woods of Suffolk County, collecting the wildflowers that Cynthia so dearly loved. Her albumed and framed collection took up much of their apartment, while Margaret chose to read, mostly romance novels. Anya Seton was her favorite and she kept a close watch on the calendar for publication of Seton's latest book.

****

One day in October 1950, in a moment of total delusion, Cynthia told Margaret she had bought tickets for them to fly to Hamburg and drive a car to Lubeck.

"I want to go to the Prien farm and find answers to all my questions about Gerhardt. Surely by now his family will not harbor bad feelings about us," she said speaking at a rapid pace. "After all, it was Hitler's Luftwaffe that ruined our cities, even if we did win the war."

Margaret cast a quizzical look at her longtime friend. "Are you really sure you want to do this? You're daft, you are. Just when you're starting to forget about the past you want to bring it back again."

"Forget about it?" Cynthia shouted. "I have never forgotten about it or my feelings for Gerhardt. I want to know why he never wrote to me. If he had had another girl, why would his father have written to me?"

****

HAMBURG, GERMANY 1950

As they left the Hamburg airport, they noticed the damage from years of war and neglect, so much like Britain. "Guess we all suffered," Cynthia said as she steered the little German car on to the highway leading to Lubeck.

They followed the map that Cynthia had so carefully saved since that first visit in 1939. Some of the roads were in dire need of repaving and when they turned to the one leading to the farm they noticed it had no visible signs of recent use. "This is strange," Margaret remarked as they bumped along and passed the overgrown vines on the black fence.

"Oh," gasped Cynthia as she stared ahead. The house had no roof, the barn was half gone and the lake was dry. There were no signs of human or animal life to be seen.

Thy got out of the car and walked to the house. The porch floor was burned out, as was the inside of the house. The fireplace bricks had crumbled into a heap. Insects, birds and other creatures had taken residence and made this their home. Outside, the trees that had shaded the house were gone, giving evidence to the fact the farm had indeed been subject to intense damage.

They drove back into the town center which had some semblance of rebuilding, and stopped at a small butcher shop. Walking into the smell of fresh meat and clean-cut sawdust, they approached the man behind the counter.

"Guten Tag. Sprechen Sie Englisch?" Cynthia asked, watching the man wipe blood onto his apron.

"Ya, I speak a little of the English. What do you want?" he said in a gruff, guttural tone.

"We are looking for German friends of ours, the Prien family. We went to the farm, but it is deserted." Searching his face for some

36

recognition, she said, "Do you know them and where we might find them?"

"Nein. During the war, when YOUR bombers came over..." here he hesitated, watching for their reaction, "...the Prien family took a direct hit from one of the bombs. I was told some of them died and the rest moved away. I don't know where they went. So many people scattered and are lost." He picked up a blood-smeared cleaver. "I hate war," he shouted, as he slammed the cleaver into the chopping block.

Cynthia and Margaret screamed, ran out of the shop and got into the car. They drove back to the airport, both trembling with fright.

Days became months, months became years, and their lives were without dimension or change. The memories of Gerhardt, Helmut, and Danny, always there, but never discussed by the two little ladies at Winch & Blatch.

CHAPTER FIVE

JEKYLL ISLAND, GEORGIA 1990

Neal Park and his wife, Louise, spent several weeks each year vacationing on Jekyll Island, in the south Georgia Golden Isles. Though his career as an FBI agent gave him little time for rest, they did manage to escape to Georgia frequently from their home in Greenville, South Carolina. The island, formerly the second home retreat for New York millionaires... Rockefellers, Vanderbilts, Pulitzers, and the J.P. Morgans, was purchased by the State of Georgia in 1947 for $675,000. The millionaires had met with loss during the Depression. The homes sat vacant and in need of repair for many years. Jekyll's natural state had been preserved and the small part of commercialism necessary for daily life, did little to detract from the beauty of the live oak trees, Spanish moss, sea oats, and white, sandy beaches. Cottages built along the palm lined streets leading to the beach, were owned by individuals on forty-nine year leases, the land being owned by the state. A large portion of the houses were duplexes where owners lived in one side and rented the other to tourists.

It was in one of those duplexes on Dexter Lane that the Parks chose to stay on their visits to the island. Two bedrooms and a sleeper sofa offered room for their son, Jordan, and his wife, Lucretia, to visit from Charleston. Jordan, a gastroenterologist at Roper Hospital, was married to Lucretia Middleton, daughter of a leading Charleston politician and patriarch of one of the oldest Charleston families. Their daughters, Annabelle and Caroline, were being raised in the old Southern tradition and would be expected to follow their mother's lead in being presented at the St. Cecilia Ball. That being several years away, they concentrated on visits to Jekyll Island and the dotage of the grandparents.

****

NEW YORK CITY 1962
Louise Prentice grew up in the society neighborhood of Charlotte, Myers Park. Her parents were disappointed that her education at Sweet Briar College and her debut at the Myers Park Country Club did not manage to persuade her to choose a husband from their circle of friends. Instead, while on holiday in New York City with her Sweet Briar roommate, Tricia Simpson, she met Neal Park.

Louise and Tricia had lunch at the Russian Tea Room, finished tasting their first bowl of borscht, and, feeling quite smug getting through this new experience, decided to shop at Bergdorf Goodman for cashmere sweaters. They paid the waiter, leaving a generous tip, and walked toward the door. Stepping onto the 57th Street sidewalk, Louise started to cross the street, when a taxi pulled quickly into the curb. She lurched back, felt someone grab her arm and found herself safely back on the sidewalk.

"Whew, that was a close one, ma'am," said the tall, dark haired man with deep set brown eyes and a warm smile. Looking into clear, green eyes, Neal Park studied the long, blond hair and shapely figure of the prettiest girl he had ever seen.

"Thank you," she gasped as she clung to his arm. Realizing one of her new alligator pumps was laying in the dirt and grime of a wet New York street, she reached down to retrieve it.

"Here, let me get that for you." Handing her the damp shoe, he paused and said, "By the way, I'm Neal Park from Savannah and if you won't think me too forward, I'd be most obliged if you ladies would let me buy you a glass of wine to calm your nerves. Know you must be a bit shook up." Grinning, he added, "Taxi drivers in this city must think pedestrians are invisible. They sure can scare the daylights out of you."

Louise glanced at Tricia, who was smiling approval, and answered, "Savannah, why I declare. We're from Charlotte. We're practically neighbors," she drawled in her best southern accent, as she fluttered her long black lashes.

Feeling more comfortable that they were not talking to a *real* stranger, she said, "That would be nice. Guess we can spare a bit of our afternoon to show our gratitude. Why, Tricia, I could have been killed if this nice gentleman from Savannah hadn't come our way."

Tricia had a difficult time keeping her composure and not laughing out loud. "'Spose you're right, Louise. I could use a glass of wine."

They walked west on 56th Street and as they turned south on Seventh Avenue, Louise apologized and introduced Tricia and herself to Neal. He held the door for them as they went into the Park Hotel. "Oh, it's not my hotel, ya'll," he laughed, "but they do have a nice wine bar and it's quiet."

Louise and Tricia never did make it to Bergdorf Goodman, as the young man from Savannah mesmerized them with his charm and his tales of ambition to be an FBI agent.

The afternoon slipped into darkness, two bottles of Chardonnay were emptied, and as the girls returned from the ladies room, Neal asked, "Would you like to join me for dinner and a show?" Before they had a chance to answer, he added, "I really hate to eat alone and I've been wanting to see the new musical, *Flower Drum Song*. A buddy of mine said it is really good, and I know a great place for Chinese food. We can set the mood for the show." He laughed as he drew a breath from speaking so fast.

Looking at each other, they shrugged their shoulders and in unison said, "Yes!"

They had the evening special at Madame Chang's in Times Square, Sea Scallops with Pea Pods and Mushrooms in a Sake sauce. *Flower Drum Song* was fast and lively with brightly colored Oriental costumes. The music and story line lived up to Neal's friend's recommendation and all three declared it a wonderful show.

Neal walked them back to their hotel, the Sheraton, and asked Louise if he could call her at Sweet Briar or at her home.

"I would like that," she replied, a sparkle in the green eyes. "Maybe you can come down to Charlotte this summer and we'll show you our version of Southern hospitality. Not that yours from Savannah wasn't nice," she laughed. "How long do you have to stay in this busy city?"

"Not quite sure. When I finished my sixteen weeks at the Training academy in Quantico, Virginia, one of my instructors asked me if I'd be interested in helping him with a special project here at the Federal Plaza," he replied. "He thought it might take three or four weeks, but we've been here six." Smiling brightly, he added, "When I'm finished here I'm set to begin some classes at the Institute of Pathology, Psychology, and Law at the University of Virginia."

"My, but you sure do move around a lot," Louise said, intent on his enthusiasm.

"Yes ma'am. In the FBI I'll be traveling right much."

"How sad, but exciting," she said.

"Oh, suits me fine. My daddy was a cotton broker in Savannah and he was gone from home a lot. We got used to it and my mother kinda liked having me and the house to herself. She said he always wanted to rearrange things when he came home and she liked things just as they were." Neal silently recalled his mother's attempts to cover her loneliness with involvement in the Ladies League. He had lots of friends from school and their fathers were usually around if he had a problem. "When I get married, I'm going to make sure my family goes with me if at all possible. Bein' in the FBI might make it hard at times, but some of the positions keep you pretty much in one place for a good while."

Neal reached for Louise's hand, gave it a gentle squeeze, and as he looked into her eyes, said, "Thank you for spending the evening with me. Other than dinner and a few beers with some of the guys, this is the first time I've had fun in New York. I'll call you when I find out if I can make it to Charlotte this summer."

"Well, you're welcome, Neal. I had a really nice time and I think Tricia did, too. Didn't you Tricia?" she asked as she looked around for Tricia, who was trying very hard to be obscure during this parting of friends.

"Oh, yes. I just loved the show and can hardly wait to tell my mother we saw Frank Sinatra at the restaurant." Tricia gave Neal a kiss on the cheek, which took him by surprise, and with a look of consternation on her face, asked, "Isn't he rumored to be mixed up with some shady characters?"

Neal quickly collected his thoughts and haltingly answered. "I, uh, heard something to that effect in training, but it's just a rumor." His recent training had instilled silence on matters like this and he was not about to address the question further.

Turning to go into the hotel lobby, Louise smiled and raised her hand to wave. "Bye, Neal. Have fun at the University of Virginia. I hear they have pretty wild parties there," she laughed.

"Not for me," he replied. "I have a heavy schedule and a short amount of time for study. No parties for me."

Walking back to his hotel, his thoughts were jagged and shot with a feeling of sudden emptiness. The recollection of the evening would have to be its own fulfillment, at least for a few months and the hope of a trip to Charlotte.

****

Neal's qualifications requiring him to be an FBI agent were secure. He was a law school graduate and had minored in accounting. He spoke fluent Spanish and had a meager understanding of German. The routine background checks revealed a good credit rating and excellent medical history. He had never been a user of illegal drugs, had no traffic violations or arrests, and he passed the polygraph test. Also to his credit, he had a work history of five years, during and after school terms. All this being in place, Neal Park left his family in Savannah, in late 1960 and took the train north to Quantico, Virginia.

****

QUANTICO, VIRGINIA 1960
Sixteen weeks at the FBI Training Academy was an intense discipline in law, firearms, investigative techniques, physical training, and self-defense, and Neal excelled in each area. When the time arrived to present credentials and favored division appointments, Neal surprised his instructors by requesting to be assigned to Investigative and Administrative Operations. Several of his teachers felt he would be an excellent special agent in foreign counterintelligence, but he knew that meant spending a significant amount of time on foreign soil. He preferred the category of applicant matters and investigations for government entities…House and Senate committees, the White House, U.S. Courts, and the Department of Justice.

At graduation Neal's sealed brown envelope of orders contained assignment to the FBI Information Technology Center in Butte, Montana, after his classes at the University of Virginia. He had hoped to be sent to the center in Savannah, but was grateful for his choice of division.

Set to depart for Virginia on May 10th, his plans were abruptly changed when Harry Watts, his instructor in interrogation, called and asked him to assist with a project investigating a civil rights movement involving New York blacks who were moving to the South to organize demonstrations. "I think you being from Savannah might be of help in interpreting some of their methods and reasoning. We

44

can cancel your summer program at UVA and you can start in the fall," Harry said, prevailing upon Neal's flexibility and loyalty.

"I'm flattered you want me to help you, sir, but are you sure I can make the class change?" He had mixed feelings of disappointment and challenge, but knew he had to agree to go. "How long will we be there?" he asked.

Recognizing the sounds of smoke blowing into the receiver, Neal heard Harry take another drag on his cigarette. "I've been given two to six weeks to gather the information we need and to complete the report. Neal, you'll be through with some time to spare before the fall classes start. Now get packin' and I'll pick you up about ten tomorrow morning. It should only take us four or five hours to drive up."

"Yes, sir," Neal said reluctantly. He had only been to New York once when he was fourteen and his parents had treated him to a visit to the Big Apple for his birthday. His most vivid memories were of the Statue of Liberty and all the traffic. "Guess I can do this," he thought as he opened the closet door and took out his suitcase.

Promptly at ten the next morning Harry knocked on his door. "Ready, guy?" Puffing on his cigarette, he reached for Neal's bag and started down the hall.

Neal followed with his briefcase and freshly pressed shirts from the hotel laundry. "Thanks for getting my bag. Where're you parked?"

The elevator doors opened.
"The doorman let me park it in front. Said if I wasn't back in ten minutes it was being towed," Harry said with a laugh.
"Guess if I showed him my I.D. he might be a bit more lenient, but the boss doesn't want us doing that unless it's official business and today really isn't."

They drove up US1 through northern Virginia, skirting Washington, and headed toward Baltimore. Harry had mentioned an old friend who lived in Middle River, just outside Baltimore, and thought they might stop there for lunch, but a fierce thunderstorm hit just as they were leaving downtown Baltimore. The wipers barely left enough visibility to see the road. Pulling under an overpass, Harry cut the engine and lit a cigarette. "Guess we'd better ride out the worst under here," he said as he took a long drag and blew the smoke out the window which he had rolled down an inch. "Let me tell you a little about this project."

Neal had been wondering when he was going to be brought into his confidence and given details of where and why. As a rookie agent, he hesitated to ask too many questions.

"Seems there's been a sizable influx of black New York activists into Georgia and some of the other Southern states. We may have a violation of civil rights law case. Groups are parading, asking for equal rights and the right to register to vote. One black guy down in Baker County, Georgia was clubbed pretty bad. The rednecks down there just turn their heads like nothin's goin' on. Then the perpetrator gets away." Harry blew more smoke out the window and continued.
"Our job in New York is to try to get information on who these transplants are, who's backing them, and what kind of agenda they're working on. Not going to be easy, but I think you'll like getting into the fire."

Neal listened intently, then asked, "I suppose most of our work will be on the street."

"Not all of it. The office downtown has some data on possible suspects. With that we can make a plan and head over to Brooklyn and up to Harlem. We think these guys are operating out of an old hangar on the Linden Airport site. They go down the New Jersey Turnpike, pick up US1 near Philadelphia, then head south to Georgia. They make stops in Trenton and Camden to pick up others in the group. Once they get to their target town in the South, they start recruiting blacks who're eager to participate."

Neal had never been bigoted, but was used to having blacks as hired hands around his family's home and in those of his friends. Some of his early childhood playmates were sons of workers at the cotton mill where his father worked. As he grew older the friendships became strained and detached, yet he maintained a congenial manner. He believed in equality for all men, but detested the aggressive and sometimes violent way in which minorities were starting to behave as they tried to receive equal rights. Now he wondered if his neutral feelings would be put to the test.

The rain let up and Harry pulled back on to the highway. "We may have lost a half hour there, but I think we'll still be in New York way before dark…early enough to have a beer and find a good Italian restaurant. You like Italian?" he asked.

"Sure," Neal said, as he studied the map. "I see we pass that Linden airport you mentioned."

"Yea, it's south of Newark airport on 95 about twenty miles before we cross over to Manhattan through the Lincoln Tunnel. That should put us somewhere near 39th street and we can drive up Broadway to our hotel. Show you the sights."

Neal was beginning to get excited about seeing New York again. "Isn't that near the garment district?" he asked.

"Yea," Harry asked, puffing on another cigarette. "During the week those streets are loaded with garment racks carrying dresses, coats, pants…I've never seen so many little shops catering to the fashion trade. Some of 'em are so small you wonder where they keep their inventory. And the trucks…they line every stretch of pavement. Sometimes you sit a long time waitin' for one of 'em to move and let you through. It's a real hassle, but ah, it's New York," he said, a big smile on his face.

"By the way, what hotel did you say we were staying at?" Neal asked.

"I booked two rooms at a small place at Seventh Avenue and 55th Street, The Wellington. It's not fancy, but close to the action and since we'll be leaving the car in a garage while we're here, we can walk to most anything from the hotel. They get a lot of foreign business there, mostly from overseas travel agents. I always find it kinda fun to watch those people. Oh yea, it's also just a coupla blocks from Carnegie Hall if you like that classical stuff."

From the beginning of their friendship Neal did not have the impression that Harry was a fan of the arts. He guessed any spare time they spent together would be bars, broads, and movies. His stash of Hemingway novels would be good excuse to miss the action.

****

The project found them researching material in the mornings and cruising neighborhoods in Harlem some days and crowded housing complexes in Brooklyn on others. Their efforts brought forth a lengthy list of names. From this list they questioned several men and women who supplied dates and places targeted for demonstrations in the coming months. Neal was beginning to feel confident in his role as an agent and Harry told him he was becoming a real "G-Man."

The original project plan of four weeks had now stretched into six and one day when Harry had decided to take time off, Neal felt inclined to go to a matinee concert at Carnegie Hall. The Boy Choir from Lincoln Cathedral in England was performing. Neal had sung in his choir as a boy and always enjoyed the clear, treble voices that gave a unique sound to the choir. He remembered reading that the choristers in England practiced twice a day from age nine to about thirteen when their voices gave way to manhood.

The great and famous hall was filled to capacity for the performance and Neal felt fortunate to get a ticket in the eleventh row. Accompanied by a harpist, the boys sang selections from Mendelssohn, Bach, Schubert, and Handel. Neal especially enjoyed *I Know That My Redeemer Liveth,* from *The Messiah.*

As he followed the crowd out of the hall, he turned right, and in front of the Russian Tea Room, started to cross the street.

Louise lurched back, felt someone grab her arm…

CHAPTER SIX

The next two years Neal had temporary duty in four field offices, honing his skills in investigation. He visited Louise in Charlotte several times. He found that he needed to hone his golfing skills to keep up with her father. On weekends he went to a local golf range and tried to improve his swing. Louise did not play golf, but as a way to gain approval from her parents, Neal made sure Mr. Prentice knew he wanted to play on each of his visits. Myers Park Country Club member's average age was fifty-five, hardly any of them played tennis or squash, which Neal would have preferred. His ability to fraternize and play a decent game found favor with Mr. Prentice and his friends, consequently, he never lacked for a game when he visited Charlotte.

Arriving in Charlotte on December 23,1962, Neal planned to spend Christmas with Louise and drive to Savannah the next day for a few days visit with his mother and father. They had both been ill with the ailments of old age and were contemplating moving into a retirement facility. Neal was going to help with selection and making the necessary moving arrangements.

As he reached for the brass door knocker, the door swung open and Louise ran into his arms. "Oh, Neal. I'm so glad to see you, but have very bad news for you," she said as she kissed his cheek. "Your mother just called to let you know that your father died last night."

Releasing his arms from around Louise's shoulders, Neal stepped down from the porch step, reached into his pocket for a handkerchief, and began to wipe his eyes. "Did she say how he died?"

"Yes, they had just finished dinner and he went into the living room to watch the news, when he laid back, gave a sigh, and died," she answered, reaching out to take his arm. "Neal, I'm so sorry. I know you must go to her at once, and I'd be glad to go with you if I can be of any help. Come in and call her, then let me know what you want to do."

He walked through the ornately decorated foyer and into the den where Mr. and Mrs. Prentice offered their condolences and left him to make the call. He spoke softly and gently to his mother, telling her that he would leave immediately and should be there in about four hours. Putting the receiver down, he turned to Louise and held out his arms. "I'll sure miss the old man. He wasn't always around much, but when he was home we had one heck of a good time." Tears came again.

She hugged him tightly. "How may I help?"

"I'm sure your folks wouldn't be too happy if you weren't here for the holidays, especially if you were traveling with a man..." Reaching into his jacket pocket, he took out a small, black velvet box and opened it. "But, do you suppose they'd make an exception if you were engaged to that man and he really needed you near him for a few days?"

Holding her hand over her mouth as she gasped, she looked at the large Tiffany-set diamond. "Neal, is this a proposal?"

"Considering the circumstances that just happened, yes, it is. Not how I had it planned, sweet one, but will you do me the honor of being my wife?" He started to kneel down, but she caught his arm, pulled him up. Their bodies met, molding to each others contours, locking their embrace. Their lips met in near savage harmony and for a moment he forgot his loss and dreamed of his gain.

"I will, yes, I will," she said as she showered kisses on his face between her words. "Oh, I must tell Mom and Dad."

Breaking from his arms, she ran down the long oak hallway to a glass-enclosed sunroom where her parents were drinking tea and reading the Charlotte Observer. "LOOK," she squealed as she held out her left hand. "My first Christmas present." She laughed as the Prentices stood up and came toward her.

"Tell us about this," Mr. Prentice said in a stern voice.

Neal entered the room, walked up to Louise, and put his arm around her waist. Noticing the questionable look in the Prentice's eyes, he apologized for not telling them about this first, but asked their understanding, given the situation at hand. "I had full intention of doing this right, but…"

"Don't fret, young man. Love isn't always as we plan. Sometimes it just takes a few twists and turns," offered Mr. Prentice, a little smile breaking on his face. "Mother and I knew this would probably happen soon anyway."

"I certainly appreciate you taking this well, but now I have to ask if you will give Louise permission to go to Savannah with me."
Waiting for a response, he looked at Louise and her mother who were admiring the ring. "We have to leave immediately. My mother has no family there and I s'pose it will be up to me to make all the arrangements. Louise could sure be a help with Mother while I'm tending to the details."

Mr. Prentice lowered his eyes to the Oriental rug under his feet, cleared his throat, and said, "I feel you are a gentleman and truly mean to care for my daughter, but I have concern."

"Sir," Neal interrupted, "You can be sure I will in no way put Louise in any jeopardy."

The Prentices helped Louise pack, adding her Christmas gifts to the already loaded car. Mr. Prentice shook Neal's hand, Mrs. Prentice gave him a hug, the first. The car left the circular driveway and they drove south toward South Carolina and the Georgia coast.

With each passing mile Neal reflected on the past and his life with his father. He also thought about how happy his mother had been the past few years since his father had retired. They were looking forward to moving to a smaller place and needed Neal to help them make the right choice. Jekyll Island had been a favorite vacation spot of theirs and a Real Estate friend told them about a new senior citizen complex on Riverview Drive, near the church they attended when they visited the island. Neal was going to go with the agent to check it out for them. "Guess now I'll be making that call for Mom."

Louise sat quietly watching the hills turn to flat sand scenery with clumps of green palmettos. Neal held tightly to her left hand, rubbing the ring with his fingers. Though deep in thought, he turned frequently to her and blew a kiss. She gave him his silence, knowing full well that this was difficult for him and the next few days would be emotionally exhausting.

****

SAVANNAH, GEORGIA
Keeping the Southern tradition, friends and neighbors filled the kitchen with homemade casseroles, cakes, and salads. Flowers were on every available table and the telephone rang with tiring consistency. Louise was amazed at the number of people who cared for this family. She kept a detailed record of each call and greeted visitors as if she was already a member of the family. Her cheerful manner and warm smile put everyone at ease and she made sure Mrs. Park was not overtaxed. "Mrs. Park, I've put a nice cup of tea on your nightstand and turned your bed down. Why don't you rest a bit before the service," Louise asked, as she led the weary lady to her room.

****

Louise unbuttoned her blouse and laid it on the bed. Slipping out of her skirt, she heard a knock on the guest room door. Opening it slightly, she saw Neal on the other side. He pushed it open, stepped into the room and closed the door. Half frightened, but aroused, Louise made no attempt to ask him to leave. Gathering her into his arms, he held her tightly, his breath against her cheek was warm. Tingling with emotion, Louise felt his lips gently tracing the curves of her neck, and his hands exploring the bare skin of her back and shoulders. His light touch gave rise to currents of desire she had never known. Until now their lovemaking had not gone beyond goodnight kisses and hugs on the porch steps and she wondered why this sudden burst of passion.

Pulling away, Neal gazed into her eyes. He held her at arms length, studying her body as his chest heaved with sighs of pleasure. "You are one evermore beautiful woman," he said as he drew her back into another embrace and kissed her, their lips blending in burning harmony.

As abruptly as he came to her, with equal abruptness he withdrew. "I'm sorry, Louise. The emotion of the past few days, and the fact that we're so close here, just overcame me and I…"

"Hush, Neal," she said, putting her fingers to his lips. "I love you and I only wish you would do this more often," Louise pleaded as she stood trembling. She gave him a quick kiss on the cheek. "No regrets, mister. Remember me? I'm the gal you're going to marry…soon, I hope."

Neal opened the door, stroked her cheek with his hand, and smiling, said, "Soon, yes. When this week's events are over we've got to sit down and make some plans, 'cause I have some interesting news to tell you." Before leaving for Charlotte he had received orders to report to the FBI Field Office in Norfolk, Virginia.

****

His father's service in the small Episcopal church was well attended, despite a chilling rain. The next day Neal took his mother to sign a lease on an apartment at Riverview Village on Jekyll Island. Several of her friends had moved there which made him feel better about leaving her alone.

Before they left Savannah for the drive back to Charlotte, Neal suggested they have lunch at a small seafood restaurant overlooking the Savannah River. They ordered crab salad and a glass of white wine. Louise sensed that Neal had something serious to tell her, but he seemed in a remote frame of mind. She made small talk, commenting about the large number of gulls flying overhead, the breeze that was picking up, and the noise from the dock across the river. Neal picked at his food, then staring intensely at her, announced, "Louise, I've been assigned to a military investigation in Norfolk and I've got to be there January fifteenth. I want you to go with me."

Dropping her fork in her plate, she opened her eyes wide and said, "January fifteenth! How can we possibly plan a wedding in two weeks?" Thoughts of shopping and parties darted through her mind.

"I know what you're thinking. There's no way you and your mother can pull it together in that time, but I'm asking you to do this for me…for us, actually," he said, as he reached across the table and took her hand. "After the other day in your room, I know I can't wait much longer. The job assignment just makes it easier to justify." He could feel her becoming tense and bewildered as she imagined how her parents would take this news. "Can't we have a small family wedding, especially since my father's just died. We don't need all that social stuff with parties and showers. 'Course I know your mother will probably never forgive me for taking that away from her, but heck, when we give her lots of cute grandchildren she'll forget all about it," he laughed, trying to make her lighten up.

Louise started to cry. She folded her napkin, got up from her chair and walked toward the door. Neal quickly put money on the table and motioned to the waiter that they were leaving.

The first hour of driving was very quiet in the car. Only the sound of the windshield wipers broke the ensuing silence. Not able to stand this any longer, Neal spoke. "Louise, I've tried to explain to you that my career is never going to be routine. It will involve time alone for you, moving frequently, and raising children mostly by yourself. Actually, it's not much different from being married to a military man."

"I know you've told me all those things, but this surprise is going to be a real problem. Mother has always dreamed of a big wedding for me and Dad would definitely want to host the reception at the club." She swallowed hard and finding it difficult to keep from crying, she continued. "I could be happy with a small wedding, but I hate to disappoint my parents."

"Hold on," Neal shouted, as he pulled onto the bumpy shoulder of the road, the car swerving sharply to the right.

Louise braced herself on the dashboard and dug her shoes into the floor. "What are you doing," she screamed.

"This," he said as he pulled her, almost violently, to him. He kissed her with an urgency that sent shivers of desire running through her body. Shocked at her own response to this unexpected splendor, she savored every moment as he continued to press closer.

"How would you like to be impulsive and become Mrs. Neal Park tonight."

"Neal, you must be crazy," she shrieked. "How could we do that and what would that solve?"

"For starters, it would soothe this fury within my soul and I could really show you how much I love you." Answering her first question, he said, "We're in Georgia and there's no waiting to get a marriage license in this state. We just go to a Justice of the Peace and he ties the knot."

"Now I think I must be crazy. Let's do it."

CHAPTER SEVEN

Justice of the Peace, Walter Hardwick, dressed in his work overalls and a flannel shirt, quickly read the service and showed them where to sign the marriage certificate. His wife wiped her hands on a soiled apron then gave her witness signature. A fire was burning in the fireplace of the small office and the smell of bean soup was coming from the adjoining kitchen. The tiny frame cottage in the town of Springfield, Georgia served as office, home and storage for this elderly couple who farmed the land as well.

Thanking him and offering a twenty dollar bill, Neal put the certificate in his coat pocket. Mrs. Hardwick gave the bride a hug and asked Neal if they'd like to stay for dinner.

"Thanks, ma'am, but we have to get on our way to Charlotte. Sure appreciate you asking us."

Walking to the car, Neal stopped and turned Louise toward him. Tears glistened on Louise's cheeks as she looked into Neal's eyes. "Never thought I'd be married in gray slacks and a black turtleneck sweater," she laughed, as Neal put his arms around her and kissed her with an intensity and hunger that sent spirals of ecstasy rushing through her body. The chill of the late afternoon air was overshadowed by the warmth of his body, firm and persuasive against hers.

Leaving Springfield, Neal took a back road to State Road 321 North to Columbia, South Carolina. They drove about an hour, not saying much, but exchanging smiles, each wanting to touch the other. Just outside Columbia, Neal pulled into the parking lot of a small motel.

"Louise, I know you must be hungry," he said with a mischievous smile on his face. "We'll never make it to Charlotte before midnight...and I don't intend to!" He reached across the seat and gave her a hug. "Let's check in here and I'll go get us something to eat. Suit you?"

The desk clerk at the Pine Motel winked at Neal as he handed him a key to room 210. "It's on the second floor, stairs to your right."

Opening the door to the room, they stepped in to find a sparsely furnished room in shades of brown, gold, and aqua. The sagging bed was covered in a chenille spread with a peacock design. Plaid drapes were hanging unevenly, and light from the blinking neon sign on the front of the building peeked in at the sides. A Danish modern chair showed signs of abusive wear and tear, and the lamp on the nightstand wore a ripped, paper shade. The bathroom floor vinyl was creeping away from the walls and the tub needed a good cleaning. Towels of extremely thin cloth were in a stack on the sink top.

"It's not the Ritz, darling, but it will have to do until I can show you better," he said, as he turned the lock on the door. Neal stood gazing at Louise as she appeared to be unable to take a step closer to him. He came forward, his broad shoulders heaving with each breath, and drew her into his arms. She inhaled quickly at the contact and felt the beating of her pulse as if it were music. Clasping her tightly to his chest, he whispered into her ear. "Darling, Mrs. Park, welcome to my world."

Louise locked herself into his embrace and marveled at the sight of this man who gave her a magnetism she had never known. Her heart was thundering, her skin rippling with shivers, and she felt bathed in passion and fury. The night became totally theirs.

****

Waking in the curve of his body, Louise was beginning to realize how hungry she really felt. She started to lift his arm from around her waist when he tightened his grasp and rolled her over to face him. His lips gently covered her mouth and then explored her velvety skin. Responding with inspired encouragement, she was surprised at her own acceptance of intimacy. Every time their eyes met it was an invitation to turn their hearts over to each other in complete abandon.

"Good morning, Mrs. Park," Neal said as he gently took her face in his hands. "Seems I promised you dinner some fourteen hours ago and all you've gotten is lovemaking. You must certainly be starved."

Hypnotized by his maleness and the magnitude of her unending desire, she sat up, reached for his arm and pulled him back on to the bed. "I am completely full…well, almost," she giggled, amazed at her newfound boldness. "But I do think some juice and a cup of coffee would be a nice departure from the activities of the day. That's not to say permanently for the day."

Astonished, and yet delighted at Louise's pleasure and reaction to lovemaking, Neal wondered if this was response due to experience or the culmination of anticipation and waiting for marriage. At any rate, it did not matter as he counted himself fortunate for finding her so in tune with his desires and emotions.

Neal took a shower, managing to overlook the hygiene of the room and quickly dressed in corduroy slacks and a wool sweater. The rain, which had been forecast, was coming down hard, mixed with gusty wind. "Better put on the old raincoat," he said, as he filled his pockets with wallet and keys. "Darling, Mrs. Park, I will only be gone a few minutes. There's a Waffle House in the next block and I'll bet they can rustle up some breakfast for a hungry bride and groom."

While he was gone, Louise realized they had not called her parents to tell them they would be delayed. She had visions of her father calling his friends at the State Road Patrol to be on the lookout. Her mother would probably take to her bed in a "southern swoon", anticipating the worst.

Neal unlocked the door, and before he could step inside Louise was frantically telling him they must call her parents immediately. "Neal, they're probably calling every hospital from here to Savannah looking for us."

"Calm down a minute, Louise." He set the Waffle House box on the little round table, and taking her by the shoulders, forced her to sit down. "Now, let me tell you what I did," he said with stern demeanor. "While you were taking a shower last night I called and spoke to both of them. They weren't exactly ecstatic over the situation, but after I explained to them about Norfolk and the time period, they seemed to calm down a bit."

Louise was wringing her hands and starting to cry.

"And yes, your mother was crying about not having a big wedding. I told them it would be nice to have a reception when I can take a leave in a few weeks. She immediately went into a vocal dissertation as to how she could use the same caterer, the same musicians and all that stuff you do for a wedding." Neal kissed Louise's cheek and said, "Don't worry, they'll get over it."

"S'pose you're right, Neal, it's just going to be hard to face them the first time. Daddy will understand more than Mother, but they're both going to be really disappointed." She finished the juice and waffle Neal had brought and started to sip the hot coffee. "Neal, are you going to have time to let me get all my belongings together before we have to go to Norfolk?"

"We can probably stay in Charlotte for three or four days, then I have to get to Norfolk and report to my supervisor. Also, we've got to find a place to stay…unless you'd like to stay in a motel like this for a while." He grinned as he watched for her reaction.

"Oh, yuk," she said with a scowl on her face. "I can hardly wait to get out of here, but I really don't want to stay at my house when we get to Charlotte." A mischievous smile and a giggle let Neal know what she was thinking.

"Tell you what," he said taking the last sip of his coffee. "We'll stay downtown at the new Mark Hopkins, part of our honeymoon. Surely your folks will understand."

Dumping the paper plates and cups in the waste can, Louise began to pack her clothes, eager to start their trip. As she turned to go to the bathroom for her cosmetic bag, Neal rushed at her, threw her on the bed and started sensuous exploration which brought immediate arousal to her passions. Whirling in a sensation of uncontrollable joy, their departure to Charlotte was intentionally delayed.

****

With amazing wonder of the future which lay ahead, they drove north, hoping to find a warm reception from the Prentices. As they pulled into the circular drive, a large, black car was leaving.

"That looks like Dr. Allen's car," said Louise, as she reached for the door handle, ready to exit.

She ran to the front door and burst in calling to her mother. "Mother, we're here," she shouted.

Ada, their maid of thirty years, rushed into the hallway. "Hush, chile. Your momma done took to her bed with a stroke."

Louise flew up the stairs and ran down the long hallway to the master bedroom. Lying on the huge four-poster bed Mrs. Prentice looked gray and was staring at the ceiling. "Oh, Mother, are you alright?" Louise asked, knowing that some dread happening occurred here. She leaned down to kiss her mother and realized that the person in the bed was oblivious to her presence. Hearing footsteps, she turned to see her father coming through the doorway, Neal behind him. "Daddy," she sobbed, "what happened to Mother? She doesn't know I'm here."

Gathering her in his arms, he tried to explain. "Yesterday at her bridge club she felt ill and came home early. Ada brought her dinner up here and found her on the floor. We called Dr. Allen immediately and he said she had a slight stroke."

"Slight, Daddy," Louise exclaimed, "it looks serious to me…and why isn't she in the hospital? Why won't she talk to me." She was beginning to be very agitated.

Neal came over and put his arm around Louise, trying to calm her. "Darling, let your father explain."

"Louise," Mr. Prentice said as he took a deep breath, "the stroke was minimal, the fact that she does not respond to you is purely by choice. You see," he continued, "she was extremely hurt by your eloping. I think it best if you and Neal go on your way to Norfolk and let this work itself out."

Neal took her arm and led her out of the massive room. She was crying and started to scream, when he put his hand over her mouth. "Don't make it worse," he said, as they started down the stairs. "There isn't anything you can do right now to change this, so let's just get your stuff and get out."

"Neal," she shouted, "this is my house and these are my parents. Getting married doesn't change all that."

"It might," he answered, "but only for a while. They'll come around, I promise."

They stayed at the Mark Hopkins that night, though the visit was strained. Had it not been for Neal's tender manner and Louise's newfound desires, the second day of their marriage would have been spoiled.

The next morning Ada helped Louise pack her clothes, sniffling the entire time. She had worked for the Prentices for a long time and felt that Louise was "her baby". "I'm shore gonna miss you, Miss Lou," using the name she called her as a young child. "Don't you worry none 'bout your momma. I'll see to it she gets good care. Why she'll be up in no time." She dabbed her eyes with a torn hanky and patted Louise on the shoulder. "You jes be happy and take care 'o that handsome young man there," she laughed, as Neal came through the door.

Neal rented a trailer from a store nearby and with Ada's help they managed to fill it with Louise's clothes and several pieces of furniture that Mr. Prentice had stored in the basement. He told Ada to let them know they were intended before Mrs. Prentice took ill.

As they got into the car, Ada came running out of the house with a big basket swinging on her arm. "Here now, I packed you some lunch for the trip. Ya'll need to eat good and stay healthy," she said, handing Neal the basket, "and Miss Lou, come into the house for a minute. Your momma done woke up and said she wants to kiss you goodbye."

Surprised by this turn of events, Louise went up to her mother's room and gingerly opened the door. "Mother, it's Louise," she said in a soft voice.

"Come over here, dear," she called out, sitting up in the bed. "I'm afraid I behaved poorly, just never did handle defeat," she said with a slight laugh. "I've thought about this all night and want you to know I'm sorry."

Hugging her mother, Louise said, "Oh, Mother, I understand. Neal and I are both sorry that you won't get to do a big wedding, but we are so happy. I never knew loving someone could be so consuming and wonderful. Mother, he is fabulous...and so smart."

She was talking fast and rolling her eyes with delight. "Why, he has already worked on some really special FBI projects and now he'll be involved in another one in Norfolk. I do hope you'll be happy for us." She danced around the bed, holding on to the posts as she turned. "And, Mother, we'll only be a few hours away. When we get settled you and Daddy can come to visit us."

Seeing her child filled with joy brought tears to her eyes.

"Louise, I pray you and Neal will have a long and happy life. Please give him my apologies, not necessary for him to come up. We'll make amends later."

Louise hugged her mother again and quickly went down the steps and to the car where Neal was patiently waiting. Mr. Prentice and Ada waved from the porch as they pulled out to the street.

"I declare, Neal, I think this has been the most emotion filled three days in my entire life," she laughed, as she recalled mostly the time alone with him.

CHAPTER EIGHT

Noon hour traffic out of Charlotte was lighter than Neal had anticipated and he was grateful, considering the heavy load they were pulling. "If the rain will hold off until later we can make some time and maybe get to Durham by sundown," Neal said, as he kept watch on his rearview mirror and the slight sway of the trailer. "How about handing me one of Ada's sandwiches. Sure hope she made some of her egg salad ones, they are the best," he said, remembering the lunches she fixed after he and Mr. Prentice came in from golf.

Louise opened the basket, the aroma of egg salad drifted out. "Here, darling. Want some iced tea?" She put the basket on the floor and opened the thermos. Handing him the sandwich and a napkin, she put his cup of tea in the beverage holder he had bought for the trip. "This sure is handy," she said and leaned over to kiss him on the cheek.

"Hey, save the dessert for later," Neal said as he took a bite of the sandwich. "Boy, nobody makes egg salad like Ada. You're going to have to get her recipe."

"Neal, dear," Louise said coyly, "I don't know too much about cooking. Mother always had Ada and I hated home economics in school."

"Guess we'll just live on love," he said, taking her hand to his lips.

The highway through North Carolina was lined with furniture manufacturer's billboards. "Neal, when we have our own house someday we can just come back here and buy our furniture. Mother and Daddy know a lot of the people who own those companies." Thomasville, Young-Hinkle, all the fine names were displayed, urging highway travelers to stop and buy.

"I'm going to bypass downtown Durham and try to find a motel on the outskirts that has a lighted parking lot." He was getting tired and knew they would have a long day of driving tomorrow. Turning off 70 he maneuvered the car and trailer under the sagging canopy of the Days Inn North.

As he opened the car door, he turned and noticed a restaurant across the street that advertised *BEST FRIED CHICKEN IN THE STATE.* "Don't suppose you'd be interested in some southern fried chicken, biscuits, and gravy before we have dessert?" he asked with a smile.

"Oh, that would be wonderful. Could you go get it and bring it back to the room?" she asked. "I'd love to take a bath before we eat." She was thinking about the pale blue, lace nightie she had packed in her suitcase with the new bottle of Chanel No. 5 that Tricia had given her for her birthday. "If this is a honeymoon, I'm going to look and smell the part," she thought to herself.

The hot water felt good as she closed her eyes and tried to imagine what life would be like in Norfolk. All she remembered reading was that it had the largest Naval installation on the East Coast. She wondered if they had country clubs in the town. "Not that we'll be able to join one," she thought. "Why, I don't even know how much money Neal is making." She decided that would be a good topic of discussion on the trip tomorrow.

The *BEST FRIED CHICKEN IN THE STATE* turned out to be far from Ada's best. The biscuits were hard and the gravy full of lumps. "Oh well, at least it's warm," Neal remarked, adding, "Say, how's the dessert coming?"

Louise placed her robe on the end of the bed as Neal came out of the bathroom with his toothbrush in his mouth. "My word, you do look good enough to eat," he exclaimed as he turned and put the toothbrush on the counter.

Later, holding her tightly in his arms, he kissed her earlobes and whispered, "What do you mean you don't know how to cook?"

****

Renting the white frame cottage near Gardens by the Sea would give Neal easy access to the military installations where he would be working…Little Creek Naval Amphibious Base, Norfolk Naval Shipyard, Oceana Naval Air Station and Langley Air Force Base which was across the bay in Hampton. The yard was filled with old oak trees and the back yard was fenced for the puppy they had talked of buying. "That will keep her company when I'm gone, since she's not going to find a job," Neal thought, as he unpacked another box of Louise's clothes.

"Neal, darling, I'm going to have to use part of your side of the closet. I just don't have enough space for all my clothes. Do you mind?" she asked, carrying an armful of dresses.

"Do I really have a choice?" he laughed, picking her up and swinging her around to face him. He moved closer, his arms tight around her waist, and devoured the softness of her lips.

"At this rate, we'll never get unpacked, you romeo!" She pulled free from him and ran around to the other side of the room, Neal giving chase. He caught her arm, locked her into another embrace, and with mutual persuasion, the boxes sat untouched for the rest of the day.

****

Rays of sun played hide and seek among the tree branches as the early morning breeze wafted in through their bedroom window. Louise had awakened early and was in the kitchen attempting to make breakfast. Neal awoke at the smell of coffee and bacon, put on his robe and came into the kitchen. "Morning, beautiful," he said as he looked through cabinets for a coffee cup. "Where did we hide the cups."

"They're in the cabinet next to the sink," she answered, jumping as bacon grease splattered on her arm. "Oh, I don't know if I'll ever learn how to do this."

"Sure you will, it just takes time. Hey, where are you going in such a hurry?" he asked, as Louise ran toward the bathroom.

She slammed the door and he could hear her heaving in abundance. Opening the door, he found her draped around the toilet, holding her stomach. "Louise, what's wrong?" He ran cold water on a washcloth and put it on her forehead. "Do you want me to help you to the bed?"

"I think I better stay here for a bit. Go eat your breakfast and leave me alone." Ordering him in such a stern tone was out of character for her and Neal was concerned.

He scrambled a couple of eggs to go with the scorched bacon and decided to forego toast. Putting the dishes in the sink he went back to the bathroom. She was not there, having chosen to go to bed. Neal pulled a blanket over her and sat down on the side of the bed. Louise was crying and staring out the window. "Neal, I don't think this was part of your plan, but there's a good possibility you're going to be a father."

Jumping up, he opened his mouth and could not make the words come out. After a few seconds he regained his composure and kneeled down beside her. "Darling, there was no real plan, just a suggestion to wait a while, but this is wonderful. Are you sure?"

"Guess so," she said, hugging him. "I've been kind of sick the past few mornings, and that's unusual for me, so...uh...guess we're going to have a baby."

He buried his face in her neck and rocked her back and forth as he laughed. "We're going to have a baby," he shouted. "Whoopee. I'm going to be a father, how 'bout that!"

****

Traveling between military installations, Neal's days were spent documenting files and doing surveillance on a suspected sabotage ring. With so many military personnel in the area, and a significant number of them traveling to foreign countries, there was opportunity to gain access to top security information and in turn offer this to enemies of the United States. Continuing hostilities were building in Viet Nam. FBI emphasis was put on activity by military and contract personnel who could attain any information that would encourage or endanger United States involvement in that part of the world. Neal never discussed his work with Louise and she never questioned his activities. Her days were filled with decorating the second bedroom as a nursery and training the Labrador puppy, *ROMEO*, that Neal had bought for her the day after she told him she was pregnant. "He can be a companion for our son."

Jordan Prentice Park made his entrance into the world ten months from the day his parents were married. Louise's pregnancy was normal, but the delivery lengthy. Her doctor waited as long as possible and after thirty hours had passed he told Neal it would be necessary to perform a Caesarian operation to save the baby. Louise was weak and lost a considerable amount of blood. During the delivery the doctor found an abnormality that would make it impossible for her to endure another pregnancy. Neal and Louise were filled with sadness, as they had hoped for at least two children. But seeing their new son changed their focus. A healthy baby, he had blond hair and brown eyes and a lusty cry that frightened Romeo into retreating to closets when they came home from the hospital. Eventually the dog accepted the new member of the family and became his serious protector, whether outside next to the playpen or in Jordan's room as he napped.

On their first anniversary Neal told Louise to find a babysitter, he was taking her to the Cavalier Hotel in Virginia Beach for dinner and dancing. Before she could ask the widow next door to sit, her parents had called and said they wanted to come for a visit to get to know their new grandson. Louise *told them* they could keep him by themselves overnight while she and Neal went to the hotel for their anniversary.

The Cavalier sat high on a hill overlooking the Atlantic Ocean. It was the scene for frequent social functions of the area and a favorite honeymoon choice for brides and grooms. "This will be a little bit nicer than our first night together," Neal said, as he turned into the long drive up to the entrance. "Of course, I'm only referring to the place!" he said with a mischievous smile on his face. "And I trust you brought dessert."

After a relaxed meal of filet mignon and a bottle of fine burgundy wine, the maitre d's suggestion, they rode the elevator to the rooftop Club Atlantic and enjoyed an hour of dancing to Lester Lanin's band. As they left the club, the host gave Louise a single red rose and wished them a pleasant evening.

"Neal, this has been so nice. It seems weeks since we've spent any time alone and I miss you," she said, as they held hands and waited for the elevator.

"Darling, I know you've been lonely, even with Jordan to keep you company now, but my job has been pretty intense and doesn't look like this will let up for a while. Please be patient, things'll change. In fact there's a good chance we might be transferred to another office in a few months."

Turning the big brass key in the lock, Neal opened the door. As he had ordered, room service delivered a chilled bottle of champagne to the room while they were out. Neal embraced Louise from behind and gently guided her toward the sofa and the glasses waiting to be filled. He opened the bottle, losing only a slight amount in bubbles and filled the glasses. Handing one to Louise, he raised his and said, "To my darling wife of one year. May our love continue to grow for many years to come. I love you."

Louise sipped the champagne, the bubbles tickling her nose, and laid her head against the sofa back. Silently counting her blessings, she constantly marveled at how even the mere touch of his hand sent shivers up her spine. With the dinner, the wine, the dancing, and now the champagne, she was filled with desire for this man who she hoped would never tire of her. "To my husband, the man who makes my heart beat faster and my love for him grow with an awareness I cannot explain."

Neal looked at her with a tenderness that belied the urgent anticipation racing through his body. He reached out to her and took her hand, leading her into the bedroom. Pausing to kiss her, he whispered his love for her entire being. Moonlight reflecting from the water below made ripples of light on the ceiling as they responded to desire and ecstasy.

****

Jordan took his first step on the day he turned nine months old. That same day his father informed his mother that they were moving. "I've been given a new assignment dealing with some Civil Rights issues in Greenville, South Carolina. It's a pretty nice town and big enough for you to get involved in some activities away from Jordan once in a while."

"I had some friends at Sweet Briar from Greenville and visited them once," she said, sounding as if this was going to be a good experience. "I think they still live there. I'll bet Tricia will know. I'll call her tonight."

CHAPTER NINE

From Albuquerque to Philadelphia, from Little Rock to San Diego, from Pittsburgh to Tampa, Noel accepted assignments on civil rights cases, organized crime, financial crime, and applicant matters. The next eighteen years they moved on an average of every two years. With the encouragement and financial assistance of the Prentices, Jordan attended boarding school at Woodward Academy in College Park, Georgia. Holidays and summers he joined Neal and Louise in their current domicile.

"Mom, I've been thinking about becoming a doctor," Jordan said to his mother during Christmas break in 1979. "I want to go to the University of Georgia and then Medical College of Georgia, that is, if I can get accepted."

Louise put down the box of ornaments she was putting on the tree. "Why Jordan, we had always hoped you would want to go to the University of Virginia to study law."

"No, Mother, that was what you and Dad had wanted for me," he shot back. "Just because your father was a lawyer doesn't mean I wanted to be one." Digging his hands into his pants pockets, he paced across the room, stepping over boxes of lights and decorations. "I'm really grateful for him sending me to Woodward, but I probably would have done just fine moving around with you and Dad. Anyway, just so you'll know, I've sent in my application to Georgia and should hear something next month."

"Am I to understand there is no changing your mind?" Louise asked.

"No, ma'am. You and my teachers taught me to be independent and make my own choices, so I have." He put his tanned, muscular arms around his mother and hugged her tightly. "Don't be too concerned, Mom. I talked it over with Dad this morning when we were jogging. He thought it was fine."

Looking up into her handsome son's face, and finding it hard to believe that he was nearly eighteen, she kissed his cheek. "Guess I can't change this, so I'll just tell you that if that's what you want, then let me know what I can do to help you."

Laughing, he volunteered, "You can keep sending me chocolate chip cookies every week." Jordan plugged in the tree lights and stepped back to admire their work. "Oh yea, the best part…I think I might get a scholarship. That late night studying is going to pay off."

****

Jordan graduated Cum Laude from the University of Georgia and was accepted in the fall class at Medical College of Georgia in Augusta. Neal's mother came up from Jekyll Island for the graduation and Louise's parents drove down from Charlotte. They repeated the trip for his graduation from medical school and the three of them agreed they could keep him in business with their ills of old age. As a new gastroenterlogist, Jordan joined four other doctors in their practice in Charleston. The practice grew and the handsome, young doctor was in demand at his associate's dinner parties and the St. Cecilia Ball. It was at one of the balls that he met Lucretia Middleton. Daughter of the patriarch of one of Charleston's oldest families, she caught his eye and his heart the first time he danced with her. Six months later their wedding at St. Philip's Church and reception at Middleton Plantation, was the society event of the season. Honeymooning in Bermuda, the happy couple returned to a carriage house behind one of the antebellum homes on the Battery. While Jordan spent long days at the office and nearby hospital, Lucretia became deeply involved in volunteer work with other young matrons of Charleston. Their first child, Annabelle, was born two years after the wedding and the second, Caroline, came eighteen months later.

****

Louise and Neal continued to spend vacation time at Jekyll Island and Charlotte visiting their families. Jordan and his family joined them at Jekyll, Annabelle and Caroline always excited to see their grandparents and hear Neal tell stories of his travels with the FBI. Protecting names and places, he managed to weave tales to hold their interest and amazement. As the girls grew into teenagers, they felt *protected* by him and his job.

"My granddad is so cool," they would tell their friends. "He knows all kinds of criminals and important people." In reality, he had usually been the support person on most projects and rarely met the individual or group being investigated. He liked it that way and had earned a reputation for dependability and loyalty to the Bureau. Serving with Hoover had not always been easy, but keeping his focus on family and his own ideals kept Neal content. The 1960s, the Kennedy era, and then Johnson, saw a major crisis of Klan activity. Following were the riots from students and activists demonstrating against the Vietnam War. Hoover died in May of 1972 after serving 48 years as FBI Director. Next came the Watergate episode. Neal was never in the forefront of FBI activity in those years, but in the 1980s he led several projects resulting in arrests of narcotics violators. In the fall of 1986, working in the Information Technology Center in Savannah, Neal started to think of retirement.

"That was a mighty good dinner, Louise." Settling into his blue leather chair, he started to read the evening paper. "Say, remember George Wilson down at Jekyll?" he asked, looking at Louise who was trying to find a news program on the television.

"You mean that man who has 12 sisters and brothers?" she answered as she found Tom Brokaw reporting the latest news.

"Yes, that's the man. He called me today and wanted to know if we might be interested in buying the brick ranch next to the duplex we rent. The owners who live in New York are retiring to Florida and want to unload it. Still has twenty-five years on the land lease."

Louise turned down the television sound and walked over to his chair. "Do you mean to buy it and move there now?" she asked as her eyes lighted up.

"Darling, I can retire now if I want. I've been giving some thought to doing just that, then taking consulting and special project assignments on a call basis." He pulled her to his lap and wrapped his arms around her waist. Her youthful glow that always enticed him was still there, as they stared longingly at each other. Remembering when she was alone for weeks at a time, when she had Jordan's difficult birth making it impossible to have more children, and when she had to pack and move frequently and usually by herself...these endurances endeared her to him with a bottomless sense of love and contentment. He always needed and wanted only Louise, and she him.

Like a child singing with delight, she spoke quickly and eagerly. "Yes, let's do it. Can we drive down tomorrow morning?" Jumping up from his lap, she blew him a kiss as she rounded the corner to the kitchen telephone. "I'm going to call Jordan and Lucretia and tell them. Oh, this will be wonderful."

"Whoa, lady," he insisted. "We don't know any of the details. We haven't even seen the house. It might be falling apart for all we know." By now he was used to her impetuousness to share everything with her son, but this would be a major move and he wanted it to be right before they told anyone.

Feeling a twinge of disappointment, she came back into the room. "Guess you're right, but you didn't answer me as to when we can go see it."

"Tomorrow morning will be fine." Gathering her into his arms, he embraced her tenderly as they stood motionless, staring into each others eyes.

****

A thunderstorm had passed over the island earlier in the day, leaving a heavy layer of humidity hanging in the air. Broken tree limbs and pieces of Spanish moss littered the road as they crossed over the Jekyll Island Causeway.

"Must have been a bad storm," commented Neal. "Did you hear about this on last night's weather report?"

"No," Louise answered, gazing across Jekyll Creek toward the marina. "It almost looks like hurricane damage and that we can do without." Fear of storms was the only resistive thought she had to moving here permanently.

Neal turned on South Riverview and then Harbor Road leading to the Jekyll Harbor Marina. Here George Wilson worked as a maintenance man. One of thirteen children, he had lived on the island all his life. Being the oldest, "my folks couldn't afford to send me to school, they needed me to work. Can't read or write," he would say, with a sense of pride in being able to help his family rather than feeling deprived of an education. His skill with tools of all kinds and his warm manner with people made him a valuable employee to the dock master who was away from the marina for lengthy periods. George and his wife, Effie, raised eight children on the island, all who moved away for more opportunity. "Proud to say," he would offer to new sets of ears, "All those young'uns, 'cept the baby, went to college." Holding the strap of his overalls, "That's okay, 'cause she married a fine boy and they done give us four of the cutest grandbabies you ever seen."

Effie worked at the marina snack shop and assumed various duties ranging from housekeeping to biscuit making. Her daily attention to the *Low Country Boil* each evening meant that diners would enjoy shrimp, sausage, corn and red skinned potatoes simmering in broth. Patrons at the snack shop were frequently boat people passing by on their way to St. Simons and Brunswick, as well as the residents and visitors on Jekyll. Effie also filled in as surrogate grandmother to the numerous children who played in the pool and around the grounds. "Raised so many children of my own, it just seems natural to always have a baby on my lap," she'd say with a hearty laugh and a wipe of her hands on her ample white apron.

"George, hello there." Neal waved as he brought the car to a stop on the sandy parking drive next to the marina storage area that was lined with oak trees and island shrubs. The huge building housing boats for repair or storage had rolling doors as tall and wide as the building.

George was hosing down the walkway that led from the building to the side of the snack shop. Hearing his name, he turned off the water spigot and came over to their car. "Howdy do. Thought I heard you call my name." Smiling as he reached to shake Neal's hand, he tipped his hat to Louise. "Afternoon, Miz Park. Glad you all took me up on comin' down to look at that house. Think you might find it real interesting."

At the word *interesting,* Louise wondered if he meant that in a curious way or as a good buy. "Certainly hope it's the latter," she thought as she followed the two men around to the snack shop door. They chose a table in the corner, overlooking the docks, ordered shrimp salad on hot dog buns and sweetened iced tea. Louise sat quietly eating her lunch, listening intently as George described the house and details regarding it's sale.

"Now Mr. Park, this here house was built 'bout 1946, right after the big war. Folks that built it were only here summers and it sat empty rest o' the year. Then those yankees from New York bought it in '62 or '63, can't remember exactly, and they came down in the winter." Building his story of the house's history, he continued. "The mister was some bigwig for a clothing company and he went back and forth, just bein' here on weekends. The missus liked to golf, so she seemed pretty happy to stay here. Didn't seem like they had much family. Nobody ever stayed here with 'em."

"How big is it, George. You know, bedrooms, baths..." Neal asked.

"Well," he said, scratching his chin and looking out the window where two large boats were pulling into the dock. "I recall there's two bedrooms and a bath in the house, and a small bedroom and bath over the garage. Think it also has a sunroom on the back. Ah, heck, let's just drive on over there and you can see for yourself."

Neal paid Effie, who was the cashier today, and followed George and Louise to the car. They drove up Beachview Drive to Austin Drive and turned right toward the beach. Three lots in on the left sat the brick ranch, its yard in dire need of attention. "A couple of loads of sand, good trim on all the shrubs, new sidewalk, paint on the shutters. Wow, this place needs work," Neal thought as he stood in the front yard waiting for George to unlock the back door and let them in the front.

Slowly walking through the house, the smell of mildew was overwhelming, forcing George and Neal to open windows in every room. The last time the house was occupied the owners neglected to leave charcoal and other forms of mildew smell prevention. "This is a wonderful house," Louise said as she studied every room. "The space over the garage would be perfect for Annabelle and Caroline. They can see the ocean from the window up there."

"George, how can we get in touch with the owners to make an offer?" Louise broke into a big smile as Neal squeezed her hand.

"Mr. Latham, he's the owner, is s'posed to be down here next week. Heck, I don't know nuthin' 'bout Real Estate, but the guy that owns the marina does. He has an office on Beachview and can probably handle what you need."

"Okay. Look, let's stop by his office and let me talk to him. I'd like to go ahead and make an offer today before we leave. Incidentally, do you know of any significant problems with the house?"

81

George scratched his chin again. "Can't rightly say I do. 'Cept the septic tank might need a good cleanin' out. Got a friend who owns a *honey bucket.* He can take care o' that in no time."

Two hours later, a copy of the offer in his pocket, Neal and Louise started the drive back to Savannah. Louise chattered on telling Neal how she would decorate the sunroom, how she would turn the second bedroom into an office for him and how she intended to plant a rose garden in the front yard that was sunny all afternoon. He had never seen her so animated and excited.

The following week a counter offer arrived in the mail. Undaunted by the change in price and terms, Neal made a few revisions, but accepted the price. His retirement pay, plus a portfolio of sound investments, would cover their expenses. Louise's inheritance from her parents who died last year, would stay invested at Neal's insistence. Their plans were made. Neal submitted his resignation with an effective date of December 31, 1994. They put the Savannah house up for sale and contacted a moving company. The house sold quickly, and they set the move to Jekyll for mid-January.

****

CHARLESTON, SOUTH CAROLINA

Neal and Louise had been with the young Parks for four days. It was customary for them to share Christmas eve and Christmas morning watching the grandgirls enjoy the holiday festivities. Lucretia and Jordan were having their annual holiday open house the day after Christmas. Her eggnog recipe, served in the family antique silver punchbowl, and sought after by friends and family, was the focal point of the highly decorated pink house on the Battery, not far from their first home in the carriage house. The dining room table was adorned in gold and pink, from the satin ribbons to the gold damask cloth. Crab balls, pecan tassies, cheese wafers, benne wafers and other traditional Charleston delicacies were on the table. From noon until eight in the evening, there would be a steady stream of friends, family, and friends of friends who wanted the chance to see the Park mansion. Lucretia's reputation for renovating and restoring the old home was becoming known throughout the South. Antique dealers along King Street often called for permission to show the house.

The morning of the open house Louise had mentioned to Neal that she felt very tired and wanted to take a nap after breakfast. A cool breeze was coming in through the upstairs guestroom, the sheers at the window were dancing. Slipping back under the embroidered satin comforter, Louise winced in pain, her head lurched back onto the pillow, and she died.

CHAPTER TEN

"Dad, I know how much you and Mom were looking forward to retiring to Jekyll, and I really think you should go ahead with your plans." Jordan sensed Neal's hesitancy in making the move and noticed his increasing depression. "There was nothing you could have done to prevent the aneurysm that hit her so fast. The doctor told Lucretia and I that he was surprised it had not happened earlier in her life. We were all lucky to have her love for so long." He tried to comfort his father, while at the same time encourage him to stick to their plans. "Come on, old man. Let's finish the packing you two had started and get you on your way to some fishing and fun."

"Jordan, just don't know if I can do it." He wiped his eyes and stared at Louise's portrait on the far wall. Painted when she was thirty, it was one of his favorite treasures. "If I do make this move, I'll have to find another house. The one we just bought is too big for me and already full of memories of her planned decorating."

"No problem, Dad. It's just the right size for my gang," Jordan said with a sense of excitement. "I'll buy if from you. We've been looking for a second home anyway and you know how much the girls love Jekyll. 'Course I will admit most of their attraction was due to the attention you and Mom gave them...not to mention all the gifts."

Neal pondered Jordan's offer and walked over to his desk. He opened a file folder and handed Jordan a large manila envelope. Opening it, Jordan began to read a letter addressed to him from Louise.

Dearest Jordan,

As you were well aware, my parents left a large estate. Your portion, which you have received, was significant. Additionally, they left in my care a fund to be used to buy a second home for Dad and me. Your dad, being a prideful man, wanted to provide this for us himself. But I, your ever persuasive mother, convinced him to let me pay for half of it, with the provision that should I die before him, you would get the house, paying him for his half. He could then buy another better suited to his needs. If he should die first, I would ask that you let me continue to live in the house until I die.

Loving you best,
MOTHER

He handed the letter to Neal. "You know about this?"

"Yes, Jordan, I knew about it. Pretty prophetic wasn't it. There are so many memories of happy times at Jekyll, I just don't know. Maybe I should stay right here in Savannah, or move near you all in Charleston," he sighed in dismay. "Or maybe I could find a nice retirement village in Florida near some of my FBI buddies."

"Heck, Dad, why would you want to do any of those things? You know you love Jekyll and have been waiting for this for a long time. Well, tomorrow is here and you have to get on with your life. Mom wouldn't want you moping around here like a sick dog." He pulled some boxes into the middle of the den floor and started putting in books from the shelves. "You're not an old man by a long shot. Do you think Mom would just sit around like this? No! She'd probably already be signed up for lessons of some sort, a trip to some exotic place, and she'd be having lunch with friends everyday. Come on."

Sighing, Neal said, "Yeh, guess you're right. Maybe I was just taking time to feel sorry for myself. I need to remember you lost someone special, too. Your mom adored you, Jordan, and I know you returned her love." Hugging Jordan, the two men gave in to tears.

Releasing their arms, Neal slapped Jordan firmly on the back. "Okay, son, let's get the rest of these boxes packed. I've got to head back down to the island and find myself a house to buy. And you, young man, have the pleasant chore of telling my beautiful granddaughters they will now have their own house near their granddaddy. 'Course you know this means I'll expect to see them more often," Neal laughed, as he taped another box.

****

JEKYLL ISLAND, GEORGIA

George Watson was hammering inside the boat storage building, the sound reverberating off the aluminum walls. Neal called out to him a second time, waiting for his response.

"How do, Neal. So sorry to hear 'bout the missus," he said, taking the cap off his bald head. "Good to see you. How can I help you?"

"Well, George, my son has convinced me that I should still make the move down here and I guess he's right. I love this island and even though it's going to be tough being here without Louise, I'm going to give it a try." He put his right foot on a boat trailer and leaned forward on his knee. Looking out at the river, he seemed to be thinking of another world. "I do need your help, George. My son's going to buy the house on Dexter from me and I've got to find a smaller place. Know of anything?"

"Mmm, seems there was some guy here last week lookin' to sell over on Austin, I believe. Don't recall the details, but like the last time, you best talk to J.D. at the marina. Think he's over there now. Saw him unload a box 'o shrimp for the boil tonight."

Thoughts of the *Low Country Boil* made Neal realize how hungry he was getting. An egg sandwich at a fast food place on the way down didn't fill the space that usually accommodated a large breakfast. "Thanks, George. I'll walk over there and talk to him. Need to get some lunch, too. Can I buy you a sandwich?"

"No sir. Effie filled my lunch box with some 'o her homemade vegetable soup and corn muffins. I'm all set. Thanks anyway."

The smell of boiling shrimp met Neal's nose as he opened the snack bar door. Effie was mopping the floor behind the bar and did not hear him come in. "Hello there," he said, as Effie turned around, putting the wet mop back into its bucket home. "How are you, Mrs. Watson?"

"My, my, Mr. Park. This is a nice surprise. We weren't expecting you and Mrs. Park...oh, I'm sorry. Please 'scuse my rudeness. Guess my memory is starting to fail," she said, obviously embarrassed. "Do hope you're doin' well since she died. We was so sorry to hear 'bout that."

"Good as can be expected, Mrs. Watson. And how are you today?" He pulled out a bar stool and sat down.

"Fine, I s'pose. Just old age ills and the like, but can't complain. Can I fix you some lunch." She washed her hands and dried them on the ample white apron.

"Sure, got any crab salad today?" He liked the way they mixed it with celery and pickles. "And by the way, is J. D. here?"

J. D. Ryan, owner of the marina and a thriving Real Estate business, heard his name and came out from the kitchen. "Hi, Mr. Park." He reached out to shake Neal's hand from across the bar. "Sure sorry to hear about your wife's passing." He cleared his throat and in a halting manner asked, "You're still moving here, aren't you?"

"Think I am, J. D. My son's going to be taking the house though, so I need to find another one. Smaller, too." Effie put the crab salad plate in front of him and asked if he wanted a beer. "No, just give me a glass of tea. Thanks."

"What did you have in mind?" J. D. asked, sitting down on the stool next to Neal.

"George mentioned that there might be a place available on Austin. Know anything about it?"

"You bet. It's not near as big as the one you bought on Dexter, but it's about five lots from the ocean and has a smaller yard. Think its two bedrooms and two baths, and I seem to recall it has a real nice family room with a fireplace." He got up and drew a coke from the draught hose. Drinking it halfway down, he added, "The lease has about forty years to go. Think that will last you?" he laughed. "How 'bout we drive over and take a look."

"Sounds good. Let me finish this salad. Real good, Effie," he called out toward the kitchen where she was dipping shrimp out of a large stock pot.

J.D. Ryan drove a shiny blue Mustang convertible which he kept in top condition. "I must get five offers a week for this baby," he said, as they drove down Beachview Drive, the breeze blowing in their faces.

"Sure runs nice," Neal remarked, as he looked at the clean interior. "I might think about selling that monster of mine and getting something sportier." For the first time in many weeks, he was enjoying talking about the future.

Eight streets north of Dexter they turned right on Austin Lane. The Mustang purred as it pulled into the circle drive at 150. Noting that this owner obviously paid for frequent yard maintenance, he quickly felt relieved that serious yardwork would not be facing him here as it would at the Dexter house. "Let Jordan have that fun," he chuckled to himself.

J. D. opened the brick red front door and ushered Neal in to the slate covered foyer. Sunlight caught Neal's eye as he took a quick circular view of the entry. A large dining room with bay window was to his left, the kitchen beyond and a huge family or living room was open from the kitchen. Here a corner fireplace of white brick invited thoughts of crackling fires on cool winter evenings. Off the hallway was a small room suitable for Neal's office and two large bedrooms, each with it's own bath. The two car garage had storage space and a laundry area. "Probably not big enough for a woman's trappings, but I think this will fit my needs just fine," he said to J.D. as he looked up at the ceilings and down at the floors. "I really like all the light in here, help keep the mildew down," he laughed, catching J.D. laughing, too.

They both sat on the hearth and Neal took a small note pad from his jacket pocket. He made a few notes…"check shutter louvers, age of water heater, appliances in warranty…" and turned to ask J.D. a question just as the door bell rang.

"Wonder who that could be?" J. D. said as he headed to the door.

"Gut day, I'm Fritz Werner from next door. I see you have someone interested in buying zee house?"

"Uh, yes," J.D. said as he looked quizzically at this man who was obviously of German descent.

Without letting J.D. continue, the man immediately went into his own sales pitch. "Dis is gut house. Man who built it many years ago used zee best of materials. I know, 'cause I bin taking gut long looks at it for number of years. Anyone who buy dis house get a gut deal, I tell you."

Neal stepped forward and offered his hand. "Hi, I'm Neal Park, and I'm thinking seriously of making an offer on this house. Your good recommendations will certainly help me make that decision."

"Ya, gut. I so glad. Now I tell Momma we have nice neighbor. You have nice wife, too?"

Before Neal could answer, Fritz Werner continued. "Momma, she like to grow roses and bake strudel. I bring you some. When you be here next time?"

"Well, I suppose that depends on how long it takes to close, assuming my offer is accepted. Then I'll have to get myself packed and moved. You see, my wife recently passed away and I'll be living by myself."

"Oh, so sorry, sir." He bowed his head and patted Neal on the shoulder. "You be okay, you see. Momma and I take good care to see you be happy. Her strudel always helps. Say, you like sauerbraten, too? She make dat almost good as strudel. You Jewish?"

"No, Mr. Werner," Neal replied, sensing a bit of leftover hostility. "Just plain old Episcopalian. But *my momma* always told me we love everybody...all God's children." Neal said as he added, "And as I recalled, she cooked just about all kind of food, German, Jewish, Chinese, we ate it all."

All three of the men laughed as J. D. orchestrated a move toward the door. "Neal, I've got an appointment at four back at the office. Mind if I take you back to the marina now? Better still, let's both go to the office and I'll fax your offer."

As they backed out of the driveway, Neal and J.D. waved to Fritz and Hildegard Werner, she in her gardening clothes, he pushing a small lawn cart toward their garage.

"Seems like a nice chap, but I hope he doesn't think I'm up for adoption." The Mustang moved swiftly on to Beachview Drive and headed south. J.D. turned into his realty office in a strip shopping center that also housed the one large grocery story on the island. Neal made a mental note to check it out before he left. "It might be smart to bring some items down from Savannah."

The acceptance offer came back the next morning and Neal was delighted, if not suprised, that there were no changes, no negotiating to be done. He called Jordan and discussed all the details, down to the grocery store.

"Dad, you're beginning to sound domestic, old man. I think this change is going to be terrific for you. When you pick a moving day let me know and I'll see if I can get a few days away from here. It'd be kinda' nice to spend some time helping you and maybe we can even sneak in a bit of fishing off the marina pier one day."

Though happy to hear his son's enthusiasm, it nonetheless was overshadowed by his loneliness for Louise. Three months had passed since she left his side, but her presence was ever with him. He imagined he heard her coming in the door, he thought he could smell the fragrance of her favorite perfume as she walked through the room, he wished he could feel the warmth of her body as he tried to sleep at night. "Got to get out of this sad state, but dear Louise, know that you will always be in my heart." He closed his eyes and prayed for peaceful sleep that he might face tomorrow and the challenges of starting a life alone.

CHAPTER ELEVEN

Jordan and Lucretia followed Neal, pulling a trailer behind their car. The movers met them in Jekyll with the furniture and after moving it in, Neal unloaded the trailer. While he and Jordan found space to lean pictures against walls, Lucretia carefully unwrapped the crystal and china that Louise so dearly loved and used so frequently.

"Okay, men, it's time to stop for a bit and have some lunch," Lucretia called out as she spread mayonnaise on rye bread slices.

Wiping his hands on a towel and tossing it to Neal, Jordan pulled a chair out from the dining room table that was piled high with silver serving pieces Lucretia had been polishing. A chore that was usually relegated to her maid, Lucretia found it a pleasant experience, and with each piece she imagined in her mind some of the dinners when Louise used these beautiful examples of silver craftsmanship.

"Mmmm, ham and cheese on rye. My favorite," Neal said with gusto as he reached into the refrigerator and took out two beers. "Jordan, you join me in a beer with those fierce looking sandwiches?"

"Sure, Dad. Here, have a seat," he answered, pulling out another chair for Neal. Lucretia sat on a stool at the kitchen counter and was picking at the ham and cheese on her plate…no bread. She maintained a trim figure and constantly watched her calories. Taking a sip of white wine, she swallowed hard and jumped up from the stool.

"Look, there's a quail family crossing the back yard."

The three of them peered out the family room window as a female quail and her covey of babies waddled through the newly cut grass. "This is going to be fun," Neal remarked as he thought of the natural beauty and wildlife on Jekyll. "I think I just might stay." They all laughed and returned to their lunch. "Jordan, I've been thinking that

I'd like to take up scuba diving. Saw an article in the Jekyll paper about a class next month. George over at the marina told me they have that class a couple of times a year and the instructor comes up from Miami to teach."

Finishing his last swallow of beer, Jordan looked up with amazement. "Why Dad, that's a great idea. You're in a good place to search for treasure," he laughed. "But before you try anything that strenuous or different to your system, I want to schedule a physical for you at the hospital."

"No problem, Jordan, I'm due for one anyway. Let me get settled here and maybe in two or three weeks I'll drive on up and do it." Making a mental note to take his shopping list of things unavailable on the island, Neal was drawn back into the day as the telephone rang.

"This is Neal Park," he answered to the inquiry from the other end of the line. "Wow, that's pretty fast, but s'pose I could get myself together." He told the caller some of the details of the past three months in his life. "Give me your number and let me have a few hours to think this out."

Neal sat back down and put his head in his hands. "Oh, me. Didn't think the Bureau would call me so soon." He turned to Jordan, who was taking the last bite of his sandwich. "Son, I've been offered an assignment in New York City and have to be there next week."

"Gee, Dad, you haven't been up there for quite a while. The trip might do you good and you can always finish sorting things out here when you get back." Jordan rinsed his plate and put it in the dishwasher, giving Lucretia a swat on her backside as he passed.

"Jordan, your dad," she squealed, jumping at the slap.

"Him? I saw him do that to Mom a million times. We're old fanny patters in this family," he said with a mischievous tone in his voice.

94

Neal laughed at the playful twosome. "Yeh, guess you're right. It'll be here for me when I get back. Can't tell you the assignment, but it shouldn't take more than a month and I can still make that diving class."

****

NEW YORK CITY
The big jet came in over Long Island Sound, passed over Rikers Island and touched down at the end of the runway at LaGuardia Airport. Late March in New York was blustery, but the sun gave forth some warmth as he stood waiting for an available taxi. The driver's medallion certificate stated that he was from Iran. Religious medals were stuck to the dashboard and his clothes did not look like they came from Bloomingdale's.

Crossing over the East River on the Queensboro Bridge, the driver honked his horn, maneuvered through the traffic, and soon came to Fifth and Central Park South. Pulling under the canopy at the Plaza Hotel, the taxi driver reached his hand over the seat, waiting for Neal to pay his fare. A uniformed doorman opened the door and offered his hand to take Neal's hanging bag.

The opulence of the decor at the Plaza had always fascinated Neal and today was no exception. Fresh flowers were on every table and housekeepers were constantly dusting or sweeping the carpets with little sweepers. Heavy drapes trimmed with ornate braid adorned each window and the upholstered furniture in the public areas was subtly, but obviously, expensive. The owners prided themselves in maintaining the reputation of the finest hotel in New York, even with several new ones coming to the market this year.

Neal gave the desk clerk his credit card, now without the FBI logo, and filled out the registration form.

"We have a nice room for you on the eighth floor, Mr. Park. Front," called the clerk as he handed Neal's key to the bellman.

His room was nice. "If you consider $350 a night nice," he sighed. Figuring his expense account would just cover this, he thought the next visit might find him across the street at the Wyndham, a converted apartment building where the actors, Jessica Tandy and Hume Cronyn, still maintained an apartment. The assignment involved a group of merchants who rented space at the Plaza, but his staying nearby, rather than here, would not make any difference in his work.

Neal hung his extra suit in the tiny closet and put his other clothes in the mahogany chest of drawers. The sink top in the bathroom was too small for his shaving kit, so he put it on top of the chest, too. "Small, but nice, And only $350 a night!" he laughed. "I really should have reserved one of those $650 rooms," he thought to himself with another chuckle.

Treating himself to a cup of coffee and a piece of cheesecake in the Palm Court, Neal enjoyed the soft music of the pianist and watched the guests come and go. Leaving a generous tip for the waiter, he walked toward the shopping corridor on the south side of the lobby.

****

Unusual amounts of foreign money, specifically Asian, had been deposited on a daily basis from the Ming Li gift shop selling high priced jade jewelry and objects 'd art. The IRS and the bank were suspicious of other trading emanating from this shop, noting that inventory and sales did not equate to the large deposits. Neal's assignment was to find out why they were making these deposits and where the money was originating. Under normal circumstances, this assignment could have been handled by a local agent, even a rookie, but there was suspicion of narcotics dealing from the East and the bureau wanted a seasoned agent assigned.

Neal strolled down the corridor, looking into the highly decorated and lighted windows of each shop. Hermes, Versace, Vittadini,

Jaeger…all had their space in this corridor walked by the rich and famous, and all displayed their finest.

Halfway down the corridor was the Ming Li jade emporium. Incense drifted through the doorway and soft sounds of oriental string instruments filled the air. Neal stared at the delicately carved jade rings nestled in velvet cases that filled the windows. Backing up the rings were various carved jade pieces displayed on teak stands. The colors were varied from pale to dark green, pink, and lavender. No prices were attached to any of the items, leaving the shopper to assume their worth. Neal walked toward the next shop and decided to go back to his room and make notes on his first observance. He was about to enter the elevator, when he realized he needed a new city map. "Surely the concierge will have one," he thought as he crossed the lobby.

"Good afternoon, sir. May I be of service?" asked the beautiful redhead sitting at the heavily gilded concierge desk. Even behind the gold rimmed reading glasses, Neal could see her deep green eyes. Noticing her name tag, he replied. "Yes, thank you, Miss Rogers. I need a city map. Do you possibly have one for a tourist from Savannah?" As yet he did not think of himself as a Jekyll resident.

"Savannah, Georgia, sir?" she asked, a slight southern drawl in her speech.

"Yes, you ever been there?"

"Been there? Why I was born there a *few* years ago," she laughed.

"Really," Neal said. "I grew up there. My dad was a cotton broker and then later I came back and worked there, too."

"This is too coincidental," she said, the green eyes flashing. "My father was also a cotton broker. "I'm Andrea Rogers. My father was John Lawrence Stanley."

"You don't mean it," Neal sputtered. "Little Andrea Stanley. The skinny little kid we all chased into the fish house at the end of the wall? I'm Neal Park, one of the chasers."

"You don't mean that," she mocked. "That seems so long ago. Well, guess it was, because I left there when I married and never returned."

They stared at each other with a mix of disbelief and curiosity.

"If I'm not being too presumptuous, would you like to join me for a drink when you finish work? Or do you need to get home to a husband and family?" He noticed the dinner ring on her left hand and wondered if it was a modern wedding ring...or a dinner ring.

"Neal, that would be nice. And no, I don't have husband or family waiting for me. Don't know if you remember Danny Rogers who was two years ahead of me in school, but we married right before he went to Viet Nam. Sadly he was killed, so I moved up here and never went back to Savannah except to visit." She nervously shuffled some papers on her desk and opening a drawer pulled out a map of New York. "This should help you find your way around the city. Is this your first visit?"

"Oh, no," he answered. I've been here on business and holiday several times, but I may need to find some unfamiliar places in my present assignment." He took the map and a pleasurable look at her stylish *basic black dress with pearls.* She was about fifteen years younger than he as best he could remember, and from the looks of it she had taken good care of herself. "What time do you finish?"

Elegantly tall, she stood up and walked around to the front of her desk. Extending her hand, she said, "I can meet you here about seven, if that suits you. My relief arrives about that time and after a few minutes wrap-up, I can leave."

He shook her hand, gave a slight bow of his head, and said, "I look forward to catching up on some stories of your life since Savannah. And, if it's not too boring, I'll tell you mine."

"Oh by the way, Neal, is your wife with you? Perhaps she could join us." Andrea did notice a ring on his left hand.

Looking down at that left hand, Neal said, "Oh, uh, I just haven't taken if off yet." He paused, realizing this was the first time he would be sharing company with a woman since Louise died, and continued. "Louise died three months ago. I'll fill you in on the details later."

****

Locking the door behind him, Neal's eyes were drawn to an envelope on the floor that someone had obviously slid under the door. He kicked off his shoes and sat down in the chair next to the television. Opening the envelope he noticed the lack of a return address and the fact that only his name and room number were on the front. "Curious, wonder where this came from?"

Inside the envelope were newspaper articles from cities around the world. All the stories dealt with current news of attempts by drug traders to conceal illegal shipments through over 250 ports of entry in at least 75 countries, the United States being one of the countries most used by the traffickers to circumvent high-tech tools now being developed. Traders were documenting legal exports that included drug shipments passed on and sold by merchants operating legitimate businesses.

Neal spread the articles out on the bed, arranging them by date. In between two stories from Boston was a slip of paper with a telephone number, but no name. "Obviously someone knows I'm here and they want me to have this information. This is not standard Bureau tactics."

CAROL SUE RAVENEL

Checking his watch, he decided to get in touch with his contact after his meeting with Andrea. Curiosity was overridden by the thought of a new social experience in his life. "Feels strange, taking a woman other than Louise out for a drink. Been a long time since I've done this." He gathered up the papers, put them back in the envelope and went into the bathroom to freshen up. The telephone rang. "Always happens when my mouth is full of toothpaste."

"Hello." He was reticent to say his name.

"Mr. Park, Neal Park?" said the husky voice on the other end.

"Uh, yes," Neal answered, with a faint recollection of the sound of the voice. "Who's this?"

Coughing spasms came through the line as the voice answered. "Guess you don't remember your old buddy, Harry Watts."

"My word, Harry. How have you been and where have you been the last few years?" Neal asked, recalling his interrogation instructor who loved his cigars.

"Retired several years ago, but like you, they call us old bucks back for the good deals." He laughed between coughs. "Didn't want to reveal myself in the envelope, but I've been following this stuff for quite some time."

"I can see that by the dates, Harry. Say, I've got a date in a few minutes, can I call you back in a couple of hours?" It was close to seven.

"A date? You and that cute Louise split? And what kind of a date is only a couple of hours?" He laughed again between coughs.

"Got a lot to tell you, Harry. First being that my darling Louise died a few months ago and this date is with the daughter of one of my father's associates. Just a drink, Harry, nothing more." Reaching his foot under the bed for his shoes, he continued. "Let me give you all the details later, okay?"

"Fine, Neal. I'm across the street from you at the Wyndham. By the way, we're on this project together. See 'ya, buddy."

"Key in pocket, hair combed, tie straight. Guess I'll do."
He pushed the elevator button and felt exhilarated with the thought of another project and his first date since Louise died.

****

He sipped a vodka martini, she sipped Chardonnay. The conversation was simple, each telling the other about their lives since growing up in Savannah. Neal felt uncomfortable and kept expecting Louise to appear and join them. "Perhaps she has," he thought to himself. He stared into Andrea's green eyes and a sense of approval swept over him. He even thought he smelled Louise's favorite perfume in the air. "Ah, dear Louise, I'll get on with it like you would want me to, but it's not going to be easy." At that moment he wished he were walking the beach at Jekyll.

"Neal, Neal. 'Scuse me," Andrea asked. "You seem in another world there, may I join you?"

Jerking himself into the present, he apologized. "Sorry. I was just thinking about all I have to do when I get back to the island. Don't think I really appreciated all Louise did when we made all those moves."

"Yes, I understand. Guess FBI moves are a lot like the military," she offered, thinking about the few short years she shared with Danny before his Navy jet crashed one day as he was headed to participate in another sortie over Korea.

Neal looked at his watch. "Wow, didn't realize it was so late. I hate to end the evening, but I have an important call to make and intended to be back in my room by nine."

"That's fine with me," Andrea said as she stood up and put her coat over her arm. "I have a group coming in early tomorrow from Spain and it's imperative that I be here to greet them and take the VIPs to their suites."

Taking the back of her chair, Neal paused for a moment. "Andrea, I really enjoyed being with you. May I possibly have the honor of taking you to dinner tomorrow night?"

"Only if we can go early and you let me take you to see Gregory Hines in *JELLY'S LAST JAM*. I have some comp tickets and want to review it before I suggest it to the guests. Just part of the job," she laughed.

"Great. I read that it's supposed to be a movin' production with lots of fast music and tap dancing and I really like that."

They walked out to the sidewalk and he hailed a taxi. Helping her in, he said, "I'll come down to get you about six. That should give us time for dinner and time enough to get to the theatre."

She squeezed his hand as she got in and gave him a big smile.

"I haven't felt like this in a long time. Oh, forget it Neal, she's much too young, and besides, she lives 750 miles away." He walked back to the Plaza and called Harry.

****

For ten days Neal spent his days with Harry and his evenings with Andrea. The drug trafficking project brought three rings to light, and with Harry and Neal's efforts enabled the Bureau to arrest several barons and their associates, mostly from the Orient. The costly jade sculptures at the Ming Li shop were quickly replaced with mass produced souvenir pieces, several of the staff were replaced with new faces, and the shop extended their hours of operation. Obviously they were now dependent on legitimate means of income.

In ten days, Neal had been cautious in showing his feelings for this beautiful and charming redhead. She was also guarded in allowing her emotions to surface in his presence. Andrea and Neal tried different restaurants each night, went to plays and concerts, and window shopped along Fifth Avenue. His last night in New York Andrea invited him to her apartment for dinner. He discovered she was not only an excellent cook…the coq au vin was superb…but she also had a unique flair for decorating. She had turned a very plain one bedroom apartment on 82nd Street into a well appointed and warm home.

"If you're finished doing whatever you're doing in that kitchen, I think there's a vacant space on this sofa waiting for you," Neal said, his anticipation for her nearness intensifying.

She hung her apron on a hook behind the door and turned off the light. Sliding in next to him, she heard the soft music he had found on the radio. Gazing into his eyes, she felt a magnetism so long forgotten, as there had been few serious men in her life since Danny died. Gently appraising her, Neal took her face in his hands, raised it to his and drew her lips to his. Locked in a passionate challenge, he was finding it hard to resist fulfilling his desires.

"Andrea, you are one tempting lady," he said as he slowly released his arms from around her. "I'm not going to fool myself and think that I don't want to go back, but…"

She put her hand to his mouth. "No, Neal. Just take the moment. This has been a wonderful ten day interlude in my life and who knows, perhaps you'll come back soon or maybe I'll make it down to Jekyll someday."

Yielding to their common desire and passion, Andrea and Neal savored the next few hours, both secretly hoping that the future would bring more moments…and memories.

CHAPTER TWELVE

JEKYLL ISLAND, GEORGIA

A knock on the door quickly jolted Neal out of a sound sleep. The clock read eight thirty. "Wonder who's here so early?" The flight from LaGuardia had been late into Savannah and the drive to Jekyll got him to the little house on Austin at two in the morning.

"Gut mornin'," said Hildegard, holding out a platter of warm rolls as he opened the door.

"Hello, Mrs. Werner. You're delivering mighty early," he said as he tied his robe.

"Ya, jus want you to have some of my gut rolls. They made with apricot and cheese, gut for you, too." She put them in his hands and turned to go back next door. "Oh, Verner say he help you move dat picnic table today. He in town getting me some flour."

The Werners had made Neal their special project and were always nearby...sometimes too near for Neal's liking, but they were pleasant people and he enjoyed their company. Hildegard was grateful for the jade bracelet he brought to her from New York and it made him feel good to return some of their generosity.

****

A seaman in Hitler's Navy, Fritz never adopted Nazi philosophy and planned for the day he could leave the Motherland. Poor eyesight prevented him from advancing to duty aboard U-Boats, causing him to spend the latter part of the war in an accounting position. Werner and Hildegard were married in 1946 and fled to the States after the Communists took over Berlin. "Dey vurse dan Nazis," Fritz would mumble under his breath.

They settled in Savannah where Fritz worked as a controller at Mason Cotton Mills. Hildegard worked in a bakery three mornings a week and took care of their two grandsons most afternoons. Their daughter, Cristel, was married to Thomas Holpath, the son of a wealthy fish merchant from Savannah. Supplying fish to hotels and fine restaurants from Charleston to Jacksonville, Holpath Fisheries was the largest supplier on the Southeast Coast and Thomas was being groomed to take over the business when his father retired.

Fritz's eyes became progressively weaker and his doctor advised retiring from his accounting job and finding something less strenuous to his eyes. Hildegard and Fritz had often discussed moving to Jekyll, having visited there many times on holiday. Always interested in having a well landscaped and cared-for yard, Werner accepted a job at the Jekyll Island Club Hotel as a gardener. Hildegard was happy with the little duplex they bought on Austin Drive, and in true German fashion, kept it neat and clean. Mornings found her sweeping the sidewalks and the driveways while her yeast dough rose in the kitchen.

The Werner's rented the other side of their duplex, mostly to friends from Germany, who, like themselves, had fled the Communist regime. Sounds of polka music and hearty laughter could frequently be heard from the house when a gathering of countrymen were on the island. Hildegard made schnitzel and special desserts, Fritz found sources for German beer and wine from a friend in Savannah. The Werner home was the center of social activity for friends and tourists alike of German descent and often they would invite Neal to join their happy group. He usually declined, as most of the conversation was in German and most of the guests older than he.

****

Neal's application for diving class was waiting in his stack of mail when he returned from New York. He sent it back with a check and made a trip to Savannah the next week to purchase the items listed necessary for participation. "Mask, fins, jacket, regulator, dive

106

computer, wetsuit, hooded vest, gloves...guess I have it all." He wrote the check, gathered his purchases, and loaded the bags into the trunk of his car. "One more thing. I've got to find a store that sells zodiaks." He had seen others using these inflatable dinghys and hoped George at the marina could help him. "This car won't hold much more...maybe I should think about something new." Picturing in his mind J.D.'s spiffy blue Mustang he knew that would never do. "Unless I don't do this diving thing," he laughed to himself. "Ah, maybe I'll just find an old pickup truck."

****

CHARLESTON, SOUTH CAROLINA
Jordan had scheduled the physical for a Tuesday morning which gave Neal time to drive up Sunday evening and spend time with Annabelle and Caroline, the lights of his life. Always ready to spoil his granddaughters, Neal filled the car trunk with toys and snacks that he knew were their favorites. While they were in school Monday, he planned to spend time with Lucretia, giving her some of Louise's jewelry from their safety deposit box.

"Dad, are you sure you want to part with these?" Lucretia asked as she carefully fondled the necklaces and earrings he had placed in her hands.

"Yes, Mom would have wanted you to have them and I know you'll pass them on to the girls someday. Just cherish them as she did, some of that stuff was her grandmother's." He reached in his back pocket for a handkerchief and wiped the tears from his eyes. "You might want some of that silver and china, too. Goodness knows, I'll probably never use it."

"How do you know, you might someday have a new lady in your life...one who would enjoy using those things?" she asked, a grin on her face.

Fleeting thoughts of Andrea crossed his mind and he momentarily wondered how she was today.

The physical took four hours and he felt like he had been picked, prodded, and looked at by the entire medical staff. Jordan had orchestrated a very thorough examination and as Neal was leaving he greeted him with good news.

"Well, old man, looks like we've got to put up with you for a long time to come. You're in excellent health and should have no problem competing with the young divers. By the way, I understand a lot of women are taking those classes these days," he laughed as he escorted his father to the parking lot. "Who knows what this new adventure might lead to."

"Jordan, what's with you and Lucretia? You anxious to dump me on some poor widow's doorstep or something?"

"Just having some fun with you, Dad. Now take it easy on the way back to Jekyll and thanks for the girls' presents…you always do too much."

Starting the car, Neal leaned out the window, "My pleasure, Doc."

Rain peppered the windshield as he turned off I-95 at Darien and picked up State Road 17 toward the island. Neal's thoughts drifted back to his ten days in New York and made a mental note to call Andrea when he got home. As he drove over the island causeway he decided to see if Effie had any of the evening's boil left. "Some shrimp and corn would sure taste good right now. Didn't realize I forgot to eat lunch after that session with the witchdoctors."

"Hello there, Mr. Park. How's that house shapin' up? You all unpacked?" She piled shrimp high in a bowl and put it in front of him. Drawing a beer from the draft tube, she asked, "Will you be havin' some of my corn bread with that?"

"Mmm, sounds good, Effie. And do you have some sauce nearby?"

"Sure thing, Mr. Park. You just about missed dinner tonight didn't you? We close in another hour."

Peeling a large pink shrimp, he dipped it in the sauce and was about to take a sip of his beer when he felt a large hand on his shoulder. He whirled around on the bar stool to face J.D.

"Hey, buddy. What you doin' out on a messy night like this?" J. D. asked.

"Been up to see my family in Charleston. Jordan arranged a physical for me before I start that diving school next week. Say, what's the instructor's name? I forgot."

"Bill Moss. He owns the Key Largo School of Diving down on the Keys. He'll be here Sunday night, ready for you guys Monday morning." Pulling out a stool, he shouted into the kitchen, "Hey, Effie, got any more shrimp?"

Neal drank the last of his beer and asked J.D. to tell him about Bill Moss.

"Well, he's owned that school down there since he finished high school in Miami and that was many a year ago," he laughed. "I think the guy must be in his late fifties, at least. But, boy howdy, he has the greatest reputation. Those classes fill up right fast and I hear tell he's a tough teacher. No monkey business. Your five days with him will be worth a month with anybody else in the water."

"I'm really looking forward to this, J. D...and hope I can keep up with the younger guys."

"Hey, man, you'll do fine," J.D. said as he got up to leave. "Gotta go. Got a cruiser comin' in from New York tomorrow and they want some maintenance before they head down the Intracoastal to Palm

Beach. Some big wigs from Spain, I hear. Need to give George a hand with this one."

"No," Neal thought. "Couldn't be the VIPs from Spain that Andrea was working with." Neal jumped up and ran to catch J.D. "Forgot to ask you, do you know where I might get a zodiak?"

"Yeh, as a matter of fact. I've got one in the shed that some rich guy bought for his sons last summer. They left it here when they went back north. Said to keep it for helping them get it launched. All we did was put the air in it. You can have it. Just needs a hosing down, pretty dusty."

****

"Well good evening, pretty lady," Neal said as she answered the telephone.

"Neal. How wonderful to hear your voice. I've been thinking about you and wondering if you've gotten all unpacked and when do you start that diving class?" she asked with rapid eagerness in her voice.

"The unpacking is finally finished. Didn't realize we had accumulated so much, but guess about forty years of buying stuff adds up before you know it. I thought moving helped us get rid of all that, guess not," he laughed. "Lucretia and Jordan were a tremendous help, couldn't have done it without them. How're you doing?"

"Fine. Spring and early summer are always busy here in the city, and despite various strikes we manage to carry on the day-to-day business without too much disruption. At the moment the taxi drivers are threatening to stop driving. Guess I'll gas up my old car that's in storage and make a few extra dollars," she said with a giggle.

"Say, Andrea, those Spanish guests you were receiving the day after I left, do you know if they were heading south, possibly down the Intracoastal Waterway in a cruiser?"

"That's funny. How do you know about that?"

"Well, the guy who owns the marina told me about them tonight and I thought it would be a real coincidence."

"No coincidence, Neal. They told me their plans and I suggested they make a stop at Jekyll. They invited me to join them, but though I was tempted, the ratio of me with five men didn't seem too smart."

"You are an interesting lady, know that? Anyway, though I'd have been glad to see you, I don't think I would have been too happy sharing you with five other men."

Smiling, she said, "Do I detect a bit of jealousy, Mr. Park?"

"Oh no, not me," he said, as he wished she was at his side. "Say, I'm going to be tied up for a few weeks with this class and then some painting and stuff I want to do around here, but why don't you try to take some vacation time later this summer and come on down here?"

They talked for another half hour. Yawning into the telephone, she said, "Neal, I think we better sign off. I have an early staff meeting tomorrow and it's almost midnight. Anyway, if I have to drive my taxi, too, it's going to be a busy day."

"Okay, pretty lady. Think of me tucking you in and have a good night's sleep."

"Good night, Neal. I'll think about your invitation." She blew a kiss into the telephone and hung up.

****

"Okay, any of you guys smoke, I suggest you quit during this class...or for good if you want to keep diving. You're gonna need all the breath you can get. And for starters, you can all jog one mile down the beach and back before we get into today's session."

Bill Moss barked orders like a Marine sergeant and had the build of one as well. Tall, muscular arms and legs, and no visible fat anywhere on his body, his hair in a crew cut, he hoisted a huge duffel bag over his shoulder and made his way to the end of the boardwalk area on the south end of the island. Moss carefully laid out six sets of books four feet from each other. In front of these arrangements he built a dais of fallen palm limbs and drift wood from which he would *lecture*. Neal thought later that if he could have made a pulpit he would have. "This man means business," Neal said to himself as he and the other five pupils gasped their way to their designated spots.

"Men, before you are books that tell you how to dive. I am going to *show* you how to dive. It's like playing golf. You can read lots of *how to* books, but until you start hitting that ball, you ain't played golf."

The next two hours they read through each of the books, scanning most of the written words, and as ordered, paying more attention to the drawings. Breaking for a half-hour lunch, Neal was glad Moss had brought some of Effie's sandwiches so he wouldn't be tempted to go home and take a quick nap. Four o'clock came soon and the exhausted six gathered up their gear and limped to their cars. Afternoon break had included another jog down the beach. "Boy, am I out of shape," Neal thought as he contemplated dropping out of this *army*. "No, I made a commitment, I'll stick."

The entire next day was spent learning terms, use of equipment, and safety measures. Neal wondered when they would get in the water, even if it was still fairly cold. "Maybe I should have signed up for an August class." His question was answered, when as Moss was handing out sandwiches he announced, "Tomorrow we dive, gentlemen."

They looked like six big, black, frogs, especially with their masks in place. They walked single file to the end of the dock and Moss watched as each of them entered their zodiaks and pushed off. Paddling out a quarter of a mile, they listened for Moss' whistle signaling the dive. Neal made sure his mask was secure, the regulator and tank in place. Over the side he went, slowly submerging into the murky Atlantic water. "Hope I can remember all Moss' instructions." After the allotted underwater time, Neal began his climb to the top…and real air. He bobbed up right next to Moss' zodiak.

"Good job, Park. You did the first dive in exactly the right time. Pat your butt with your fin. Ha, ha."

The next two days Neal felt more confident and began to think this was not as difficult as he had thought. "But I think for a while I'll just dive close to home…around this island," said his cautious self.

Friday afternoon, as a late spring storm was moving in, Moss arranged his pupils in a circle on the beach, facing the ocean. He paced up and down in front of them, Patton fashion, then circled around them. Stopping in front of Neal, he pulled a plastic gift tube from his hip pocket and popped Neal on the head with the tip of it. "You, sir, are our star student."

Neal looked up. "What does that mean?"

"It means, Park, that you are number one in the class and this certificate entitles you to an advanced class at the Key Largo School of Diving, should you ever get that far south. Ha, ha."

"Thank you, sir."

They toasted each other with warm beer and packed up their gear. No apparent long-lasting friendships were made. Each seemed happy that they learned to dive, and happier yet for the class to end.

Neal told J.D. that he enjoyed the class and Moss was a good teacher. He did not elaborate on his sternness or strange sense of humor, especially after J.D. told him they were cousins.

CHAPTER THIRTEEN

The morning sun shone through the glass doors, shadows from the sheer curtains giving illusion of clouds on the family room carpet. Neal finished the last piece of Hildegard's weekly pastry offering and put his plate in the dishwasher. "Almost full, guess I'll have to run a load tonight," he said, closing the door and reaching for a dish cloth. It took three or four days for him to fill the appliance, as he studiously avoided washing dishes in the sink. "Another reason I really miss you, Louise," he thought. During their life together she rarely called on him for help in the kitchen, preferring to do those chores herself.

Louise's mahogany grandfather clock had fit perfectly in the hallway across from Neal's office and was now striking eight, its clear tones none the worse for so many moves during their marriage. "I'd better throw my gear in the car and head for the beach if I'm going to practice what I learned last week," he murmured, recalling the intense, yet satisfying, diving class with Bill Moss. Eager to try his newfound skills under the sea, Neal took his diving equipment off the garage shelves, placed it in the trunk of the car, and went back into the house. The telephone was ringing as he came in.

"Neal, George here at the marina."

"Morning, George. What can I do for you?" Neal asked.

"Some ferin' fellas from somewheres abroad…Spain I think, was here yesterday and left a package for ya. Thought ya might wanna stop by an pick it up soon. Got a fancy wrappin' on it." He gave a chuckle into the telephone.

"Thanks, George. I'll probably drop by this afternoon. I was just on my way to the beach. Goin' to try some diving." Knowing that the package had to be from Andrea, Neal made a mental note to go by the marina later today…"right about dinner time and I'll have some of Effie's low country boil."

115

****

He parked the car on the shoulder of the road near a path through the sea oats and other beach vegetation. Prickly plants scratched his legs as he made his way down to the beach. Checking each piece of diving gear before he put them on, Neal felt good doing something new.

He walked to the water's edge, put on his fins and walked slowly out into the surf, choosing not to go out in the zodiac this time. The sun was warm and the water sparkled as he went under. Visibility was not as good as he would have liked, the movement of the surf having created a murky situation, but he swam on out and kept going deeper as he swam. After about five minutes and a depth of thirty feet, Neal checked the compass to get his bearings. "I want to stay fairly close to shore," he thought to himself with a slight fear of being alone on this first dive since class. It was easier to see at this depth and he enjoyed watching the antics of sea urchins and other creatures he'd only seen in photographs. A school of mackerel passed within six feet of him and he saw fins of some dolphins.

Approaching a large outcropping of rocks, he saw what looked like a square piece of wood, wedged between two very large rocks. Swimming closer he realized it was some sort of box. He could now see that it was a metal box, not wood. He reached down and tried to free it from its prison. The box would not budge. Still harder he tried, pushing the box, while at the same time trying to move the rocks. Finally one rock moved slightly and he was able to change the position of the box, but still it held hard to its place. Time was catching up with him and he knew he would have to surface immediately. Putting his foot on one rock and his hand on the other, he gave one last shove and the box came free. He put it under his arm and made an attempt to surface using his legs and the fins for motion.

Neal popped to the surface facing the bright sun and rolled on to his back. The effort expended in freeing the box had taxed his energy and he took a few moments to catch his breath. "Whew, sure hope there's buried treasure in here after all that," he laughed to himself. He made his way back to the beach, walked on to the sand and slipped the fins from his feet. He sat there for a few minutes just staring at the box which was about eight inches long, eight inches wide and three inches deep. It had German markings and writing on the lid.

"My God," Neal choked, "this could be from a sunken U-Boat." He recalled that many were sunk in Atlantic waters during World War II. "If it's that old, I'd better get it back in water to keep it from rusting." He ran to his car, took out a styrofoam cooler he kept in the trunk for beer and sodas, and took it back to the beach. Filling it with beach water, he placed the box inside and put the lid on securely. Not knowing if his thoughts were true, he felt it wouldn't hurt to make the effort to preserve his find. "Ah, it's probably just a piece of junk one of those German tourists threw overboard." Still, he carefully carried the cooler back to the car. Little did he know that the parcel he carried had been in the sea for over fifty years.

Neal lowered the garage door before he opened the car trunk. Gingerly lifting the lid on the cooler, he studied the top of the box. *OL G. PRIE* was barely visible under the faded swastika. He had forgotten most of his German from college and immediately thought of asking Fritz to take a look at the box. "No, I've got to think this out. I'm not sure how he would react, considering his feelings for the Nazis. And a lot depends on what's in the box."

He placed the cooler on top of his workbench and went in to the house. Most men's normal curiosity would have seen the box opened. Neal's FBI training taught him to evaluate the situation first and act second. "I'll leave it there until I get back from the marina," he said to himself as he went back outside and to the mailbox. "Looks like nothing but bills today. Had hoped for a letter from Jordan." The father and son were planning a few days of fishing and Jordan was to let him know the dates he could be away from patients and hospital. His practice had grown rapidly in the past few years, and though he liked the increased income, he held to keeping time for himself. In between two pieces of junk mail Neal found Jordan's letter.

Dear Dad,

Checked my schedule today and it looks like I can come down next Tuesday and Wednesday. I'll try to leave early Tuesday so we can fish all afternoon. Maybe you can show me how to dive, too. Put some beer on ice and buy baloney and bread for sandwiches! Lucretia and the girls send their love. The girls are trying to find ways to tag along. Sorry, this is our time, Dad.

Love, Jordan

"Hooray, he's going to come down," Neal said out loud. Still not used to living alone, he frequently spoke out loud as if Louise was within hearing distance. "I'd better check the larder and get some groceries in." He quickly thought of getting out the fishing poles and locating some diving gear for Jordan.

Neal tossed the rest of the mail on the kitchen desk and headed for the bathroom and a much needed shower. "Think I'll take a nap before I head over to the marina. I've got a lot to get ready for Jordan's visit. Let's see, beer, baloney, bread and bait. And in that order," he laughed to himself, as the warm water flowed over his newly tanned back. Yardwork and the beach had added color to his formerly pale complexion. He threw the towel into the clothes hamper and laid across the unmade bed. A cool breeze blew in the window and in a few minutes he was deep in sleep.

The ringing door bell woke him and he quickly pulled his terry bathrobe on as he headed for the front door. There stood Hildegard, her hands holding a casserole of pork and sauerkraut. "Thought you'd like some kraut and pork for dinner," she said as she raised the dish to him. "You need some hearty food."

"Thanks, Hildegard. I was going to eat at the marina tonight, but this sure smells tempting. You are just too good to me."

"Is gut to be gut to you, Neal. You gut friend to me and Fritz." She turned and walked through the grass to her house next door, waving as she left.

"Didn't realize I slept so long." The clock was striking five and he decided it would be a good idea to have a drink, eat Hildegard's meal, and watch some TV. Then he remembered the package at the marina. "Oh well, that kraut will be good for lunch tomorrow." He dressed in khakis and a black turtleneck shirt and locking the door, went into the garage. He stared at the cooler and started to open it, his hand reaching for the lid. "No. I'll have dinner and do this when I get back, or maybe tomorrow when I'm not so tired."

J.D. was sitting at a corner table with some tourists. Neal noticed the maps they had spread out and decided they were getting directions for water travel. Their laughter gave him a feeling of loneliness and he suddenly realized how little socializing he had experienced in recent weeks, compared with how he had lived for so many years. If not being with co-workers, he and Louise were with friends. They had a full social calendar and he now missed that part of his past. "I'm going to call Andrea tonight and get her down here soon."

Effie's dinner was consistently tasty and filling, and after two beers and second helpings on his plate, he felt satisfied. He was about to pay and leave, when Effie appeared from the kitchen with a large piece of key lime pie. "Neal, looks like you just might need a piece o' my pie. Baked it this mornin' and we haven't been too busy tonight, so you got to help me finish it. Don't keep too long, ya know, with all those eggs."

"Effie, I swear, you're gonna put pounds on me yet. After all that shrimp I just ate, I'll need the whole bottle of Tums," he said, as he put his fork into the fluffy meringue. "Mmmm, this is too good for words."

Neal was almost out the door when he remembered the package. "Effie, George said those men from Spain left a package here for me. You know where it might be?"

"Right here, Neal. Been keepin' it under the counter 'til you came round." She handed him a large, square box wrapped in shiny red paper, tied with blue and white ribbons.

"Wow, looks like Fourth of July. Come to think of it, that's just around the corner, huh," he said as he took the box and walked out to the deck and over the shell and gravel drive to his car. The island evening was warm with a slight breeze and he looked for stars as he drove down Beachview Drive.

Neal stared at the cooler as he passed his workbench. Again, he lifted the lid and peered at the mysterious box. "Like Scarlett...I'll think about that tomorrow." He went to bed.

****

The bacon was frying as Neal whisked eggs and added salt and pepper. He transferred the bacon to a paper towel, put the eggs in the skillet, and buttered toast while the eggs cooked. He poured a cup of coffee and sat down at the counter, reading the morning newspaper as he ate his breakfast.

His mind wandered as he looked out the window at bluebirds round a feeder. His curiosity over the box's contents was heightening as he went out to the garage. "Okay, now or never," he said as he lifted the lid and gently took the box in his hands. Using an old towel, he dried it, being careful not to rub off the markings.

Akin to lifting a baby, he cautiously put his fingers on the lid of the box and raised the rusty and corroded steel top. To his surprise, the inside was totally dry, attesting to the tightness of the container. Taking a deep breath, Neal looked at the contents and gently lifted each one out, placing it on a dry towel.

First he took out a small, black velvet box, deciding to open it when he had retrieved all of the intriguing matter within the confines of this watery coffin. Next was a lace edged, linen handkerchief embroidered with the initial "P". Under these were a dozen folded pieces of paper that appeared to be letters all stuffed into one envelope. He picked up the velvet box, the nap falling off into his hands. "This must be very old and the air is causing disintegration," he thought as he put his thumb and forefinger around the top. Opening the box, he was stunned to gaze upon a very beautiful gold ring set with two small pearls and flanked by two deep red rubies. Taking it from its satin bed, he looked for an inscription. One had been there, but time or a woman's finger had obviously worn it to invisibility and it was too faint for identification. Almost afraid to put his hands on the handkerchief again for fear of it falling apart, he went to his desk and found a large manila envelope into which he slid the cloth. The lace was surprisingly white and the intial showed the marks of hand stitching.

Neatly wrapped in a piece of thin paper much like tissue, was a photograph of a young girl who appeared to be in her late teens. Though faded, the picture showed her with dark blond or light brown hair and a happy smile. It looked like she was in a garden setting and on the back of the photo was written *Cyn...1..9.* Neal next studiously took time to unfold the first piece of paper from the envelope. Fully opened, the paper was a piece of 6"x9" stationery with the faded initials "GP" at the top. He ascertained that they may have been originally in black, but were now a very light brown. The ink was equally, if not more faded, and the words were hardly legible. Neal put all of them in a box top he found in the garage and took them into the kitchen where he had brighter light.

Spread before him on the dining table he searched for something decipherable that might help him identify either the sender or intended recipient. A few words...*Lieberhaber*...this he knew was the partial of *lover*...a partial paragraph referring to a *project...the farm*...and in several places he made out the letters *Sud*. Could that be a person, a place, was it the girl in the garden? Was the partial name of *Prie*...the same as the initial on the handkerchief? And surely the initials on the letterhead were the same. But who were these letters to? And who was *OL G. Prie*...? He remembered that *OL* was German abbreviation for *Oberleutnant*, a senior lieutenant. At the top of some of the letters he could make out the date "1942". Neal pondered all this and tried to use his investigative skills to make some sense of his find. He kept looking at the letters and found a very faint *Dear Cyn...,* but no more in the name. On one letter were last letters of a name or place...*beck* and another seemed to make referrence to an airfield in England...*at the base in Lav...in U.K.*

Neal found a framed print of which he had never been fond and took the glass out of the frame. He cleaned it well and placed it over the letters, hoping to protect them until he could make out more of the contents. Locating a small silver framed picture of himself from Louise's collection, he removed his photo and slipped the girl's picture under the glass for safekeeping.

Finding it hard to get to sleep that night he got up and went back to the table. He made a list of the words that were legible and planned to make a concentrated effort to solve this puzzle. The clock struck two and he decided to make another attempt to sleep. Glancing across the room he saw the package from Andrea. "I almost forgot about that," he said, as he put it on the kitchen counter and began to untie the ribbons. "Boy, almost like Christmas. First the box and now Andrea's present."

Lifting the top, he found two cups emblazoned with gold crests of the Plaza Hotel. "For our morning coffee," read the attached card. Also in the box was a package of sparklers. "For making some sparks fly next time we're together," read this card. He wanted to call her, but it was after two and he knew she would be asleep. "Gosh, I really miss her. Should I tell her about the box?" he thought as he poured a glass of milk. "No, not yet. Gotta think this out. Anyway, it could just be mementos lost by one of our German tourists." The milk helped and he soon fell asleep.

****

Despite the approaching visit of Jordan, Neal was preoccupied with finding out the who, what, where, and why of his find. He drove to Brunswick and spent Saturday morning at the library searching German and English maps. His efforts brought forth fruit as he ascertained that...*beck* could possibly be Lubeck, which was only thirty miles from Kiel, the largest naval installation in Germany, and home to U-Boat fleets during World War II. This would be good information, providing the find had been from a sunken U-Boat, and not a German tourist. On the English side, he checked World War II airbases and the one that seemed to fit *Lav...* was Lavenham, not far from *Sud...* Sudbury. But the names were still a mystery. He wrote all this in a spiral bound notebook and put it, with several books on U-Boats and the war, in a backpack that he had taken to using lately. His next effort would be to identify the correlation between Lubeck and Lavenham. A sense of anxiety and anticipation flooded his spirit and he was feeling fulfilled for the first time since Louise died. Even meeting Andrea had not had this same effect on him in lifting his despair. But she had made it interesting. "Better call her when I get home."

CHAPTER FOURTEEN

Jordan's visit gave Neal the chance to tell him about the find and ask for his suggestions on how he should follow up to find the recipient of the contents...or, if he should even attempt to do this. Between baiting hooks and making dives, the two men stayed deep in conversation. The two days went by far too quickly for Neal and he sorely wished his son could stay longer.

Jordan dropped his travel bag on the floor near the kitchen door and sat down at the kitchen counter, where Neal had just placed two plates of macaroni and cheese. "Not much of a cook, but I do stay healthy, thanks in part to Hildegard's rich pastry and other goodies."

"This is fine, Dad. We eat a lot of macaroni and cheese. You know how much the girls like it, too," he responded, as he buttered a piece of bread. "Dad, as we discussed, I really think you're right about that box being in the water for a very long time. And I don't think it was dropped there by a German tourist. See if you can find out what U-Boats may have been sunk near here, or even north of here." Continuing with enthusiasm, he added, "It's very feasible that it could have come from one sunk north of here and the currents carried it down this far. I'd sure give it a try."

"Guess you're right, Jordan. And if you don't think I'm completely stupid, or getting senile, I may make a trip over to Germany and England to see what I can find. I need some adventure in my life," he laughed, "and it could be kind of interesting to see if I can find who this stuff was meant for."

"Ha! From what you told me about this Andrea gal, seems you've got a good start on adventure. Don't overexert yourself, old man. She's a lot younger than you." He finished the last of his glass of milk and rose to put his dishes in the sink.

They hugged and Jordan got into his car. "Call me later this week, Dad, and let me know what you find. I won't say anything to anyone as you asked, but I will sure be darned curious to hear your news."

****

Neal's call to Andrea, prior to Jordan's visit, ended with her telling him she just might appear on his doorstep one day soon. He asked her to please give him some notice as he was involved in a local project and would not want to disappoint her with his absence.

Jordan barely had time to get over the causeway bridge when Neal's telephone rang, Andrea at the other end.

"It's all arranged. I asked for a week off and my boss said it was fine. I have a flight arriving in Savannah tomorrow afternoon at four. Please say you will meet me and I'll cook us an old fashioned meat loaf dinner."

Her breathless message caught him off guard and he stumbled on his words. "Uh, I, uh...yeh, guess that's okay, Andrea. We'll have to stop by the store in Savannah for groceries, I'm about out. Jordan just left and I found out he hasn't lost a bit of his boyish appetite for food...or fishing."

"Wonderful. My flight is on Delta and I'll have a red rose in my mouth," she laughed. "Now don't bother to clean up from your son's visit. I can help you do that. Oh, Neal, guess it's alright if I bring a bikini for the beach, or will that embarrass you in front of your neighbors?"

He was beginning to wonder if he might be getting in too deep. She seemed a bit pushy, or maybe it was just excitement. "Oh well," he thought, "it's only a week's visit."

The flight was an hour late. As they headed south, Neal turned to Andrea. "Let's get groceries tomorrow. I have enough stuff for breakfast." He turned toward the beach and pulled into *The Crab Caddy,* a small seafood restaurant on the water. They sat near a window and enjoyed a dinner of raw oysters, crab soup, and broiled grouper. "Surely not as good as your meat loaf, but at least you won't have to clean up the kitchen," he laughed as they left the rustic building with its smell of fruits from the sea.

Andrea immediately found *her places* around the house, in particular the bathroom, and in short time it looked like she had always lived there. Somehow Neal liked the look of female things around his new home and was not bothered by the intrusion.

Their days were spent exploring Jekyll, trips to St. Simon, and a cruise to Cumberland Island, where she delighted at seeing the wild horses romp. The bikini got good use. She wore it most of the day…her evening *garments* being equally brief.

As her week drew to a close, Neal informed her he had bought a ticket for her to accompany him to Europe and she was to call her boss today and tell him she would be gone for a month.

"Neal, have you gone batty?" she squealed. "I can't do that. He'll fire me."

"Then let him. You can live here on Jekyll. We have hotels. Small, but in no time you'd have a Days Inn looking like the Plaza," he said with a loud laugh. His offer surprised him, too, but their week together and the ease with which they lived was the life he wanted…again. "'Life is for the living' is what the minister said, and dammit, I want to live again." He did not regret his offer to Andrea.

Andrea did call her boss and he emphatically said, "NO," reminding her of an upcoming convention that would be filling the hotel…and the city.

"Neal, dear as you are, I can't do this. I've worked so hard at my job and this is just too sudden for me. Guess I come across as impulsive, but I really do give long thought to my decisions, especially one as lasting as this sounds. Forgive me if I've led you on. I do care for you and this has been a wonderful week. But, wow, that would be a big step to take right now."

Looking up into his eyes, she put her arms around his neck and kissed him with an urgency that belied her reluctance to go with him. He led her into the bedroom. Suddenly twisting in his arms, she struggled to get free.

"Andrea, I don't understand. We're lovers in New York, we've been lovers here, and now you push away. What gives? Are you afraid of change, of making a commitment?"

Tears rolled down her cheeks and a cold shiver spread over her body as she remembered how many times she had come so close to giving herself totally to another human being. "Neal, I'm sorry. I can't explain it. Perhaps I've been alone for so long that I can't even imagine how it would be to be part of a pair again. It's not you. You're a kind, gentle man and I adore you, but I'm..." She ran out of the room and to the bar, where she began to fill a glass with ice and vodka.

Neal followed her, stopping to watch as she sat down on the sofa and gazed out the window. He fixed himself a drink and sat in his recliner chair, looking across the room at this crying woman. "Funny," he said, "thought I'd be the one to bolt if we got too close so soon. I almost felt like I was betraying Louise, but you made me feel like it was good...and right." He sat upright in his chair and continued. "Okay, I'm sorry. Maybe I pushed too hard and too fast, but I thought we had a good thing going and I wanted you with me."

They both sat quietly, not saying another word for a long time. She got up, poured the ice from her glass into the sink and went into the bedroom. Neal gave her time to be alone and in about twenty minutes he went into the room. She was in the bed, her face toward the wall. He reached down, kissed her on the cheek, and said, "Goodnight, Andrea. I'll sleep in the guestroom."

****

Neal spent the next two days organizing all of the information he had gathered at the library and from his own books. He met with George Wilson for a couple of hours one afternoon, trying to find out if there might be some German tourists of questionable intent who could have possibly tried to get rid of the box. Using his career tactics of questioning, searching, and evaluating, he drew a blank. George knew of no one. "All we get here on the island is some of those Germans who only come to see the Werners. Most time they stay to themselves an' don't bother nobody. Heck, they don't even come eat Effie's good boil." Laughing, he continued, "I think all they like is that stinky kraut stuff."

Next he talked to Hildegard and Fritz who assured him their friends "would not have ever had any Nazi stuff." He told them he was not sure if it was from a Nazi or not, but did look like it had something to do with an officer and someone from England. By now he was not as guarded with his find, since he did not feel it had any significant value to anyone but the intended recipient. "Certainly it was of no military or political value."

****

HARTSFIELD ATLANTA INTERNATIONAL AIRPORT
As the L-1011 rolled down the runway, Neal Park, seated in his usual row twelve window seat, watched as the black tarmac passed beneath the wings. He held tightly to the small, grey, canvas carry-on bag at his side and closed his eyes. Trying hard to imagine the events of over fifty years ago that prompted this flight today to Europe and the hopeful delivery of the bag's contents, he drifted off into slumber.

"Excuse me sir, "said the flight attendant bending over him. "Do you wish to have dinner?"

"Oh, yes, just dozing." He sat up and watched as she put a steak dinner on his tray table. "Mmm, not too bad," he thought as he surveyed the salad, vegetables and chocolate cake. "Guess a nice meal would be good before I try to catch some more sleep."

He finished the steak, which was tasty but tough, and slowly sipped a glass of Merlot. Looking out at the approaching darkness he mentally went over the events of the past two weeks. Neal's thoughts turned to the day he found the box and the ensuing days when he tried to figure out to whom it might have belonged. With only a few clues on names, dates, and places, he put his faith into action and made the choice to find out. "It's not the obvious small value of the items, but perhaps just my curiosity that's driving me to do this. Who knows, I might meet some interesting people, and for sure I'll visit some places I've never been."

He laid back his head and drifted into a state of dreamy euphoria. Visions of a young girl running through a garden were interrupted by sounds of gunfire and much crying. He saw a German officer holding up a box and trying to catch the girl. The officer opened the box and was waving its contents in the air. The girl disappeared over a hill and the officer fell into a lake and went under.

"Would you like a headset to watch the movie, sir?" asked the flight attendant.

"No thanks, but I would like a glass of sherry before I try to nap."

She returned with the sherry and he turned again toward the window, this time watching the stars appear as the plane flew high above the Atlantic Ocean. "Perhaps the box came over this same route," he thought, constantly trying to figure out the mystery. Putting the glass on the tray table of the empty seat next to him, Neal fluffed a pillow and closed his eyes.

A tap on the shoulder aroused him from a deep sleep and he took one of the warm lemon-scented towels being offered by the flight attendant. "We'll be serving breakfast in a few minutes, sir, and should be landing in Gatwick in about an hour."

He went back to one of the plane's bathrooms. The cold tap water helped him wake up and he tried to comb his hair into neatness. "I sure look tired," he said to himself as he looked in the mirror.

His breakfast was on his tray table and he made haste to eat some cereal and a scone. The hot tea tasted good. "Guess I'd better get used to this," he said, "the English do like their *cuppa.*"

The first officer announced their approach into Gatwick as Neal was watching the neat green patches of farmland with white dots that were obviously grazing sheep. Puffy, white clouds seemed to float between the plane's altitude and the ground. The sun was starting to rise and it's rays were reflected in the many ponds throughout the countryside. It was three a.m. at home and eight a.m. in London. Cars were lining all of the roads leading into the busy city, taking workers to the many places of commerce that made this one of the great and thriving cities of the world. From high in the sky the cars looked like little toys and the occasional thatched roof houses appeared as broom-topped boxes. Boundaries of land were marked by neatly trimmed hedgerows.

The sound of heavy metal signaled lowering of the landing gear and Neal checked to make sure his seat belt was secure. He took the canvas bag from its resting place in the vacant seat and once again held it close to his side. He checked his coat pocket for the few pounds he had exchanged at the airport, making sure he had enough for the train ride to Victoria Station.

With only a small jolt, the landing was smooth and within a few minutes Neal stepped onto the jetway leading to the gates and immigration. After being on what seemed like ten miles of moving sidewalk, he made his way to immigration and took his place in line.

Posters along the way warned passengers to keep their belongings with them at all times. Neal held tight to the canvas bag.

The uniformed agent looked at Neal's passport, asked him where he would be staying, how long was he going to be in the U.K. and what was the nature of his visit. He responded with, "I'm delivering some gifts to friends." The agent had a quizzical look and Neal realized he may have aroused some suspicion. Taking out his wallet he showed the man his FBI identification which was valid due to his contract work of late. This satisfied the man and he stamped the passport and told him to have a nice visit.

He found his large suitcase and headed for the *"Nothing to Claim"* aisle in the Customs Hall. He walked still further and came out into the lobby area of the terminal which was lined with coffee shops, newsstands, exchange vendors and tobacco shops. Looking up he spotted the *taxi rank*, but decided it might be more interesting to take the train to Victoria station and then a taxi to his hotel.

Settling into a window seat on the train, Neal saw the refreshment cart being pushed down the aisle. He bought a cup of tea and a package of *biscuits*..."cookies to me," he thought, and enjoyed watching the passing scenery. Making their way through small London suburbs, Neal could see into backyards where most every family had a rose garden mixed with clothes lines, aluminum furniture and toys of all description. Here and there lights could be seen in kitchen windows behind lace curtains. It was almost ten thirty and Neal was thinking how nice a hot bath and a nap would be once he got to his hotel.

Planning to spend a few days in London before going to Sudbury, he checked with one of his FBI buddies who had been stationed in London for several years. He gave Neal information on a small hotel in South Kensington, *The Tramore.* Only ten rooms, it was moderately priced and within walking distance of the tube, museums, bookstores, restaurants and even *Christies,* should he want to look at antiques.

The train pulled into Victoria Station alongside dozens of other trains heading to or from various cities in England. Neal loaded his bags on a cart and made his way to the front of the old, grey building and got into the taxi rank, waiting his turn for one of the shiny, black taxis so symbolic of English travel. Telling the driver he wished to go to Number 10 Cranley Place, Neal settled back and watched the morning traffic as they inched their way across town.

He paid the driver, who made no conversation the entire trip, and walked toward the front door of *The Tramore.* Sitting behind the desk in reception was a lady with her red hair in a knot at the back of her neck.

"Good Morning, Sir. Do you be havin' a reservation?" asked the neatly groomed lady.

"Yes, I'm Neal Park, and I'll be staying here for three days." Watching her write in a large leather-bound book, he asked, "Guess you're not computerized here yet?"

"Oh, no. I've been here for several years and the owners just don't think we be needin' it." She looked up, smiled, and continued to write. Standing up, she handed him a large brass key marked "350". "'Tis on the third floor, sir, but ya look like a fit man and suppose the bit o' exercise won't do ya no harm."

From this statement he surmised there was no elevator and he'd have to climb the stairs.

He entered the room and had a feeling of *being at home*. Along one wall was a fireplace and opposite was a window overlooking a neighboring garden. The bed, covered with a bright, flowered spread, looked comfortable and looking into the bathroom he knew the deep bathtub would indeed feel good…"and soon." Neal stored his clothes in the old fashioned armoire, put his toiletries on the sink counter and started running hot water into the tub. Watching the water and steam rise, he was snapped out of his euphoric daze upon hearing a firm knock on the door. Almost tripping on the bedspread as he maneuvered around the bed, he wondered who could be at his door. He looked through the peephole and saw the red haired lady from reception, an envelope in her hand.

"Excuse me, sir. The manager is invitin' ya to be his guest at dinner tonight and he be askin' me to give ya this invitation." She smiled, placed the envelope in his hand and turned to go down the stairs.

"Thank you." She was almost halfway down the stairs when he called out, "By the way, what's his name?"

"Oh, he's Colin Wadsworth, he is…" and with another broad smile, she said, "And I'm Maureen."

Neal shut the door, opened the envelope and read the invitation. He went back to the bathroom, soaked for a half hour and laid down on the bed, slipping into his dreams for tomorrow.

****

Colin Wadsworth had been the manager of the Tramore for as many years as Maureen had been there, and together they ran a quiet and respectable hotel in what had been a townhouse. Talk of the owners' turning it back into a private home had not materialized, and at this moment Neal was grateful. He found it to be comfortable, reasonable and very well located. The dinner with Colin turned into an interesting mix of conversation from art, to politics, to history, and finally to his revealing a past infatuation with an American from Cleveland who now lived in Kersey, near Sudbury.

"Sudbury!" Neal shouted. "Are you sure? I'm trying to find some people who have some sort of connection with Sudbury and it would be wonderful to have a contact there."

"Right. I haven't spoken to Patti in a long time. She lived there for a few months and then returned to the States. Divorced her husband

and came back here." Scratching his chin, he continued. "Was a bit mysterious, I must say. Sad for me, but she fell in love with the Rector in Kersey and they were married. Went to the wedding, glad I did. Now, if you see her, give her my best. She was a lovely lady."

Neal was excited just to hear the word "Sudbury" and could hardly contain his anxiety in wanting to pursue this further, but his instincts told him he should ease off and try for more information tomorrow. "Interesting," Neal said. "Perhaps we can pick this conversation up again in the morning. I'm beginning to feel a bit of the jet lag, so guess I'll turn in. Thanks again for a fine dinner."

The reception area was dark as he started up the stairs. He was glad, as he did not want to confront what seemed to be Maureen's interest in him. "She's attractive enough, but right now I'm not about to get involved with anyone." Still unable to understand Andrea's change of attitude, he vowed to stay focused on the find.

The bed felt good again and in a few short minutes he was sound asleep, a cool breeze from the open window floating over his body.

CHAPTER FIFTEEN

Having heard so much about the Portobello Market, Neal woke thinking that would be a fun thing to do this Saturday morning. "I need to mix with the people, feel the flavor of the city, and maybe that will give me more ideas on how to proceed with my quest," he thought as he started to shave. "Gosh, I'm beginning to sound like Don Quixote...my quest. Next thing you know I'll be looking for windmills and starting to practice tilting."

Passing reception, Neal observed Maureen arranging a large bouquet of flowers on the coffee table. "Good morning, Maureen. Is there a money exchange place nearby?"

"Ah, and a good mornin' to ya', Mr. Park. Right, you'd be findin' one next to the bookstore at the corner," she answered with a lilt in her voice and another big smile. "But if ya' be headin' to Portobello Market, there's one at the entrance road, though I hear they charge a bit more."

"Thanks, Maureen. By the way, those sure are pretty flowers." He walked to the front door as she called out.

"Have a nice day, Mr. Park. And don't be forgettin' to have some fish 'n chips for your lunch," she laughed.

Neal found the exchange shop on Old Brompton Road and putting the British money in his money belt, he walked down toward the tube, passing travel agencies, luggage stores, music shops, pubs, and *Europa,* one of a chain of neighborhood grocery stores. "I must remember to stop here on the way home for some wine and cheese."

He descended the stairs to the tube tracks and waited for the next train. Seeing the light in the distance, Neal walked closer to the edge of the tracks. The doors slid open, he jumped on board and grabbed a leather strap to get his balance. "Seems like a full train. Wonder if they're all going to Portobello Market?"

The train pulled into *Notting Hill Gate* station and he followed the departing masses as the doors opened. Following the signs, he found a map on the front of a shop window. Noting that Portobello Market extended "from Chepstow Villas to Elgin Crescent," he decided this would be a morning of walking and proceeded to become totally engrossed in surveying the unusual wares in the shop windows. Turning a corner, he was startled to see the sight of so many shoppers jamming the streets. Car traffic was banned on the market streets, as they were filled with booths and trolleys manned by vendors of fruit, clothing, toys, old books, war paraphernalia, and anything that would sell. The street side arcades and trading booths sold linens, housewares, silver, china, and other goods. Sales seemed to be brisk, as shoppers had full bags on their arms.

Neal walked slowly through the maze, watching street entertainers give forth with music, magic, trained monkeys and mime. He stopped in the Grouse and Feather pub and had a pint of bitter. Hardly one to drink so early in the day, he said to himself, "It's just part of being here, and I like being here, so there!" Finished with the bitter, he walked on and was looking in a glass-topped case at some jewelry when all of a sudden he could not believe his eyes. It was an exact duplicate of the "girl in the garden" picture from the box. The frame was dark wood and had cuts and gashes, as if it had been dropped or caught between something. "How much is that picture of the girl?" he asked the elderly lady behind the counter.

She lifted the glass lid and pulled the picture close to her face. Squinting, she answered, "That'd be three pounds, sir."

Quickly tallying up the price, he thought, "That's five dollars for an old battered picture." Taking a step back, he asked, "Isn't that a bit much for it's poor condition?"

"Now, be on with ya' or buy it," she said. "I'll have no slang-matchin' here."

"Guess she means she won't bargain," he surmised.

He paid her the three pounds and took the torn plastic bag holding his purchase. Thanking her in spite of her unpleasantness, he continued down the road and came upon a World War II memorabilia booth and began to search through a table of old books. The man behind the booth was dressed in camouflage fatigues, a vest with numerous medals and wore a stainless steel helmet on his head.

"Pardon me, but do you have any items that would relate to U-Boats?" Neal hoped he could find some books that would help him.

"Right, mate," the man answered as he put down his tea cup, though Neal wondered if tea was in the cup. "Over here on this table ya' might be lucky and make good with a couple of old ones." He pulled two books out of a lineup on the table and handed them to Neal. They had seen better days, but Neal's delight in just finding them made that no contest.

He flipped through *The U-Boat Peril* and *U-Boats Under The Swastika.* "These are great. How much, my friend?"

"Well, I'll not be grousin' if you hit me with two pounds."

"Sold." Neal added the books to his bag and looked around for another pub. "I need another pint and a bit of lunch. This has been a most profitable morning." His stomach calling for sustenance was totally overcome by his anxiousness to sit down and look through the books. As he was crossing the street, he heard someone calling out.

"Hey, mate. Don't ya' need a German dictionary to go with those books?" It was the man from the booth. Neal turned around and came back.

"Guess I might be needing a dictionary at that. I'll give you a pound for that blue one there," he said as he reached for the thick book. Putting it also in the bag that was growing heavy, a metal pair of wings caught his eye. He seemed to feel he had seen them before. "How much for those wings?"

"Right. Those are German Oberleutnant wings. Solid silver those are," he said as he lifted them up to catch the sun. "I be thinkin' that might be like your Senior Lieutenant or somethin'. Not sure though, I didn't do much at school...didn't like to swot."

Neal assumed he was trying to tell him he wasn't a good student. "Fine, but how much do you want for them?" He realized that was what the "OL" on his box must have stood for.

"Tell ya' what, mate. Since ya' seem really into this, and I've had me a pretty good mornin', I'll let ya' have 'em for fifteen pounds."

"Twelve and you've got a deal," Neal retorted, figuring twenty dollars was plenty to pay for old, tarnished wings.

"Righto. They're yours mate." He wrapped them in a piece of tissue paper and handed them to Neal. "By the way, what's your fascination with this stuff?"

"Long story, buddy. But to make it short, I found a box of stuff off the coast of Georgia...U.S., that is...may have come from a U-Boat. It had some letters in it that I think were meant for someone in England. So here I am...a hunter."

"Good huntin', mate. Stop back by and let me know how ya' make out." He went back to arranging a pile of old medals.

Pleased beyond belief with his purchases and the thought that they could bring him closer to unraveling the mystery of the box, Neal remembered, with the help of intestinal growling, that he was heading to a pub for lunch when he found the German booth. He found a vacant table near the door of The Spotted Rabbit. As he waited for his order to be filled, Neal looked around the room, studying the patrons. Across from him sat a disgruntled looking man sucking on his ale, while the lady with him chewed voraciously on a beef sandwich. Next to them was a bobby, obviously taking his lunch break. He drank tea and seemed to be enjoying a plate of bangers and mash. The man behind the counter called out to Neal that his order was ready. Spreading Branston pickle on the bread, he broke a piece of cheese and placed it on top. "So this is what they call a *Ploughman's lunch*," he said to himself. With the bread, cheese, and pickle, his plate also held lettuce, sliced tomato, and a pickled onion. It went down well with another glass of bitter and he felt sufficiently fed and ready to tackle more of the market.

The noise level and the amount of people walking the streets had seemed to increase since he had eaten lunch and he found it harder to navigate into the arcade shops. Inching his way block by block, he stopped to look in an interesting shop, *Chelsea Galleries*. The windows were full of antique jewelry and most of the items looked expensive. As he walked inside, a well groomed lady with her black hair in a knot at her neck, approached and said, "May I be of service, sir?"

"Just looking, ma'am," Neal answered. "You have a nice shop here."

"Thank you. We also have a shop in Hampstead Heath if you ever be in that neighborhood."

"I'm only visiting for a few days. Heading up to Suffolk County."

"Really. Why, we have an agent in that area who sends us many fine pieces. Are you looking for anything in particular?" she asked.

"No, just having a good time being here," he responded, as his eyes were drawn to a ring exactly like the one he found in the box. Breathlessly, he said, "Please, may I see that ring in the last row?"

The lady gently placed the ring in his hand and said, "This came from an estate near Dover. We were told it was found with some belongings of a German officer shot down near there during the war. It's not of the best quality," she added as he rubbed his fingers over the pearls and rubies. "I understand that this style ring was duplicated in large quantities prior to the war and was usually an engagement gift." Noting his interest and her eagerness to make a sale, she continued. "However, I do feel this is an exception, as you can see the fine cut of the rubies and the color of the pearls. If you are interested, I can offer you a good price."

He wondered what her idea of "good" would be, and answered. "It's pretty, but nothing special," he said, secretly thinking that he would like to have it for comparison to the one in his bag in the safe at the hotel. "I have a couple of granddaughters that might have fun with it when they play dress up," he said, not wanting to sound too anxious.

"Right," she responded in true British fashion. "Would ten pounds be reasonable?"

"Mmm, s'pose so. Eight might be better," he answered, enjoying the trading game.

She took his eight pounds, put the ring back in its black velvet box, and slid it into a small bag. "Thank you very much. I do hope your granddaughters have fun with the ring." She felt she had made a very good deal indeed, considering she had only paid the agent two pounds for it last week. And Neal felt he made a very good deal, if the ring was as authentic as the one from the box.

"I think I've done all the damage I'd better for one day," he thought as he made his way back to the tube station.

****

Colin Wadsworth was coming down the steps as Neal turned the corner at Cranley and Old Brompton Road. "Hello, Neal," he called out as he waved his hand. "How was the market?"

Meeting him halfway, Neal reached to shake his hand. "Fine, fine. I had a really nice time. By the way, you didn't tell me it would be so crowded," he laughed.

"Right. Well, Saturday is always busy there as the locals and the visitors try to find bits and bobs." They entered the front door and Colin added, "I say old man, why don't you come back down and have a gin with me. And if you don't have any dinner plans we can walk over to Drake's for a bit of food. You might enjoy it. It's bare brick in the basement and serves up a good spit roast boar. If you like that kind of thing," he said with a robust chuckle.

The four block walk was pleasant, the cool night breeze sliding over their faces. Neal even found he liked roasted boar. "Tastes an awful lot like a moose roast I once had in Montana," he remarked.

When Colin inquired about his reason for being in Montana, Neal shared with him some of his FBI adventures. Fascinated with each other's pasts, the two men drank several brandies as they laughed and enjoyed the evening. Walking back to the hotel Colin asked, "Where did you say you were going from here?"

"I have some personal investigative work to do in Suffolk County, around Sudbury and Lavenham. You know the area?"

"A bit. As I briefly mentioned during dinner the other night, I once had a terrible infatuation with an American lady who stayed here before she moved up there. She was from Ohio, I do recall. Fell in love with the priest in Kersey and lives there now." He stared up at the sky, thinking about Patti and his brief time with her. "When she came here she was having an unpleasant time in her life. I gathered she was unhappy with her husband and wanted to get away to sort it all out. The owner of the art gallery nearby saw her before she went back to the States, said she told him she was going back to have her baby." Shaking his head, he continued. "I didn't even know she was going to have a child. Perhaps she didn't know herself at the time. I only know I was very attracted to her and would like to have pursued a relationship, but she was very proper." Staring again at the sky, he said remorsefully, "Her name was Patti."

"Say, don't feel so bad. Maybe you've been saved some trouble," Neal laughed as they walked up the stairs and into the hotel. "But if I get to Kersey and run into her I'll let you know."

Waking the next morning, he heard the sound of rain coming in through the open window. "Ah, a typical English day, and I wanted to do some more sightseeing. Oh well, that's what slickers and umbrellas are for." He dressed and went down to the basement dining room for a bowl of oatmeal and some toast. The strong tea in his cup tasted good and he walked over to the serving counter for a refill. Colin came through the door, poured a cup of tea and sat down with Neal.

"Say, old man, would you like to take a bit of a stroll over to my friend's gallery. Don't know if you are interested in any of the Victorian artists, but he has quite a selection...Girtin, Grimshaw, Cottman."

"Listen, Colin, what I know about art you could put in your tea cup, but I do enjoy looking at it and yes, I'd like to go to the gallery. When did you have in mind?"

"After lunch would be good. I have to go over some orders with Maureen." Standing up he said, "See you in reception about two."

Neal walked four blocks from the hotel to St. Augustine's Anglican Church. The service was brief and the attendance was small, but he felt spiritually refreshed and ready to continue his "quest". Turning off Queen's Gate and on to Old Brompton road, he went into a small patisserie, ordered a curried chicken salad sandwich and a glass of

white wine. Colin was waiting for him in reception as he entered.
"Am I early, late, or on time?" Neal asked.

"On time, old man. Put your umbrella back up and let's see if I can
educate you on art in the Victorian era," he said with a hearty laugh.

Entering under a bright red awning, Neal was impressed with the red,
black and white polished interior of the gallery. Large track lighting
fixtures illuminated the paintings lining all four walls of the small
shop. Colin gave a running commentary as they passed each work of
art. "This is Grimshaw's painting of the *Knostrop Hall* mansion he
rented before he died.   Here he did some of his best work."
Proceeding further, "And this is *Kirkshall Abbey* by Thomas Girtin."
Hearing his name, Colin turned around.

"Hello, Colin. What brings you out on this nasty day?" said the
owner.   Colin introduced Neal, the three exchanged small talk.
Finished viewing the paintings, they went back out into the rain.

"Do I now consider myself a Victorian art expert?" Neal asked with a
laugh. "Seriously, I did enjoy the education and you've inspired me to
increase my interest in art."

"Glad you liked it, old man. Why don't we head back and have a gin
before dinner. I heard the chef say he was serving plaice tonight and
his famous "Fruits of the Forest" dessert. I never miss that."

"Sounds good to me," Neal answered, as they walked toward the
hotel.

The chef's dinner was no disappointment and Neal was almost
embarrassed at how much he ate. "My compliments to your chef,
Colin. You made no mistake in your recommendation of his work."

Maureen served a tray of sherry and brandy to Colin, Neal, and two
couples from Belgium who were also Tramore guests.   After a
brandy, Neal thanked his host and went to his room.

"Tomorrow I shall give British Rail my time and my money as I find my way to Suffolk County." He packed most of his clothes, and drew a tub of hot water. "Wonder if I could install a deep tub like this at Jekyll," he thought as he slid into the slippery water, enhanced by some mild bath oil. "Sure do like submerging."

****

With a last look at The Tramore, Neal got into the black taxi for his trip to Victoria Station where he would take another train, then still another at the Liverpool Street Station which would take him to Sudbury. Maureen gave him a big smile and waved as the taxi pulled away.

The sound of the windshield wipers clicking in rhythm lulled Neal into a state of quiet solitude. But the honking of horns in the heavy morning traffic kept him from dozing. He watched the Londoners on their way to places of commerce and began to think how it would be to live here.

Approaching the circle drive at Victoria Station, Neal dug in his pocket for the fare and prepared to hop out of the taxi. The driver handed him his bags, thanked him, and got back in the taxi. He found a luggage cart, loaded his bags and looked for the overhead sign showing his departure track. "Track eighteen, Marks Tey and Colchester. That's it. Wonder if I can find a close place to get a cup of coffee," he thought as he pushed the cart toward a counter nearby. Cautiously carrying the coffee, he found a vacant table and sat down. Minutes later the sign was flashing for his train. He made his way to track eighteen, loaded his bags on the front of the third car and found a seat. He unfolded a copy of the London Times and read until the train pulled out of the station. As the car began to move he watched the train yard pass with its stacks of pallets, lined up carts, spare wheels and other equipment that kept this immense industry on the move.

After changing trains at Liverpool Street Station, Neal looked at one of his maps and ascertained that they would make possibly nineteen stops before reaching Marks Tey, where he would change again to a two-car open-window train, then travel the last twelve miles. Passing little villages with strange names...Ilford, Gidea Park, Hatfield Peverel, Tiptree...he enjoyed watching the sights of the countryside.

"Marks Tey. All off to change to Chappel & Wakes Colne, Bures and Sudbury," came the conductor's loud announcement. Gathering up his bags again, he got off the train.

As he sat on a bench with peeling green paint, from the distance he could hear the clickety clack of the little two-car train pulling into the station. The windows were all open and the conductor changed seats from front of the train to back of the train, depending on which direction they were headed. Passenger seats also reversed to face to Sudbury or Marks Tey.

Leaving the two room station, the train slowly made its way west to Sudbury, passing fields and patches of trees hanging over the tracks and the River Stour. Remembering something Colin said, "You'll be going through Constable country.", Neal seemed to recall seeing a print of one of Constable's paintings when they were at the gallery. "Maybe I can find some literature here about that," he thought, putting it second after *the box* on his priority list.

CHAPTER SIXTEEN

SUDBURY

What Neal surmised to be the only taxi in town, took him to the Mill Hotel on Walnuttree Lane, a block from Gainsborough's home. At seventy-five dollars a night, the fifty-six rooms were advertised as spacious and light with the River Stour running directly under the hotel. The one hundred year old mill wheel turned here. Encased in glass screens separating the restaurant and bars, the wheel was young compared to the three hundred year old restaurant. The Mill Pond across from the hotel had benches on its banks where families and lovers stopped to enjoy the solitude and watch graceful swans swimming.

Walking the flight of stairs to his room on the second floor, Neal was grateful it was only the second, as his baggage had increased by a few pounds since he left London. He found the room, unlocked the door, and placed his bags inside the small closet. After unpacking he went downstairs to the restaurant and ordered a fish salad lunch. "Think I'll walk around town for a while before I settle in," he thought, as he signed his lunch check and thanked the waitress.

Gainsborough's home was not open this day, though tourists were peering through the iron fence at the back gardens which contained several metal sculptures among the shrubs and flowers. He walked on toward the center of town, passing shops of all kinds. At Market Hill he saw stalls with vendors stocking tables as the shoppers filled their net bags and totes with purchases. He passed the old Town Hall, built in 1828, now the Mayor's Parlour. The brochure he picked up at the hotel boasted of Sudbury's past as a center for weavers in the wool industry, which was significant to most of the towns and villages in this part of Suffolk County.

He crossed the street from the Town Hall and went into a department store, Winch and Blatch. Wondering if they had a luggage department, deciding he would need another bag to carry the numerous items he was beginning to collect and would surely be accumulating more in the ensuing weeks, Neal went in. As he walked up the steps into the small, but apparently well stocked store, he was approached by two white-haired ladies in dark printed dresses. One on each side of him, they said in tandem, "May we be serving you, sir?"

"Guess so," he responded with a big smile. "I'm just getting too many gifts to take back to my granddaughters, so I need another bag," he laughed.

Walking in small, but quick steps, the two diminutive ladies led him to the back of the store where he saw shelves of bags, a wide variety of sizes, colors, and prices. He felt like an honored guest with the hovering attention of these two interesting ladies who apparently had not had much business this day, the store being void of other customers. They chattered about the weather, John Major's latest news…"We might be best friends," said the more vivacious of the two, "but I don't be likin' his attitude on the new train fares," and began asking Neal questions about himself.

He told them he was from Georgia and at first they thought he was Russian. After he explained where his Georgia was, they giggled, putting their hands to their mouths and giving forth with a shyness belying their ages, which he guessed to be in the seventies. He introduced himself and they said they were glad to meet him, but did not give him their names. Putting the package over his shoulder, he thanked them and said he hoped to shop here again. "Do come back, Mr. Park. We'll be more than happy to be servin' you again."

His throat feeling dry, Neal turned into the Orwell Hotel whose sandwich board sign at the front door advertised the best bar in town. "I could go for an ale," he thought, as he walked toward a large room paneled in dark, carved wood. "I'll have a bitter," he said to the bartender as he settled himself on a stool. "Say, how old is this building?" he asked, admiring the detail of the carving.

"Right. It's a bit old, I'd say. Think it was built 'bout 1845," said the man as he put the ale in front of Neal. "Ya' be here on holiday or business?"

"Oh, a little of both," Neal answered. "I have some research to do in the area so I might be here for a month or two."

"Right," the man again replied, wiping the bar with a wet rag that had seen many wipes.

"Would you by chance know of an Estate Agent nearby? I think I might want to lease a place."

"Right. Charles Abbott is just down the lane and he usually has places to let. Just walk out tha' door and down three blocks. Ya' won't be missin' it."

Neal thanked the man, paid for his ale, and started down the street. He shifted the bag from Winch and Blatch to his other shoulder and though it was not heavy…"until I fill it with all this stuff I'm accumulating,"…it was clumsy and he looked eagerly for a sign of Charles Abbott's office. "Be glad to put this bag down," he said to himself as he looked left and saw the shingle hanging out from the front door. *Charles Abbott, Estate Agent Specializing in Lease.* He knocked on the door and tried the knob. The door was unlocked. Neal stepped in and called out, "Hello, anyone here?"

"Yes, yes. Be right out," answered the deep male voice. Charles Abbott appeared from another room and reached out his hand to Neal. "I'm Charles Abbott. How may I be helpin' ya'?"

"Good afternoon, Mr. Abbott. My name is Neal Park. I'm here on business and holiday and think I just might be needing a place to lease for a couple of months."

"Sit down, Mr. Park. I'd be pleased to be showin' ya' some of my listings. See some ya' like and we can go take a look."

They talked for a few minutes, Neal telling Charles that he only needed a small place and wanted to be fairly close to Lavenham and Sudbury.

"Now why would ya' be wantin' to be near there?" asked the tall man as he put fresh tobacco in his pipe.

"Oh, it's for some research I'm doing. I found some interesting things recently and I believe they're from this area or were intended for someone in this area. At any rate, I have a lot of digging to do to solve my mystery. Probably just a wild goose chase, but thought a trip here would be interesting anyway."

Taking a deep draw on the heavily carved pipe, Charles asked, "You got a wife with ya' on this scavenger hunt?"

"No, sorry to say, she died several months ago and guess I'm just filling time." He was flipping through the pages of a notebook showing properties and their rates. "Couple of these look nice. 'Specially this one in Kersey. Think I'd like to take a look."

Charles took the notebook to his desk, picked up the telephone and dialed a number. "Hello, Patti. Charles Abbott here. How are all the bairns? And the good Father, too?"

"Mmm, Patti, Kersey...I wonder. Maybe just a coincidence," Neal thought to himself as he listened to the conversation.

"Right. Have a nice chap from America...Georgia, I think, who needs a little place for a couple of months. The cottage is available, right?" Neal shook his head in affirmation hearing Georgia. "Right, right. We'll motor over now. Hope I get to see those bairns and get me hugs," he said, as he laughed and hung up the telephone.

Noting that most Brits drove small cars, Neal wondered, "when Americans were going to wise up and do the same. I'm going to really consider gas consumption when I trade in that guzzler in my garage," he thought, as they got into Charles' little car. They drove out the A1071, through Boxford, and at Hadleigh turned north. Nearing Kersey, the top of a stone church came into view. "What's the name of the church?"

"Oh, that's St. Mary's Church. In fact, the cottage we're goin' ta' see is his...that is, Father Tom is the rector there. It's Anglican, ya' know." They turned at the old landmark pump, passed the Bell Pub, the weaver's cottages with window boxes and pots on their steps, the Kersey Pottery, and crossed the watersplash where ducks were preening themselves with water from the stream.

"What's the name of this street," Neal asked, surmising that it was the main street.

"The street," Charles answered.

"No, the *name* of the street."

"That is the name, The Street," he laughed.

Turning right at Brett Lane, Charles drove to the end and turned left next to a salmon colored house with a thatched roof. They went down a long driveway and into a turnaround beside a small, white, stone cottage that had shutters of dark brown, almost black.

"Here we be," he announced, slamming the car door. English lace curtains hung at the windows and the front door knocker of brass had been recently polished. The door opened and a pretty woman with dark blond hair and blue eyes stepped back as she greeted them.

"Hello, Charles. It's so good to see you again." Looking out at the car, she asked, "Did Priscilla come with you."

He gave her a big hug and answered. "No, she's at her ladies' book group and doesn't know I'm here. This is Neal Park, the man from the States. Mr. Park, Mrs. Beacham."

"How do you do, Mr. Park. Please come in. Tommy take the kitty outside," she said to a small, blond, boy of about four who had a tiny, gray kitten in his arms. "Please excuse my son, but he always has an animal of some variety with him. Do hope he'll grow up to be a veterinarian," she laughed, as she closed the door behind them. "Let me show you around. I need to do a bit of cleaning before you move in." She explained that the fireplace worked well, should he be here into winter and, "the stove and refrigerator are only a year old." She proudly gave him a tour of the tiny cottage and he knew immediately it would be right for his visit. He noticed right off that the bathroom had a deep tub and the thought of soaking seemed very appealing at this moment. Well trimmed shrubs and rose bushes of many varieties created inviting space for two chairs under the trees. He could imagine sitting here on cool evenings, contemplating his day's findings on solving the mystery of the box.

"This looks fine," he said, as he took a seat on the sofa. "You've done a nice job of decorating, and the yard is great. Did you plant all those rose bushes?" Not waiting for her answer, he asked, "Would it be possible to move in next week?"

"Why I think that would be fine," she said, fluffing up the pillows the ladies at Winch and Blatch said she *"had to have."* "If next Monday suits you, then we can settle now."

"Sure, I only have time," he said with a laugh. "Incidentally, I note you don't speak like a Brit. Where are you from?"

She smiled broadly. "You're right. I've been here about eight years now. My original home was in Cleveland." Hesitating she continued. "Seems very long ago." A sad look permeated her face as she stared up at the sky. Abruptly she stood up, showed them to the door, and said, "I'll tell you my story someday. Not today."

They thanked her, got into Charles' car and drove out onto Brett Lane.

****

Neal spent the next few days gathering domestic items for his move. He shopped several times at Winch and Blatch, the two ladies courteously insisting he take blue towels and sheets. "I don't want to buy too many things since I'm not going to be here but a couple of months, and Mrs. Beacham has furnished most of what I'll need."

"Oh, but you just might be likin' it here and want to stay longer," said the more vocal of the two.

"Well, ladies, I already like it a lot and part of that is due to how nice you've both been to help me. By the way, what are your names?"

Shyly looking down, they then glanced at each other. "I'm Miss Stiles and this is Miss Overstreet," said Cynthia.

He was amused at their proper manner and accepted their hands to shake, letting them be first to extend the gesture. "I'm pleased to meet you both and want you to know how much I appreciate your assistance. Perhaps after I get settled you will allow me to take you to lunch one day."

Giggling, Miss Stiles answered. "That would be ever so kind of you Mr. Park. Do let us know when you will be calling."

He laughed to himself. "Almost sounds like I've asked them for a date."

In an earlier conversation they had mentioned living in this area all of their lives. Neal felt this would be a good opportunity to start some local research. "Maybe they can help me find some people who might have information that will solve my mystery."

CHAPTER SEVENTEEN

From his visit to the *Mighty Eighth Air Force Heritage Museum* in Savannah, Neal had learned there had been 350,000 men and women who had served in the U.S. Eighth Air Force during World War II at 60 hastily constructed bases in Britain, and many were stationed at one time in Lavenham, specifically the 487th Bomb Group. He also remembered that of the 350,000 who served, 26,000 never came home. Many gave their lives, but while being away from home they made lasting friendships, some married British citizens, and many who survived came back to live in England after the war. It was one of these people that Neal hoped would be the key to reveal the mystery of the box.

Inquiries at the Tourist Centre, and from Charles Abbott, gave Neal information on car rentals. Taking the early morning train back to Marks Tey and changing on to Colchester, he found his way to the car rental office. Remembering the cost of *petrol* in Britain, he chose a small, blue, two-door car that was ten years old. "It'll suit me fine, just want wheels to get around," he mused to himself as he signed the papers and received the keys from the pretty red-haired girl behind the counter. She handed him a packet of papers, and told him it contained emergency numbers and insurance information. "Details, details," he thought as he walked out to the lot next to the office. Starting the car, he put it in gear and eased out on to the street. "Better take it easy and try to concentrate on staying on the left side."

Neal pulled into the car park across the street from the hotel, locked the doors, and crossed over Walnuttree Lane. He walked past the front door and continued toward the river. Six cows were standing half on the bank and half in the water, drinking from the deep, blue water. Further down the bank two young boys were dangling lines with wiggling worms. The warm afternoon sun, mixed with a slight breeze, gave Neal the inclination to find a spot on the grass where he could take a nap. With hands behind his head, and drifting into a pleasant euphoria, he thought of John Constable's painting he had seen with Colin Wadsworth in London.

Shrill screeching pierced his ears and he sat bolt upright as five white swans fluttered past him on the water. They looked as if trying to fly, but were only inches above the water flapping their wings ferociously, seeming to be chased by something below. He walked closer to the edge of the water and saw what appeared to be a beaver or woodchuck chasing the swans. "Ah, nature," he thought as he made his way back up the bank and headed toward the hotel.

Neal nodded a greeting to the reception clerk and went into the bar adjoining the restaurant. With a mix of wood and stone flooring, the room was warm and inviting with large sofas and a collection of assorted antiques on walls and tables. A massive oak armoire housed an impressive array of wines and he made a note to ask for the wine list at dinner. Two groups of people were enjoying drinks and appeared to be business associates. Neal remembered seeing some conference rooms as he went to the elevator and surmised they were being used by these same people.

"Good afternoon, sir. Whot'l it be today?" asked the white coated man behind the bar as Neal took a seat on a burgundy covered stool.

"Thanks. Uh, think I'll have a scotch and water," he answered. "And please put extra ice in it, too."

He tried to engage the bartender in conversation, but the man seemed preoccupied with restocking his glassware and paid little attention to Neal's efforts. "Guess I'll go on in and have dinner."

After a meal of baked fish, asparagus tips, and a glass of Pinot Noir, he ordered a bread pudding for dessert, signed his bill, and went back to his room.

Television selection was limited and he found himself watching a taped speech given by the Prince of Wales. The Prince, a proponent of preserving architecture, gave forth with boring facts regarding saving old buildings instead of demolition for new construction. Neal changed the channel and fell asleep watching two British comedians entertaining children at a circus.

The next morning Neal finished breakfast listening to the rain as it got heavier. "Darn, I wanted to take a drive over to Lavenham, and walk around," he thought as the sky became darker. "Maybe I'll just go upstairs and read for a few hours until this ends...if it does."

The desk was spread with maps and notes he had made at the Brunswick library. Disappointed with the weather delaying his plans, he took a book out of his suitcase, laid down on the bed and read. *RED MERCURY,* a newly released novel about an explosion at the Summer Olympics, would prove to be prophetic. Neal liked to read thrillers, especially if they dealt with a plot he could relate to...one with FBI involvement. After two hours of reading, his eyes closed and he slept until the telephone ringing woke him.

"Hello," he answered with sleep-induced huskiness in his voice.

"Neal, it's Andrea. How are you, darling?" came the voice from far away.

"Why, Andrea," he answered, "Nice surprise to hear your voice. I'm fine, but how are you?"

"Oh, very well. I had a day off today and was thinking of you, so thought I'd call. It's just morning here. Isn't it after lunch there?"

Looking at his watch, he said, "Mmm, yes, as a matter of fact it is. I was reading and fell asleep. Glad you called or I'd have slept through a meal!" He laughed. "Anything exciting happening in old New York?"

"No, not really. I just miss you and wanted you to know. Maybe I'm having regrets that I didn't come with you," she said, a sad tone to her voice.

He told her about the hotel, the town, and the cottage he had rented in Kersey. "Oh yea, there are these two little ladies at the department store who've adopted me and keep trying to sell me all sorts of stuff I don't need. You should see them, typical old maids in dowdy clothes, sensible shoes and giggles all day long.

They sound charming, darling, just so they're *old* ladies and not cute young Brits," she said, sounding very possessive.

"Well," he responded, "You could come over and see for yourself. As a matter of fact, there's a sofa in the cottage living room where you could sleep."

"Neal, you are a tease," she said. "Just don't be surprised if I show up on your doorstep one day soon. That is, if my dear old boss will give me more than two days off at a time. Better go, I have to get my hair done and do some shopping. Miss you, darling."

Hanging up, he wondered if she meant it. "Will she really come over, or is she just trying to hang on?"

The rain had stopped and he walked down Stour Street to Gainsborough Street, past Gainsborough's house, and crossed over to a little tearoom where he had a curried chicken sandwich and a cup of tea. He asked the waitress about directions to Lavenham and showing her his map, she gave him instructions.

"Right, sir. Ya' be goin' out the B1115 north and it will take ya' to B1071 and right in to Lavenham, it will. 'Tis only about 10 kilometers I should think."

Back at the car park, he put the grey canvas bag on the seat and pulled out on to Walnuttree Lane toward the town center where he would pick up B1115. The rain had stopped and the afternoon turned out to be cool, but sunny, for which he was grateful. Approaching Lavenham, he was interested to see so many half-timbered houses standing at cock-eyed angles looking as if they'd roll down the street. He found the Tourist Information Centre and picked up some brochures. The attendant at the center told him the air field was one mile north and he could make the arrangements for him to tour.

Neal made a tour appointment for the next morning, as he wanted to walk around the town today before dark.

"Right, right," answered the attendant. "The people at the field are usually there to do tours about ten in the mornin'. I'll ring them up and let them know you'll be comin'."

Neal followed the map and walked for an hour, winding up on Church Street at the Swan Hotel, built in 1425. Here Big Band leader, Glenn Miller was reported to have had his last drink prior to being lost on a flight to France in 1944. Neal ordered a scotch and water, "Extra ice, please," and amused himself looking at the walls of pictures and autographs from flyers in the 487th. The bartender was also the manager of the hotel and ran between reception and the bar on a frequent basis. Neal wanted to engage him in conversation and hopefully gain some information. Noticing his empty glass, the man approached Neal and spoke.

"See your glass is empty, sir. Might I be fillin' it for ya'?"

Neal smiled and answered. "You sure can. And while you're here I'd like to ask you some questions. You got a minute?"

"Right. Most of my guests are checked in for the night, so s'pose I can chat a bit." It was nearing dark and Neal hoped he'd find his way back to Sudbury.

Without disclosing all of the details, Neal shared with him some of the information about the contents of the box. The man looked to be in his sixties.

"Were you living here during the war?" Neal asked.

"Right, but I was a wee bairn. My father was in the war, was in Normandy, he was. Lived through it, too," he said proudly. "But I only remember what he told me about it. Me mum has some pictures she saved from the war days. Got 'em in her dowry chest, she has."

Excitement was growing in his heart and he boldly asked, "Would it be possible for me to speak with her and see the pictures? Maybe she can help me figure out some names."

"Right. She's gettin' on poorly now, don't be seein' too good and such, but her hearing is keen. You be comin' round tomorrow?"

"Oh yes, I have a tour set up at the airfield at ten. Could I come back by here after lunch and meet her?"

"I'll be askin' her tonight and let ya' know. Me telephone's ringin' at the desk. I gotta go."

With that he left. Neal put some money on the bar and went to find his little blue car.

The next morning he anxiously drove back to Lavenham. Half a century prior to his visit, the countryside was dotted with air bases. Now the land had gone back to farms, forests, and business parks. It looked like the outskirts of many small towns in the States. Here, where once tractors plowed, then bombers landed, now tractors were plowing again. As he got closer, he saw in the distance the control tower, finding out later that it was to be preserved in tribute to the 487th Bomb Group. The runways had long since been dug up and left in weathering piles, some of the farm owners giving chunks of the concrete as souvenirs to visiting veterans.

Farm implements and necessary tools were being stored in quonset huts that the airmen had used for theaters, mess halls, kitchens and maintenance shops. Closing his eyes for a moment, Neal tried to imagine the hustle and bustle that must have occurred during the war days, when on a moments notice, pilots and crews would have to be ready to become airborne and meet the enemy. He imagined he could hear the Jeeps rushing to deliver the flight crews, the cough and eventual start of the B-17 engines, and the roar as they lumbered down the runway and climbed into the puffy sky over Lavenham. He tried even harder to picture them high above enemy lines, perhaps over Dusseldorf, or Osnabruck, or Bremerhaven, dropping their bombs, and returning to the air field.

As he parked the car, a man walked toward him and waved. "Hullo," he yelled as Neal approached. "You must the man from the States who wants a tour."

"Yessir. Guess you get a lot of us." Neal answered. "I'm probably different from most of those guys, though. I was too young to be in the war, but I do have a curiosity to be satisfied."

"Well, now young man, just follow me and I'll be trying to cure your curiosity." He laughed as they shook hands and walked toward one of the quonset huts. "Don't be gettin' webs in your hair," he said as his hands pulled at some spider webs covering the top of the doorway. "This hut was barracks for some of tha men. You see tha drawings painted on tha walls?" pointing to amateur sketches of pinups of the day. "Sort of reminds one of your Betty Grable, eh?"

They walked through the hut that was the Officer's Club, the man pointing out where a movie screen would have been, where the bar was set up...remains of a cabinet still nailed to the wall, told him of the blackout curtains always pulled shut, and described a typical evening in the club.

"Oh, they would be havin' a great time, not knowin' if tomorrow they would go out and not come back. But they were young, they were, and not afraid of anythin'." He wiped a tear from his eye. "Sorry, I lost some in tha war. Near 'bout got it meself, but me bad eyes kept me home. We just dodged tha bombs here and prayed for you Yanks to get it over with."

Neal made some notes and as they seemed to be ending the tour, he asked the man if it would be in order to ask him some questions.

"Right. But I'm gettin' on in time, and sometimes me mind don't tell me everythin'."

Like with the Swan Hotel manager, Neal asked the tour guide the same questions. Neither one could help him with the German name, though they both knew Germans had been here working on a secret project. Nor could they shed light on the "Cyn..." on the letters. The tour guide told him there were some records he could see at the Tourist Information Centre and he would show them to him.

The tour guide followed Neal back to Lavenham and at the Centre he took some old battered notebooks from a file cabinet.

"These might be helpin' ya'. Thars a lot of names in thar. Might be you could be findin' the ones ya' want." He said goodbye and told Neal to take his time, "The Centre is open until five. Cheerio."

He pored over the old documents, searching for anything that would be close to "Cyn..." or "Prien". Just as he was about to make his leave, his eyes focused on a billeting list from August 1939. Barely able to make out the faded names printed on the list, he scarcely detected a name..."Ger...Pri..., Fahnric..." His memory told him that *Fahnrich* had something to do with an officer's designation in the Luftwaffe.

"Wow, could the "Pri..." be the one I'm looking for?" he quickly thought. "But now how do I find out where he was from and what he was doing here?"

Staying another hour, he could find no other reference to this name. He located the guide and asked if there was any other place he might search.

"Well, tha' old Corpus Christi Guildhall has some local history information. It's on Market Place. And there just might be some war stuff at St. Peter and Paul Church on Church Street. That's 'bout best I can tell ya, Mr. Park."

Neal thanked the man, got into his car and drove back into town. "Guess I'll have lunch at the hotel and try to see the manager's mother." Feeling good after eating a plate of fish and chips, washed down by a pint of ale, Neal pursued his request to see the old woman's pictures. "S'pose it would be convenient to visit with your mother now?" he asked the manager.

"Right. Let me ring her up and see if we can be walkin' over to her house."

The lady agreed to see them and they walked down to her house on Water Street. Her son opened the dark, weathered door and motioned for Neal to come in. A stooped, tiny lady approached them. With a starched white apron over her flowered cotton dress, she gave them a big smile and said, "Hullo, sir. Me son tells me you be wantin' to see me old war pictures."

"Yes, ma'am, if it's not too much trouble." He told her why he wanted to see them and assured her he would not take much of her time.

"Oh, that's fine. I'll be puttin' on the tea and you can join us. Do you be likin' biscuits with your tea?"

He remembered that biscuits were cookies, and never one to turn down cookies, he replied. "Yes, ma'am. I love cookies. My granddaughters and I try to see who can eat the most."

"You a grandfather?" she exclaimed. "I don't be believin' it."

"Oh yes," he said proudly. "They're the lights of my life."

She served the tea in thin china cups painted with tiny red roses. The biscuits were on a silver tray and the spoons glistened as if polished that morning. Despite the humble furnishings of the house, the tea service was proper and well received.

"Mmm, these are sure good biscuits, ma'am. What are they called?" he asked, reaching for another.

Smiling brightly, she answered, "They be shortbread, sir. Not much for those that be a dietin' 'cause they be full of butter."

Folding the napkin and placing it back on the tray, Neal hesitantly spoke. "Uh, perhaps you could show me those pictures. I don't want to take up too much of your time."

"Right," she said, picking up the tray and carrying it to the kitchen. "Come on after me and I be showin' you what I saved from those sad days." The son excused himself and said he had to return to the hotel and would see Neal later.

Neal followed her up a very narrow flight of steps that ended on an open landing above the living room. Two large upholstered chairs faced the back wall. Neal sat down in one of the chairs. Against the wall was a large hinged blanket chest. Its top was scratched and dented, evidence of many moves or busy children. She took a key from her pocket and unlocked the chest. Lifting the top released a strong smell of lavender and Neal thought of how his own mother loved the same fragrance. The old woman gently lifted a well worn album out of the chest. It's corners and edges were frayed and the top layer of paper was peeling back. Carefully placing it on Neal's lap she sat beside him and opened the cover. *Norman in his new uniform. June 1, 1939* was written in white ink on black paper beneath a picture of a tall man in an RAF uniform. The next pictures were of a pretty, blond girl and a small boy of about five. Neal surmised they were the manager and his mother. He looked at six or seven pages of this same threesome and finally came to some photographs of a large group of men in uniform. He recognized that all were not wearing the same uniform.

"Who were these men?" he asked, pointing to three who looked to be wearing German uniforms. His heart began to race as he waited for her answer.

"Oh. Those be tha damn Nazi flyers were here workin' on a British project. Not here long though. Our men be findin' out tha no good Lord Haw-Haw had some bad plans, he did. Next we knew he took Poland."

Neal looked closely at the writing on the photograph. "Who wrote these names on the picture, ma'am?"

"That must have been one of tha men in Norman's unit. He got some o' tha pictures when the poor bloke was killed. Happened right at the base, it did. A bomb went off in the plane and he was workin' right under it, he was."

Getting very close Neal thought he could see the letters "Pri" under one of the men. "Oh, could I be so lucky," he thought. "Ma'am, would you mind if I borrowed this picture for a few days? I'd like to have a copy made. I'll be very careful and return it."

A quizzical look on her face, she stared at him for a moment. "Now I don' be understandin' why this old picture has meanin' to ya'. It's just a bunch 'o men, most dead, me sure, and you want to copy it?"

He told her briefly again of his interest and let her know that he would be most grateful.

"S'pose would do no harm. Right, you can take it. I didn' know any of those blokes anyway and me Norman is gone. Guess won' make no difference."

He put the picture in his upper pocket, thanked the old woman and walked back to the hotel. There he told her son what he was about to do and thanked him also. Before leaving, he downed a half pint of bitter and ate some crisps.

The sun was setting as he pulled into the car park. Looking at the grey canvas bag, which now contained the picture, he took a deep breath. "Perhaps it's starting to break for me," he thought, as he got out of the car and walked to the hotel front entrance. An unexplainable feeling of accomplishment ripped through his body. Holding his head high, he entered the hotel.

"Mr. Park," called out the girl behind the reception desk. "You have a message."

Opening the envelope, he laughed as he read the message.

> *Neal dear, I will be arriving Gatwick Airport next Wednesday morning at 5:40 A.M. Don't worry, I'll have breakfast while I wait for you to arrive. Just page me in the Crown Room. Surprise!*
>
> *Love, Andrea*

"Oh, brother," he thought. "I move into the cottage on Monday and she gets here Wednesday. Oh well, I can do it, and anyway it'll be nice to have some company…and some help."

Walking up the stairs to the second floor, he wondered, "She didn't mention how long she was planning to stay. Not that it really matters, but it would be nice to know."

CHAPTER EIGHTEEN

The morning noises of birds and traffic invaded Neal's thoughts as he walked into the center of town where he had seen a photographer's studio. *Wilkinson Photoart,* painted in red letters on a large white sign, listed the services of the business. *Portraits, Reprints, and Framing.* He opened the door and a small bell tinkled.

"Hello, anyone here?" Neal called into the empty room whose walls were lined with examples of the owner's talent. He noted a diverse interest in nature, people, and inanimate objects. But interestingly, all of the photographs were framed in the same silver framing, giving the room a feeling of structure and variety at the same time.

From behind blue curtains stepped a petite, dark haired, woman, dressed in a long black skirt and a white peasant blouse loosely tied at the neckline. She pulled the curtains to one side, smiled, and said, "Good morning, sir. And how might I be helping you?"

Stunned at her beauty and soft voice, Neal paused and haltingly asked, "I have an old photograph that I'd like to have reproduced. Do you do this type work?"

Her unique, dark, violet eyes sparkled as she walked toward him and took the picture in her long-fingered hands. Holding it close to her face, she studied it and then held it up to the light coming in from the front window.

"This is quite old, perhaps fifty years or more, but I see no reason why we cannot reproduce it." She handed it back to him and was aware that he was staring at her in a curious manner.

Neal could not stop looking at her until he realized she knew what he was doing. "Mmm, sorry. I was just admiring the exceptional necklace you're wearing," he said, mentally grateful that he was able to pull out of his trance. "Is that a star sapphire?"

169

"Yes it is. My brother is a collector of jewels and he frequently gives me something that is different. This one is, wouldn't you agree?" She delicately lifted the setting and leaned closer to Neal, a view of her porcelain cleavage greeting him.

Realizing he was breathing heavily, he pulled back. "Yes, that is a fine piece."

Georgette Wilkinson laughed at his embarrassment and twirled around. "Here, won't you please sit and have some tea with me?" Extending her hands toward a small table and two carved chairs, she went back through the blue curtains and he could hear the water running into a tea kettle.

In a few minutes she reappeared with the tea tray. A small silver basket, lined with a pink linen napkin, held small chocolate cookies. "Biscuits, I think," he mumbled to himself.

"Do you take cream or lemon, Mr...uh, I do not know your name."

"Oh, I'm Neal Park, staying up the street at the Mill Hotel."

"How do you do, Mr. Park. I'm Georgette Wilkinson, and I own this humble little shop. Cream or lemon?"

Still mesmerized by her delicate and flawless beauty, he stuttered, "Ca, ca, cream, thank you."

For the next thirty minutes she entertained him with animated stories of how she became a photographer. "Couldn't imagine keeping all the images of things I love in my little brain, but photographs would help." How she came to live in Sudbury. "Stopped here on my way to Cambridge and became thoroughly enchanted with the town and the lovely people." How she hoped to travel someday to the States. "My deceased husband was from Florida and I'd like to meet his relatives. He died before we got to make our big trip across."

Neal hardly said a word, just kept smiling and nodding his head. When at last she seemed to be finished, he told her he was here on a search for information and the picture could be key to his work. Reluctant to tell her too much, he nonetheless wanted her to know about his life. Some mysterious magnetism drew him near to this gorgeous creature and he had barely been in her presence for more than forty-five minutes. But he held back his thoughts, stood up, thanked her for the tea, and asked when he could pick up the photograph.

"Mr. Park, I must go to London tomorrow to visit a sick friend, but I should be able to have it ready for you early next week."

"Fine. Uh, I'm uh," he hesistated, "Moving into a cottage in Kersey on Monday. Have to pick up a friend at Gatwick airport on Wednesday, could I get it that afternoon on my way back?"

"Indeed. It will be ready for you then. Cheerio, Mr. Park." She shut the door behind him. The little bell tinkled.

He stood on the steps outside the shop for a few minutes, trying to decipher why he had these feelings of anxiety and perplexity. "I've never felt like this before. What is it about that woman?" he asked himself as he started back to the hotel. He abruptly turned around and walked up Gainsborough Street toward Market Hill to Winch & Blatch. "Maybe a chat with those ladies will calm me a bit."

Miss Stiles and Miss Overstreet were not there. The store manager said that Miss Stiles had a very ill cousin in Norwich and the two ladies would be there for an extended time. "Have no mind how long they might be. Seems the dear cousin is in a very poor way, she is."

He thanked the man and went back to the hotel. As he was about to walk out the door, he turned and asked, "What do you know about the lady photographer down the street? Is she a gypsy or something?"

The manager laughed. "Indeed no, bless Pat. She's just a very artistic and different lady, she is. Shame she be alone. 'Tis been a long time, too, it has. I seem to recall they were only wed a short time when he died. Poor soul."

Try as he might, Neal had a hard time putting Georgette Wilkinson out of his mind. Jolting back into reality, he remembered that he had planned to drive back to Lavenham this morning for visits to the guildhall and the church.

Turning the little blue car out of the car park, Neal drove out East Street, the B1115 and headed to Lavenham. Coming into town on Church street he pulled into a wooded area, the sign reading, *The Parish Church of Saints Peter and Paul.* Sitting on a slight hill overlooking the town, it was most impressive with high arches and clerestory windows. Neal parked the car and walked inside. Greeting him were decorated windows and pinnacled stair turrets, the nave and aisles of limestone were base for brasses and inscriptions, and the original pulpit, a three deck structure, was now replaced with a carved mahogany "preacher squeezer" enclosure.

"Might I help you, sir?" asked a voice from behind.

Turning, Neal met eyes with a man he presumed to be the rector of the church. "Yes, I was told you store records here from World War II…something that might tell me about people who lived or worked in this area at that time."

"Right. Follow me," said the man, his long frock making a swishing noise as he led Neal to a room on the north side of the building. "This is our excuse for an archives, but you might find somethin' of value here. Is there anythin' of particular interest that I might be helpin' you with?"

"Actually," Neal replied, "I'm looking for information about some Germans who were here at the beginning of the war."

The man of the cloth shook his head, "Don' be knowin if we have anythin' of that nature. Most of those blokes were Lutheran."

He left and Neal began to look through files and books in drawers and cabinets that lined the walls of the small room. Three hours later, his eyes tiring and his stomach growling, he decided to quit his search. Just as he started to close the last book, he saw a picture similar to the one he'd left at Georgette's shop. "Good grief," he exclaimed, "that's the same group of Germans." And, much to his delight, there were legible names beneath the picture.

LUFTWAFFE PILOTS VISITING LAVENHAM, AUGUST 1939
KAPITANLEUTNANT REINHARD SCHREDER
OBERLEUTNANT JURGEN HARTENSTEIN
OBERLEUTNANT OTTO WERNER
OBERLEUTNANT FELIX GREGER
OBERLEUTNANT GERHARDT PRIEN

"PRIEN," shouted Neal, forgetting that he was in a church. "Pay dirt. That's got to be him," he said to himself as he read the last name under the picture. "The name on the box…*OL G Pri*…it has to be the same person." The man in the middle appeared to be the senior of the flyers. Barely visible were the words, *Kleiner Spion Project with U.K.* "Now I have something to go on. Wonder how I find out about this project?"

He copied down the names and put the last book away. "My next stop will be the guildhall. Maybe they'll have some stuff on this *project.*"

Driving out Church Street, he turned left on the High Street and found a parking place on the street near the Corpus Christi Guildhall, a timber-framed building that was built in 1520. A sign on the door said it was owned by the National Trust and open to the public from ten a.m. until five p.m. Checking his watch and looking for a close pub, he decided to have a quick lunch before resuming the quest. He crossed the street and went into The Sword and Feather pub, where he ordered a ploughman's lunch and a glass of bitter.

Neal introduced himself to the agent on duty at the guildhall who put a stack of books on the table. The books were a weak attempt at chronicling events from the war years. Mostly newspaper clippings and faded photographs, Neal found they related almost exclusively to hometown boys who were serving abroad, those who had died, and children waiting for fathers to come home. He spent two hours trying to find anything that would lead him to more information on GERHARDT PRIEN.

"One more of these sad albums and then I'm going back to the hotel," he thought, disappointment invading his spirit. Just as he was about to put the books back the agent approached his table.

"Sir, I thought I heard ya' say a bit about a special project at the beginnin' of the war. That right?"

"Yes," he responded. "It was something that was scrapped when Germany invaded Poland…least that's what an elderly lady here in town told me."

"Right, right, right," the man said enthusiastically. "Think I be rememberin' me mum tellin' me 'bout that. They was doing somethin' with a secret airplane out there at the airbase. You been out thar yet?" he asked.

"Yea, I was out there yesterday. Nothing left but concrete parts and those old quonset huts. No paper stuff to look at, just the place and some old buildings," he answered dejectedly. "Say, how could I find someone in the RAF, or today's air force that could help me?"

"Beats me, mate. Ya' might give it a go somewheres in London for that."

"Okay. Thanks for your help." He found the car and drove back to Sudbury. "I'm tired. It's been a good day, but guess I was looking for all the answers at one time. Well, now I have a good reason to go down to London before I pick up Andrea."

He stopped in the bar and ordered a scotch and water..."Extra ice, please"...and watched the swans on the pond outside. "Georgette, that's a pretty name. Something about that lady though. Didn't she say she was going to London...was it tomorrow? Mmmm, no I couldn't ask her if she wants a ride. Could I? Maybe I'll just wait until Andrea leaves before I go down there..."

The restaurant was featuring plaice and creamed potatoes. It was good and the chardonnay he ordered did not disappoint his taste buds. A small band was playing in the bar and after dinner he went in, had a brandy, and an hour later went up to his room. The memory of the star sapphire pendant and it's holding area haunted his sleep. A dream of two fairies dancing in the woods invaded his dreams. One had long red hair, the other black. Both were in filmy, silk gauze gowns and they were waving at him. He woke in a cold sweat, hearing himself say, "Andrea, Georgette, Andrea, Georgette..."

CHAPTER NINETEEN

The Sudbury sun was streaming into his window as he stretched and made his way to the bathroom. After a hot shower Neal dressed in khaki slacks, ivory turtleneck shirt and a navy jacket. He dialed the Beacham residence and Patti answered. "Good morning, Mrs. Beacham. This is Neal Park."

"Good morning, Neal, and please do call me Patti. And how are you today?"

"Fine thanks," he said. "I was wondering if it might be possible to move in today. I need to go to London for a couple of days and have to do it before Wednesday."

"Mmm, I s'pose so. We only have to do the windows yet and your moving in wouldn't hinder that chore."

"Gosh, that would be great. I don't want to impose on you and as you know, I only have clothes and a few other items to move. You've seen to making a very comfortable cottage there," he said. "By the way," he added, "I have a lady friend from New York coming in on Wednesday and she'll be staying with me for a few days. Do hope that's okay."

"Neal, that is your business, but thank you for letting me know."

The tone in her voice had noticeably changed and she came across as uncomfortable with this arrangement. He wondered if it was because of the children or the church. He hung up the telephone and checking the time, he thought, "Well, maybe it might help if I attend services at Father Beacham's church before I move in." Realizing he did not know where to get the key, he called Patti back.

"Patti, I forgot to ask you how I might get the key. If it will be of any help, I'll be attending services at the church this morning. Could I get the key from you there?"

"Indeed, Neal. That will be fine. See you at church. Oh, by the way, the service starts at eleven. Cheerio."

"Hope the chef made some muffins for breakfast today," he thought, remembering the ones he had had a few mornings ago. "Never thought gooseberries could be so good. And I'll have to eat fast to make it over to Kersey by eleven." At the last minute he changed into a navy blue suit, white shirt, and tie. "The turtleneck won't do for church."

In lieu of the time situation, he chose the shorter Lavenham route, knowing he'd have many opportunities in the weeks to come for trying new routes with new adventures. Right now he needed to get to church on time.

Pulling into the gravel parking lot next to St. Mary's Church, Neal looked down the hill at The Street where groups of people were walking up the old stone steps. The church bell pealed, calling the worshipers to service in this church which was restored in the 19th century. He went through the huge carved wooden doors beneath the bell tower. Inside the sun streamed through stained-glass windows and cast colorful shadows on the old wooden pews. An usher, dressed in a grey suit with a flower in his lapel, smiled and offered Neal a program.

Patti and her four children were seated in the second row. The two boys and two girls were neatly dressed and rose as the organ began to play the processional. A young boy acolyte carried the cross, followed by the lay readers and finally the rector, Father Nigel Thomas Beacham, who walked up to and behind the lectern which was carved with an eagle over 500 years ago. The Anglican morning prayer service ended fifty minutes later with the congregation singing *Faith*

Of Our Fathers as the acolyte, lay readers, and rector recessed to the back of the church.

Neal waited at the end of his row until Patti passed. Stepping out behind her, he spoke her name. She turned, smiled, and stopped.

"Good morning, Neal. These are my children...John, Tommy, Catherine, and Elizabeth. Each one nodded as she called their name and the boys extended their hands to shake.

"My, what a handsome little flock you have, Patti," Neal said as he shook the boy's hands. "And don't you little ladies look pretty today."

They walked toward the door where Tom was greeting his parishioners. Patti and the children bypassed Tom and walked out into the front courtyard. Neal spoke with Tom and told him he was looking forward to being their tenant and also told him he enjoyed the sermon.

Catching up with Patti, Neal asked her if she had the cottage key.

"Oh, yes. With this troop pushing me for lunch, I almost forgot. Here it is. You may have to jiggle it a bit, but it does work."

She was polite, but reserved, and he hoped he was reading more into her attitude than was really there. He also hoped Andrea would not be a problem.

Neal drove back behind the big house on Brett Lane and unlocked the trunk of his little car. "Or as they say here, *the boot.*" He took out his bags and went up the steps to the cottage door. Jiggling the key in the lock as Patti advised, he opened the door and stepped in. Surprised, he found she had left a bouquet of flowers on the coffee table and some fresh scones on the kitchen counter. "Now isn't that nice," he said to himself as he carried his bags into the bedroom. "Think I'll make a pot of tea while I unpack. Will sure taste good with those scones."

Neal put his clothes away, lined his toiletries up on the back of the bathroom counter, and stored his bags in the back of the closet. He found the few linens he had bought at Winch & Blatch were unnecessary, as Patti had furnished the cottage with most everything but food. She even had staples of sugar, flour, spices, and napkins in the kitchen. A quick trip back to the bathroom found an ample supply of toilet tissue as well. "Guess all I'll need to buy is weekly groceries." He had already decided to check out the pub for his dinner tonight.

Moving in was finished sooner than he had anticipated. After reading the *Sunday Times* he had bought in Sudbury, he put his head back on the sofa and drifted off to sleep. Two hours later he was awakened by a knock at the door. Standing on the stone steps were the four Beacham children. The oldest, John, spoke. "Our mum said to give you this," he said as he handed a plate to Neal. On the china plate was a loaf of fresh baked bread, still warm. "You have any boys or girls?" asked the little blond girl who looked to be four or five.

"Well, I do have two granddaughters back in the States. They're a little older than you, but sure not any prettier!"

After putting the bread in the kitchen, he went outside and sat in one of the yard chairs. The children sat on the grass and looked at him and asked him questions as if he were from another planet. They wanted to know where he lived, if he had a big boat, did he fly an airplane, "You all sure have a lot of questions." Pretty soon they got up and started chasing each other around the big yard. Neal realized how much he missed Annabelle and Caroline. "Maybe I can get them to come over before I have to go back."

Later that afternoon he walked down Brett Lane to The Street and went into the pub.

"Afternoon, mate. Wot can I be gettin' for ya'?" said the chubby red-haired man behind the bar.

"I think a pint of bitter might be a good idea," he answered, as he sat down on one of the bar stools.

"You're new here, right?" the man said, placing a foamy glass of ale in front of Neal.

"Right," Neal answered, proud that he was picking up the local slang. "I'm renting the Beacham cottage for a couple of months while I do some research. Neal Park," he said, extending his hand.

"Welcome to Kersey. You be needin' anythin', just give us a holler. Me wife and I are here everyday. She's Rosie and I'm Paddy. Paddy Houlehan's me name."

The two men discussed the weather, national news, and the status of the British pound. Neal looked at the menu and gave Paddy his order for dinner.

"Right. You'll like Rosie's lamb stew. It's full of vegetables and she's even made a pudding for dessert, she has."

Paddy was *right*. The stew was hot and thick and the soda bread fresh from the oven. After a cup of coffee and two brandies, Neal paid Paddy and walked back to the cottage. The evening air was misty and the sound of night birds gave him a feeling of peace. "I think I really like it here."

****

"Good Afternoon. Tramore Hotel." answered Maureen.

"Good Afternoon, Maureen. This is Neal Park."

"Oh, hullo, Mr. Park. How might I be helpin' ya' today."

"I'm coming in to London tomorrow and need a room for two nights. Do you think you might be able to accommodate me?" he asked.

"Yes we can, Mr. Park. And you say you only be needin' the room for two nights?"

"That's right. I'll be there around lunchtime."

He next checked his train schedule and figured he should take the early train to insure arriving in London by lunch.

After a dinner of soup, a glass of milk, and a piece of Patti's bread, Neal went into the bedroom and started packing. He checked to be sure the grey canvas bag contained his notes and London maps. He also put the photographs Georgette copied for him in the bag. "Wonder where she'll be staying in London?" he thought to himself. "Oh well, I've got to focus on my research, and with Andrea coming to town things could get complicated.

****

The little two-car train pulled away from the Sudbury station at exactly nine a.m. and made it's way through the countryside, paralleling the River Stour, it's deep blue water sparkling from sunlight between the leaves above. Neal put his head back on the cracked leather seat and tried to imagine what life was like here a few centuries ago. He wondered if Constable or Gainsborough had thoughts of what life would be like now. "Interesting," he mumbled to himself as the train pulled into the Marks Tey station for connecting to his London train. One hour later the conductor announced their arrival at Liverpool station. The taxi rank was nearly empty, the commuting workers having already made their way to offices and places of commerce. Neal stepped into a shiny black taxi and gave the driver the Tramore address. "Ten Cranley Place, driver."

As they passed Harrod's, Neal made a mental note to find some stuffed animals for Caroline and Annabelle. "I know they're growing up, but their beds still have space for a few more animals." He and Louise had always tried to find unusual ones for them when they traveled, and the girls looked forward to this grandparenting indulgence.

They turned on to Cranley Place and the taxi stopped half-way down the block. Neal paid the driver, checked in with Maureen at reception, and walked up to his room on the third floor. He quickly put his clothes in the armoire and went back downstairs, the grey canvas bag under his arm. "Maureen, I'll see you later. Going to grab a bite of lunch at the corner pub and then find my way to the Ministry of Information," he said, heading for the door. "By the way, how far is Malet Street from here?"

"Oh, it's not too far on the Tube, Mr. Park," Maureen replied. "I think ya' should be takin' the Circle Line to Embankment and then change to the Northern Line. Should drop you off at Tottenham Court, it should," she said. "That would be puttin' ya' only a short walk to Malet Street."

He had a Ploughman's lunch and a pint of bitter, then walked the block to the South Kensington tube station. "I have no idea what I'm going to find, or how I'll even get started," he said to himself as he watched the train light appear in the distance. "Guess I'll just take one step at a time and hope for the best." Stepping off the train at Tottenham Court, Neal looked around to catch his bearings and took a quick glance at his map. "Okay, guess I walk three blocks north to Store Street and two blocks east to Malet."

A light mist was falling and he liked the feel on his face. At Malet Street he saw the huge British Museum to his right and hoped to have time to go there today. *Hours 10 A.M. until 5 P.M.* read the sign on the front of the grey stone building. He walked up the short flight of stairs and entered into a circular rotunda with glass topped cabinets containing directions to the rooms within. Finding the room for Military Information, he took an elevator to level three. A matronly looking lady sat behind the desk and gave him directions to the area he was seeking.

He pored through volumes of journals about British Military history, famous battles, and their leaders. Searching deeper, Neal finally found reference to Britain's affiliation with Germany on several secret projects prior to the Invasion of Poland. One in particular caught his curiosity. It was named *Kleiner Spion,* and the report gave a brief account of this endeavor involving the Royal Air Force and the German Luftwaffe. In it's brevity a reference was made to the involvement of Unterseeboots…U-Boats.

Neal was beginning to think he had stumbled on to the right track. He took copious notes and wrote down names, addresses, and titles of books and documents that were mentioned as references. Several listed were to be found at the RAF Museum, his next stop.

A ringing bell caught his attention, and looking at his watch, he realized the museum was closing. "So much for the British Museum today!" He put his notepad into the grey canvas bag and took the elevator down to the main floor. The intense concentration had given him a headache, and seeing the long ques at the tube station, he decided to walk for a few blocks. At the end of Charing Cross Road he looked up and saw St. Martin-in-the-Fields Church. Neal went inside and took a seat, listening to the orchestra rehearsing a selection of Baroque music. Not expecting the good fortune, but grateful for the privilege, he watched Sir Neville Mariner conduct the orchestra. Looking up, Neal drank in the majesty of the church's architecture and magnificent stained glass windows. In this moment of peace and tranquility, he closed his eyes and thought of Louise, remembering how much she loved music…and him.

It was beginning to get dark and again he referred to his tube map. "Guess I can get the Circle Line in the next block and head back to Cranley Place." The tube was full of workers on their way home, some reading *The Times,* some dozing, others just staring ahead.

He stopped at the pub on the corner, ordered a pint of bitter and a Shepherd's Pie for his dinner. The walk back to the hotel culminated a day of travel and enlightenment and he had no trouble getting to sleep that night.

Waking to the sound of the gardener's shovel scraping the ground in the mews next door, Neal called down to reception for coffee and toast. As he waited, he looked at his maps and was pleased to find that he would be taking the same tube lines today to get to the Royal Air Force Museum in Hendon, just north of Hampstead Heath. "Hope I can find some positive information today," he thought, as he poured cream into his coffee. "I'm beginning to think a trip to Germany might be more enlightening. Maybe that's what I'll do next." Then he remembered. "Andrea!" he gasped. "She'll be here tomorrow. Wonder how she'd feel about going to Germany instead of Kersey?" His excitement of getting nearer to the answers he sought, made Neal resent the fact that he might have to interrupt his momentum and entertain Andrea before he could continue. "Aw, heck. Don't project," he thought. Picking up the grey canvas bag he went down the stairs, greeted Maureen in reception, and walked to the South Kensington tube station for his trip to the Royal Air Force Museum.

The morning air was typically misty and the cloud cover cast a grey pallor on the streets as he made his way to the museum. A lady in a docent's uniform greeted him and gave him directions to the World War II section.

Books describing U-Boat activity during the war listed sinkings in the English Channel, near Cornwall and Sussex, the Isles of Scilly and in Brest, France. Most met their demise from mines or torpedoes. None of the books listed information that he could use regarding Germans in Britain prior to the war. "Let's see. I found the billeting list and the photos, but nothing to connect the air part with the U-Boat. There's got to be something in here that will tell me more." Just as Neal was closing the last book from a large stack he had checked out, he looked across from the table and saw a book in a glass case that was facing him. *Classified and Special Air Projects 1935-1939.* Literally flying across the table, he opened the glass door and reached for the book. Bound in black linen with scorched gold lettering, it looked as if it had been in a fire. "Perhaps it was rescued from a fire," he thought to himself as he gently placed it on the table and opened to read the Table of Contents. As if lifting off the pages and into his brain, he rapidly read the list. "There it is. This has to be what I'm looking for.

KLEINER SPION, RAF AND LUFTWAFFE SPECIAL PROJECT NUMBER Z81.

Neal couldn't read fast enough. He devoured every word as it described a joint project involving a small reconnaissance aircraft that would be launched from a U-Boat. "How would they do that?" he asked himself as he continued to read. Then he realized that he must have copies of this information since no books were allowed to leave the museum and he doubted this was a book he could buy off the shelf or order from Waterstones.

"May I help you?" asked the lady in uniform.

"Yes, please. Is there some place in the building where I might make copies of a couple of chapters from this book?"

"I'll be happy to do that for you, sir, but it will be 35p for a page. That be alright, sir?"

He told the lady that was fine and mentally calculated he'd be paying the British government about $75 to make copies that he could get done for about $9 back home. "Well, I've come this far. If I'm going to complain about money at this point, I have no business being here." Satisfied that he had justified his decision, Neal went back to the table and waited for his copies.

The documents were safely stashed in the grey canvas bag as he walked to the tube station and his ride back to the Tramore. As he exited the South Kensington station he stopped to buy a bouquet of pink tulips from the flower vendor and a *Times* at the newsstand. His next stop was at the *Europa* market where he bought cheese, crackers, and a decent bottle of Merlot, remembering Andrea's fondness for red wine.

"Afternoon, Maureen," Neal said, entering reception. "Would you be kind enough to have some tea and biscuits sent to my room. I have a lot of work to do before dinner and don't want to go back out. Oh, yes, please make my reservation for dinner here. Thank you." He climbed the stairs, entered his room, placed the grey canvas bag on the table by the window, put the tulips in a vase he found under the bathroom sink, and waited for his tea to arrive.

The dining room waiter delivered the tea and told him dinner would be served at "Eight tonight, sir. A bit later than usual, but Mr. Wadsworth has chef roasting a rather large leg of lamb. Do hope you'll enjoy it, sir."

"Thanks." He poured a cup of tea and unzipped the grey canvas bag, lifting out the newly copied information.

For the rest of the afternoon Neal read and reread the chapters about *Kleiner Spion.* The project was jointly sponsored, but the British pulled out when they received intelligence that Germany was going to invade Poland, knowing that it was only a matter of time before they too would be in the conflict in some manner. He made notes and pieced together a rough outline from the information he had gathered so far.

1. G. PRIEN, from Lubeck, Germany (written on photo).
2. G. PRIEN, Luftwaffe pilot assigned to project and sent to Lavenham to work with Brits. (from billeting list).
3. G. PRIEN, sent back to Germany? (RAF records show U-352 sunk off Cape Lookout, North Carolina after leaving U-Boat base in Neustadt. Crew listed.)

Leaning back in the deep-cushioned chair, Neal looked out the window at the garden below. His mind wandered as he tried to imagine who G. PRIEN was. "Was he a career Luftaffe officer? Or was he a Naval Officer? Is he still alive? Who was the blond girl in the garden in the photo marked "Cyn…" on the back? Did she live in Sudbury, and was she still there, or even still alive? Was she perhaps from Lavenham?"

A breeze came in through the window and he sat upright, startled that he had drifted of to sleep. "Guess I needed that. Gosh, so much to absorb, but I'm going to solve this. Someone is going to get that ring." He bathed and dressed in a suit and went down to dinner. New guests had arrived during the day and the dining room was noisy with conversation of the guests waiting for their first course to be served. Neal excused himself after the dessert, wanting to tidy the room before he went to sleep, since he would be heading to Gatwick early in the day to pick up Andrea. Passing reception he asked Maureen to give him a wake-up call at five.

"Andrea. Andrea. Wonder how I can amuse her and still get on with my search?"

CHAPTER TWENTY

Maureen's pleasant voice at the other end of the telephone line announced that it was "Five a.m., Mr. Park. Hope you have a very pleasant day."

Dressing quickly, Neal decided to pick up coffee and a roll at Victoria Station. "For that matter, I could even get a bit of breakfast on the train out to Gatwick." Refreshment trolleys rolled through all cars during the trip and passengers could purchase juices, candies, fruit, cigarettes and even liquor.

The train to Gatwick left on time as usual and after finishing his coffee, Neal put his head back on the leather seat and dozed. The squeal of metal wheels braking on the tracks woke him at seven-thirty and he prepared to depart the coach. Business people and travelers hurried to their destinations and Neal found himself studying lighted boards for directions to the airline lounge. He headed toward the lift bank, as the lounge was on the third level of the terminal. "Guess she should be through immigration in a short while," he thought as he stopped at a flower stand and bought a small bouquet of white Lilies of the Valley for Andrea. Their fragrance was much sweeter than he had remembered. The last time he had bought them had been several years ago for Louise.

"May I help you sir?" asked the agent inside the lounge door.

"Yes, thank you. I'm meeting Andrea Rogers. She just came in from New York on Flight 12. Have they cleared immigration yet?"

"Yes, sir. Your party should be here in about twenty minutes. Won't you please help yourself to tea or coffee at the bar?"

Gatwick was busy this time of the morning with numerous flights coming in from the States and Canada. He watched through the large glass windows as tiny airplanes landing far down the field now came

189

into view as giant birds. The hot coffee tasted good and he was swallowing the last tasty drop when he saw her approach.

"Neal," she shouted across the room. Attired in a navy blue pantsuit and white, silk shirt, she was turning heads of the men in the lounge, not only with her high pitched greeting, but with her auburn beauty and glamorous grooming. Almost embarrassed at the scene, he nonetheless got up and held out his arms to this beautiful woman.

Hugging him tightly, she kissed him firmly on the lips and then sat down next to his chair. "Oh, I am so excited to be here. I don't believe I slept more than ten minutes the whole trip over. Oh," she breathlessly continued, "please get me a cup of tea. I'm not going to have another cup of coffee until I go home to New York." Her babbling continued as she gave Neal all the details of her trip to Kennedy Airport. "The driver spoke no English and I really thought I'd have to draw him a map with pictures of planes. Then when we got to the airport, he didn't have any change and I had to find a skycap to change a fifty dollar bill, then I almost left my carry-on bag on the taxi seat, then I couldn't find my passport…okay, though." She took a deep breath. "It was in the zippered part of my handbag, next to my Paris cologne. Oh, Neal, am I just talking too much?" she giggled as she reached for his hand.

"No darling," he answered, "It's wonderful to see you so happy and animated. In fact, it's just wonderful to see you, period."

Startled as they walked into the lift, Neal breathed deep. "Hello, Georgette. What a surprise to see you here."

"Well, hello, Neal. Are you leaving London today?" she asked, surprised as he. "What pretty flowers," she said, looking at the lilies Andrea was clutching to her bosom.

"No, no. This is Andrea Rogers, a friend of mine from New York. Andrea, this is Georgette Wilkinson," he said as he introduced the two women. "Andrea just arrived and we're on our way back to London.

We'll be coming to Sudbury and then over to Kersey day after tomorrow."

"How nice," Georgette said politely, yet with a bit of coolness in her voice. "Please bring Miss Rogers by my shop. I am introducing a line of unique jewelry and I think she just might find some of the pieces to her liking."

"Oh, that would be wonderful," Andrea said, smiling sweetly at Neal as she draped her arm over his arm. "I just love jewelry."

Mixed emotions flooded his being as he looked from one beautiful woman to the other. "I wonder if Georgette thinks this is someone very special...a significant other," he thought to himself. He quickly added, "Andrea's father and mine were in business together and I invited her to come over and visit while I'm here, so she did."

"How lovely," said Georgette, as she picked up a small bag. "I'm on my way home to Sudbury. I've been visiting with an old friend also. He lives in Edinburgh and I flew up for a few days." She wondered if he cared. "Ring me up before you come, and I'll prepare tea. Toodleoo." She walked out of the lift and toward the train station, her long silk skirt blowing in the breeze. Interestingly, they were on the same train from Gatwick to Victoria Station, yet none of the three saw each other.

"Andrea, let's store your luggage in a locker," Neal said as they got off the train. "I'd like you to see Westminster Cathedral and then we can get a bite of lunch before we go to the hotel. It's just down the street from here."

The grey stone plaza in front of the cathedral was scattered with people. Some were eating, others studying, still others just sitting and enjoying the mid-day warmth. Neal and Andrea walked into the dimly lit cathedral with its white stone floor. To the left was the traditional book store and souvenir shop. Straight ahead, the stark, black seats faced the altar. Heavy, ornate, wrought iron chandeliers hung from the three story ceiling, their lights low. To the left of the altar was a bank of candles, some lit in memory of loved ones, some in thanksgiving, some in asking, and others awaiting the offering and charge of worshipers. The two tourists gently sat down. He held her hand as he bowed his head. But his thoughts drifted back to Louise and their life together. She felt his warmth, but her thoughts ran back to a young man in uniform, a very long time ago.

They walked slowly down the aisle to the back of the church and out onto the plaza. Two blocks past the cathedral they found a small tea room and went inside. He ordered for both of them, choosing curried chicken sandwiches and fresh fruit. The tea pot came first and she thanked him for remembering. A plate of date bars finished the meal, and leaving a generous tip, they walked back out onto the sidewalk. Neal found an American Express office and they went inside to exchange some dollars for pounds. "I might need those pounds to buy some of your friend's jewelry," she said with mischief in her voice. He started to swat her on the backside, changing his mind as he counted the faces staring at them in the office.

At the hotel Maureen greeted them and took a piece of Andrea's luggage, Neal carrying the largest bag. After unpacking, Andrea said she'd like to take a bath and relax for a while. Neal told her that was fine as he had some copying to do and would have to go to an office in the next block.

"Don't you want to rest, too?" she coyly asked.

"Andrea, don't get your feelings hurt, but I'm here on a special mission and there'll be time for *resting* later." He heard the tub water running as he closed the door and went down the stairs.

Next to Waterstone's Book Store Neal found a solicitor's office, and ringing the bell, he opened the door and went in. "Hello, anyone here?" he asked. The room was sparsely furnished and unlike most offices, there were few books and papers on desks or tables. "I suppose they really do practice law here, curious."

"May I help you, sir?" said the thin, dark, girl with large brown eyes. She spoke with the eloquent speech of Indians living in England.

"Yes, thank you. I'm doing some research and need to make some copies of about ten pages of text. Do you possibly have a copy machine?"

The girl took his pages, went into another office and made his copies. He thanked her and offered to pay. She bowed, told him it was not necessary, and bid him good day.

Andrea was deep in sleep when he came back to the room. Trying to be quiet, he sat in the chair by the window and spread his papers out on the table. Looking at them another time made him feel intensely involved in this mystery and fueled his efforts to find answers. Even the gardener's spade scraping the drive down below in the mews could not break his concentration. "I feel so close to unlocking something...but what?"

Pulling the sheet back to reveal a thin, yellow nightgown, Andrea motioned to Neal with her little finger. "Come see how rested I am," she said. His concentration broke.

****

Walking down Old Brompton Road, they went into Harrod's. Andrea was overwhelmed with the amount of inventory and the small range of price. "My, they certainly aren't bashful about charging twenty dollars for a perfectly good ten dollar pair of hose," she exclaimed as they walked through the store. Her fascination however, overrode the prices when she came to the toy floor. "Oh, I do have to buy this stuffed lamb for my new niece. It's so cuddly and she'll love it." The clerk accepted her credit card and rang up the thirty pound charge. "Can't believe I'm spending so much on a toy, but Neal you must see her. She is a darling baby."

Continuing their walk back to the hotel, they stopped at a silver shop where she bought coffee spoons. "Aren't these the most precious little spoons you have ever seen?" Next his hands were being filled with bags of Wedgewood from the discount china store. "No one will ever know they came from the discount store, I'll just tell them we went to the factory and saw it being made. Wish we could do that. Maybe next time." Passing a Boots pharmacy she pulled him into the doorway. "Neal, a friend told me about the most wonderful and sensuous bath oil they sell here. I must get some. Come to think of it, "sensuous" is in the name, too." She laughed as she kept a continual flow of chatter going during their walk.

"Andrea, it's getting late. We'd better head back to the hotel. I've made reservations for our dinner at a place nearby called Boswell's. Do hope you'll like it."

She did like the dinner. She did like the bottle of red wine he ordered, and she did drink more of it than intended. He found out later how "rested" she was. It had been a good day.

****

Andrea was unusually quiet on the train to Marks Tey. She read from the travel books they had bought at Waterstone's the day before. Neal told her of his plan to take her to Gainsborough's house and Georgette's studio before they drove to Kersey and the cottage.

"Didn't she say she was introducing a new line of jewelry?" Andrea asked, looking up from a copy of *Constable by* Michael Rosenthal.

"Think so," he answered. He was beginning to have those mixed feelings again. "We won't have too much time to shop. I have some work to do before we go to Lavenham tomorrow morning."

His rental car, parked in front of the Sudbury train station, was wet from the morning mist. He put Andrea's bags in the *boot* and drove the few blocks to Georgette's studio. "We'll leave the car here and

194

walk across to Gainsborough's house later," he said, parking at the front door. A hand released the sheer window curtain of the studio window just as he looked up. "Wonder if we're being watched?" he thought to himself.

Georgette was patronizingly polite to them both as she opened several cases of handmade jewelry, most set with semi-precious stones in gold and silver. Andrea chose two rings and two necklaces, both gold with aquamarine stones. "These are beautiful, Georgette," she said. "The workmanship is very nice. Do you plan to market this line outside Great Britain?"

"That would be a possibility if I had a reliable agent," she responded as she smiled at Neal.

"Ha," he said with a nervous laugh. "Surely you'll have all the market you need in this country. However, Tiffany's might be interested." Again he laughed.

"By the way, Neal. Your photograph copy is ready. Here it is. Do hope the quality is satisfactory." Handing him the wrapped package, Georgette again smiled deeply at him.

They bid goodbye, but not before Georgette asked Andrea how long she was staying.

"Oh, I'm only here for three more days. Then I fly back to New York. We're getting ready for a very busy summer season at The Plaza," she answered, with heavy emphasis on *The Plaza.*

Neal felt somehow he was in the middle of a contest. "Oh well, just my ego imagining they're both interested in me." His feelings told him he was definitely interested in both of them.

They toured Gainsborough's house, had tea at the tea room across the street, then drove to Kersey. The four Beacham children were playing in the yard as they drove in and stopped to wave.

"Neal, this is charming. However did you find it?" she said as he opened the cottage's front door and led her in.

"An Estate Agent in Sudbury brought me here, and interestingly enough, the owner's wife is from the States, Cleveland. The owner is rector of that big church we saw as we came in."

After finding space for Andrea's things, Neal suggested they walk to the pub, telling her about Rosie and Paddy Houlehan, the owners. "She makes the best lamb stew and he pours a great brandy."

****

There was enough cool in the air for Neal to build a fire in the cottage fireplace. "Want to warm the little cockles in your heart," he said with a laugh. "Would you be liken' another brandy, me lady? Would be a fine finish to that hearty meal."

"Neal, you are a tease and you do seem to be picking up the accent here," she said, curling her feet under her skirt as she sat on the sofa. "This is such a wonderful and cozy place. We may never get you back to the States. Oh, what a horrible thought."

Watching the coals become embers, Neal put his arms around her shoulders, pulled her close to him, and kissed her. "We'd better turn in. I have a lot to show you in Lavenham tomorrow and I want to check out a few more places that might have some information I need." A cool breeze came in through the open bedroom window. He pulled the blanket up over them both, kissed her gently and turned to go to sleep.

"Neal," she whispered in his ear, curling into the curve of his body, her ample breasts pushing through the folds in her nightgown. "Do we have to get up real early?"

He turned, seeing her glistening eyes reflecting from the outside moonlight. Lightly exploring the soft lines of her body, his eagerness to sleep gave way to a sensuous path to ecstasy.
"Not too early."

****

The little rental car moved swiftly down the Suffolk roads as they made their way from Kersey to Lavenham. He pulled into the parking area next to the airbase museum, helped Andrea out, and they walked toward one of the quonset huts.

"Mornin' there," yelled the tour guide who had shown him the base last week. "You back again with your wife?"

"Hello. No, this is a friend from the States and I told her about the base. She's helping me with my research," he said, wondering if the old man would really believe that statement.

"Right. Well, you two just be helpin' yourselves to lookin'. I'll be goin' back home for me lunch." He got into a small car and drove out of the parking area.

Neal and Andrea walked around for a half hour. He told her the same things the old man had told him. He showed her the Officer's Club, the barracks with the pinups on the walls, and then they stood looking at the control tower.

"It must have been a terrible time for these people," Andrea said as they walked away from the tower.

"Darling, it was a terrible time for the whole world."

Back at the cottage he showed her all of his notes, photos and copies of documents he had collected since he arrived. She studied every piece. Looking up at him she said, "Neal, you must go to Germany to find out more. There you might find the key."

"I know you're right, I just want to be sure I'm finding out all I can around here first."

They walked to the pub again that evening and this time enjoyed a dinner of Rosie's shepherd's pie. As they turned into the drive on Brett Lane, Neal noticed Patti and Tom sitting on the porch of the big house. Walking up to the porch, Neal said, "Good evening. This is my friend, Andrea Rogers, from New York. We've just had two nice days in the area and she's leaving tomorrow. Andrea, this is Father Tom Beacham and Mrs. Beacham."

"Patti and Tom, please." Patti and Tom came down the porch steps and shook hands with Andrea, asking if they would like to come in for tea or a brandy.

"Think we better pass. She has a mid-afternoon flight, so we'll be taking the early train to Victoria and then Gatwick," Neal answered, hoping they wouldn't insist. "Thanks, anyway."

CHAPTER TWENTY-ONE

The train ride from Gatwick to Victoria and on to Colchester was uneventful. Neal was not happy that he had to take a taxi from Colchester to Kersey, but the Sudbury line stopped running at seven and he did not leave London until six. A cold sandwich and a glass of wine that he bought on the Colchester train was his dinner and he vowed to fix a big breakfast for himself the next morning.

While at Gatwick, Neal made a reservation for the next week to Germany. *Lufthansa* had a direct flight to Hamburg and he reserved a rental car for the drive to Kiel and Lubeck. The airline agent assured him he would have no problem finding lodging. "It will be part of my adventure to find quaint German hotels," he thought, anxious to continue his search.

Pulling into the driveway back to the cottage, he noticed the lights on in the front room of the big house. He stopped the car and went up to the front door. After a quick knock, Father Tom opened the door.

"Good evening, Neal. Your lady friend get off to the States alright?"

"Yes, thank you. But I forgot the Sudbury line stops at seven and had to taxi in from Colchester," he answered. "Not a problem though. Gave me time to organize my thoughts for this coming week. Wanted to let you and Patti know that I'm flying to Germany on Friday and will probably be gone four or five days."

"I don't mean to sound as though I am prying, but Patti mentioned you are here on a search," Tom said, a quizzical look on his face.

"Yes. Some weeks ago I found a box in the ocean off Georgia and it contained some stuff from a sunken U-Boat. I'm trying to find out who lost it and return the contents."

Father Tom asked him to sit down. Neal told him the entire story and asked him if he could shed any light on the search, specifically the girl in the picture. "I'll drop by tomorrow and show you the picture. Also have one of the German fliers. Think one of them is the person who owned the box and wrote the letters. That's why I'm going to Germany. I want to find out who this man was, and who was the girl."

Father Tom thanked him for sharing his story and said he would be glad to help him if he could. "I'll check some of our old directories and books at St. Mary's to see if something there might be of value."

Neal slept well that night and did not awake until nine the next morning. After a big breakfast of eggs, toast, and orange juice, he poured a second cup of coffee and proceeded to clear the small table. "Guess there's not enough room here to spread out all my stuff. Think I'll put some on the sofa and the rest on the coffee table." With piles of paper, maps, and a small stack of photographs in front of him, he began the process of organizing his collection. He started with German documents on the left side of the sofa and British documents on the right side.

Three hours later Neal's own snoring woke him up. He had fallen asleep on the sofa, papers on his lap, a pencil in his hand. "Whew," he said. "Must have dozed off." Getting up, he looked at the clock. "It's one-thirty already. But who cares," he laughed. "I don't have to be anywhere at any special time."

The past months since Louise's death, the move to his little Jekyll house, and now this trip, had hardly given him time to stop and rest. Every day had been full and he liked it that way. "I'm not on a schedule now, except for the flight to Germany, so think I'll just try real hard to take it easy. No rush to find the recipient of this stuff either. After all," he again laughed to himself, "it's been in the ocean over fifty years."

That afternoon he walked up the hill to St. Mary's. Father Tom was in his office and invited him in. "Do sit down, Neal. Did you bring the photograph?" he asked.

"Here," Neal said, handing him the faded picture he had put in a plastic sleeve.

"Mmm, doesn't look like someone I would know, but this is over fifty years old as you said, so by now this girl would be a mature lady. That is, if she is still alive." He studied it in the light coming in his office window. "Did you say you think she would have been from Lavenham?"

"That's where Prien was based and I just surmised he would have met her there."

Father Tom looked again at the photograph. "You know, old man, Suffolk County had, and still has, a lot of pretty girls. She could have been from right here," he said with a hearty laugh. "I remember my mother telling me she went to dances in Lavenham at the airfield. And she lived south of here in Stoke-by-Nyland. Seems the young girls would get as many of them as possible into one car and pool their money for petrol to make the trip. It was about a twenty kilometer drive each way. Not far, but petrol was scarce then."

Seizing an opportunity to learn more, Neal asked, "Is your mother still in Stoke-by-Nyland?"

"Oh, no. She died ten years ago from a stroke. She had a hard time during the war and never really regained her strength. Her home was bombed, family members died, and she took sick soon after. How she ever managed to marry and have children I do not know."

"I'm sorry. Know you probably miss her a lot. I lost my mother right before my wife and I married and I still miss her terribly." Neal felt disappointed that he would not have had yet another person to talk to about that time in Suffolk County.

For the next three days Neal slowly and methodically cataloged and chronologically noted his documents. Thursday evening he had an early dinner at *The Bell Pub* and enjoyed a brandy with Paddy. Back at the cottage, he packed his bag, took a hot soak in the tub, and sat down on the sofa with his notebook in hand. "Okay, let's see if I can do a summary outline of all this stuff so I don't have to take it all out each time I need a reference." Starting, he wrote down the date he found the box. His following entries were:

   I. Gerhardt Prien (?) from Lubeck, Germany.
      Uncle, Guenther Prien, U-Boat ace in WWII.
  II. Prien part of Ger/UK special project *Kleiner Spion*, in Lavenham.
 III. Project scuttled. Germany invaded Poland.
 IV. Prien had British sweetheart from Lavenham (?).
  V. Prien writes to girl in picture. Letters, etc. in box.
 VI. Prien goes down off NC on U-352, May 9, 1942.

On the next page he listed his objectives for the German trip.
   a. Visit German naval yard in Kiel.
   b. Search for *Kleiner Spion* and Prien info.
   a. Talk to townspeople in Lubeck.
   b. Locate Prien home/farm.
   c. Find Prien relatives.
   d. Find out who "Cyn..." was, and where she lived.

Excited and exhausted, Neal went to bed, dreaming again of Andrea and Georgette. In this dream they were being chased by Louise.

OVER THE ATLANTIC OCEAN
Neal studied his German maps and silently wished he had taken the time to sign up for a speedy German language course before he left Jekyll. "I'll never understand this language...too many haus', and schweis', and wigs, and burgs, and steins. And, I've never seen so many towns in one small country. Every landowner must call his space a town," he laughed, as he read on. Almost lulling himself into

a nice afternoon nap, he was jolted into awareness of landing as the flight attendant announced their descent into Hamburg.

Clearing customs was without delay and he made his way to the car rental area of the terminal. Keys in hand, Neal followed the signs to the parking area and found his little rental car, a red one this time. He loaded his bags in the trunk, put the map from the rental agency on the front seat and started the engine. The roads were well marked out of the airport area and he easily found his way to the highway and drove north toward Kiel. Turning east at Bad Bramstedt he wanted to get to Bad Segeberg early enough to check into *The Romantik Wald,* a small roadside inn he had read about in a travel magazine. Owned by the same family since the seventeenth century it was in a forest and beside a stream. Driving down what seemed like an unending road with heavy growth on both sides, he finally found the inn. He parked the car on the gravel drive in front of the thatched roof building and went inside.

"Guten Tag," greeted the lady behind the desk, her long blond hair braided in a crown on top of her head.

"No sprechen sie deutsch," Neal responded.

"Mmm," she mumbled. "I speak a bit of de English, so I help you."

"Thanks. I need a room for tonight, please." He watched as she looked down at a large ledger on the desk.

"Ein Zimmer mit Bad…oh, mistake…you want room mit bath. I have one on second floor. Is nice. You vill like it."

She handed him a large brass key on a leather strap and a small brochure. The inn's dining room menu listed fresh game and other fruits of the forest cooked daily. He checked his watch and noted that he would have time for a quick nap before dinner. The brochure described the antiques that decorated each guest room and boasted of many original paintings that had also survived the big war. "Guess they mean WW two," he thought to himself.

As he walked up the heavily carved stairway, he noticed the beamed walls, the wainscoting, and he was aware of the aura of old and mold. The carpeting showed need of replacement, but gave the inn a feeling of its place in time. He could not imagine anything new in this building.

Opening the door, he found a cheerful room decorated in dark wood furniture, with bright yellow curtains and bed covering. The window overlooked the creek he read about and he was not disappointed with his choice. He opened the window and a cool breeze met him. "Now I'll take that little nap and get ready for my first real German dinner." Thinking about Hildegard and Fritz back home in Jekyll he realized he didn't even know where in Germany they were from. It had seemed curious to him that they rarely talked about their life here.

The dining room was near empty as Neal walked to a table by the window. He ordered the daily special of roast pork with spaetzel and kraut, topped with a pepperkorn sauce. His red wine was served in a painted crystal decanter. For dessert he had an apple strudel and did not think it was as good as Hildegard's. "I'll have to remember to tell her so." Sitting down at the bar, Neal ordered a brandy and began talking to the bartender who told him he was one of the owners. Neal gave him a brief outline of his reason for being in Germany and asked if he by chance knew the name Prien. The young man shook his head, "Nein, but mein pater vas in dat war. He could maybe talk mit you."

In short order a tall, grey haired man came into the bar. He introduced himself as Otto Schmidt, telling Neal that he and his wife, Gerda, were now the owners like his parents before him. He listened intently to Neal, did not interrupt, scratched his chin, and finally said, "Yah, I knew dis man, Prien."

Neal could hardly contain himself when he heard this. "You mean you really knew Gerhardt Prien?"

"Nein, nein," Otto said in a gruff voice. "I knew who he vas because I served mit his Uncle Guenther on U-47. I vas U-Boat man, too," he said with a proud smile. "Ve sunk many ships, but I leave before his boat go down. Got measles." At this he lowered his head as if in shame. "Ich liebe dee see," he said, wiping his eyes. Neal could tell the man did indeed love the sea.

Neal continued to ask him questions. "Nein," he did not know what happened to Gerhardt, but had heard he died at sea also. "Yah," they had a farm not far from here, but he didn't know exactly where. "Tink it vas near Ponitz. Dey vas farmers. Sold vegetables to places like dis. Mein pater bought from Gerhardt's pater. De vas friends. But after war, he no hear from him."

Otto suggested Neal drive to Ponitz and talk to townspeople. "You vill find many of dos people dead or moved to other places. Bombing vas very bad around here and people move to forget and start over. Wir lucky, no bombs come here in wald...er, forest." He drew a map for Neal, detailing roads not on the rental agency map and added names of some families who he thought were still in the area. "Been so long. Ve all try to forget. Don' talk much about dat war."

With the cool breeze and a thick quilt, Neal slept soundly that night and hated to hear the ring of his little bedside alarm clock the next morning. The heavy meal and the profound information had put him into deep schlaf...sleep. For breakfast he had a large helping of Ruhreier and Speck...scrambled eggs and bacon. The coffee was strong and the toast lavishly buttered with butter from a local dairy. Neal thanked the Schmidts for their hospitality and the information they gave him. He told them he would try to stop for a night on his way back. "I really feel comfortable here," he said as he shook their hands. Passing through the lobby with a tray of clean glasses, the son nodded his head and bid Neal goodbye. "Leben Sie wohl."

The gravel crunched under the little red car's wheels as Neal pulled out onto the paved road. He stopped, backed up, and turned off the engine. Taking out his rental car map, he made a decision to drive north to Kiel and then southeast to Ponitz in a day or so. "Ponitz will wait. I want to learn more about the German Navy and the U-Boats before I venture into finding the Prien family," he thought to himself as he again started the engine.

The highway to Kiel had signs advertising resorts in Trappenkamp and Wankendorf along this route. From his reading he had noted that Germans loved to holiday, and enjoyed swimming and shore activities. "S'pose these people play as hard as they obviously work," he thought, as he neared the city center. His travel directory listed the *Wiking Hotel* as "near city center attractions and commerce". He checked into the hotel, a 42 room property that showed signs of recent renovation. His room, small but clean, had only a bed, dresser, lounge chair, and a TV on a small table. "For $60 a night I shouldn't complain," he said to himself as he put his clothes in the tiny closet with varnished folding doors.

The clerk at reception pointed him in the direction of the seawalk along *Hindenburgufer* that led to the *Holtenhau* locks. From the seawalk he could see not only the canal, but an impressive view of harbor activity and the surrounding shipyards. The Kiel Canal, 62 miles long, connecting the Baltic Sea to the North Sea, "the most traveled canal in the world," as stated in his directory was the main tourist attraction in Kiel, second only to the naval installations. The entire city suffered massive damage during World War II. Eighty percent of the city was destroyed and much of it was never rebuilt. One building of note, the *Rathaus*, or City Hall, originally built in 1907, had been restored. Shipping remained active, with 50,000 ships a year passing through the locks. Today being a Saturday, *Samstag,* the shipyards were void of human activity, but the many ships docked were evidence that come Monday, *Montag,* work would resume.

Neal walked around the *Holstenstrasse,* the pedestrian area and stopped in an open-air cafe for lunch. He ordered *Kohl mit Pinkel,* cabbage with coarse sausage and potatoes. "A bit heavy for lunch, but I think I might need the sustenance if I plan to walk all afternoon." He finished a large stein of beer and paid the waitress, a large woman with a crown of braids. She was wearing a bright red skirt, white blouse, and an embroidered vest of black velvet. She told Neal the average German consumes about 35 gallons of beer a year and most of the hops are grown in an area from Nuremberg to Munich. He secretly wished it were closer to Oktoberfest so he could sample some of the beer from the more than 1,500 breweries in the country. "Next visit," he promised himself.

A few blocks from the cafe Neal stood in front of a small bookstore. Looking into the windows he could tell it contained many very old volumes and he hoped he might find some with reference to World War II and the U-Boat effort. A small bell tinkled as he opened the door and for a moment his thoughts were of another small door bell in Sudbury...and Georgette.

From behind a faded, brown, curtain hanging on an opening in the back of the shop appeared a stooped, old man wearing pince-nez. "Guten Tag," greeted the man.

"No Sprechen Sie Deutsch," answered Neal as he walked closer to the old man.

He told the shopkeeper what he was looking for and the man directed him to a tiny room at the top of the stairs. In very good English, the man told him that Germans are still reticent to acknowledge losing the war and do not like reminders of the fighting. He showed him the dark, almost hidden shelves that held the books Neal so longed to see. Poring over dusty books with torn covers and mildewed pages, he learned that the Deutsche Werke yards, nearby, built and repaired the majority of the U-Boats used during the war. Making a mental note to see if anything of this installation still existed, he went on to find several books that listed each U-Boat, with commissioning dates and dates of decommissioning or when it was sunk. "Ah, here it is. U-47. Commissioned December, 17, 1938, Sunk March 8, 1941," he anxiously read. Further pages told of the commanding officer, Guenther Prien, born near Ponitz am See, who was credited with sneaking undetected into Britain's Scapa Flow Naval base and sinking the Royal Navy's largest battleship, *Royal Oak,* then retreating undetected as it sank. It would remain to this day one of the most famous of naval actions. Checking the indexes of each book, Neal finally found one book that listed *Kleiner Spion.* He was beginning to feel a rush of adrenaline as he scanned the pages for the name Prien. "There it is," he shouted in a booming voice. The old man came running up the stairs.

"Are you alright, sir?" he asked.

"Yes, yes. I'm just so delighted to find the information I've been seeking," showing the man the page with Gerhardt's name.

The man grabbed the back of a chair as color seemed to drain from his face. "You have been looking for the man Prien?"

"Why, yes. Did you know Gerhardt Prien?"

His breathing coming in short pants, the old man sat down in the chair and stared down at the table. He looked into Neal's eyes and said, "I vas on U-352 ven Prien and Kleiner Spion vent down. Mein commander and thirty-two of us ver rescued at sea. Dey took us to Charleston, South Carolina for interrogation. Most of us ver badly hurt, but American doctors took gut care of us. You know ver Charleston is?" he asked as he took out a handerchief and wiped his eyes.

"Oh, I do, Yes, I do. My son is a doctor there and I live about 120 miles south in Georgia. Actually, on Jekyll Island. Ever heard of it?" Without allowing the old man to answer, Neal started asking him how well he knew Gerhardt, did he ever hear him speak of a sweetheart in England, where did he live…he hardly took a breath, his enthusiasm was so overwhelming. He showed him the picture of the German officers that Georgette had copied for him and the one of the girl he had found in the box.

"Nein, nein," answered the old man. "Ve crewmen ver not close mit de officers. He vas beeg man, had secret mission to do, and ve did not know about dat."

Crestfallen that this man could not answer all his questions, Neal asked him if he could buy some of the books.

"Ya, vy not. Nobody here interested in dat var anyvay."

Together they descended the stairs and the man wrapped up the books Neal bought. He told him about a small museum near the shipyards, and a memorial and museum in Laboe about fifteen miles north. Neal thanked him for his time and walked out into the afternoon sun. He felt like he was making progress, if only with confirmation of what he had already found. He drove to Laboe and walked through the museum. A tall, stone, contemporary structure in the form of a ship's stern, it commemorated the war dead from both world wars. The museum housed many rooms of documents, maps, and dioramas of battle sites from World Wars I&II. Neal made notes and was surprised to find that visitors could make copies of many documents on the museum copy machine.

In the front yard of the *Marine-Ehrenmal* museum, and on the water's edge, was a beached U-Boat...U-995. The marker beside the huge vessel stated that it was put into commission on September 16, 1943 and decommissioned on May 8, 1945, in service a mere twenty months, operating in Norwegian waters and the Barents Sea. It was part of the last one hundred U-Boats Germany built before the end of World War II. As he stood there looking across the expanse of this great, grey sea vessel, he tried to imagine the faces of the many men who served aboard these boats. Just like him, they had sweethearts or wives, parents, children, and love of their country. "God, war is so awful. Why do men do this to each other?"

He drove back to Kiel, and after a dinner of sauerbraten and kraut in the Bauerenstrube Restaurant at the hotel, he went back to his room. After a long, hot shower, he laid out all his findings from the box and from his research on the bed. "Got to make some sense of this. I know who he was, where he may have lived, how he died, but who was the girl in the garden? Tomorrow I'll drive to Ponitz and see if I can find any Priens."

CHAPTER TWENTY-TWO

The map showed a road from Kiel through Preetz, Plon, and Eutin, and then to Ponitz. Along this route were many lakes with long German names, like *Erholungsgebiet Ponitzer Seenplatte*. He enjoyed the cool morning air and the sights of the farms along the way. "Now, if I can only find the Prien farm and hopefully some of Gerhardt's family," he thought as he drove.

In Eutin he stopped at the *Hotel Voss Haus,* which his tour directory said was over 300 years old. Knowing he was quite near Ponitz he checked in and told the innkeeper he would be back later in the day. The hotel was on a lake, *Eutiner See,* and had five dining rooms. "Certainly won't go hungry here," though at the moment his thoughts were focused on his search and not his appetite.

Back in the little red car, Neal had a feeling of excitement as he went the next eight miles toward Ponitz. He slowly drove into the center of the small town and parked in front of a row of shops on *Ahrensbaker Strasse.* He strolled down the broken sidewalks, looking into the shops…a bakery with tempting delicacies, a tailor's where the tailor was hemming wool trousers, a bookshop featuring pornographic magazines, a photographer's studio with pictures of snow scenes in the window, and finally, a butcher shop where the fresh smell of sausages caught his attention. He went in and at the back of the shop saw a huge man wielding a meat cleaver over a butcher block that held a large piece of fresh beef.

"Good morning," Neal said, as the man's arm lowered the cleaver into the red muscle. "Sure smells good in here."

"Danke," replied the man as he put down the cleaver and wiped his bloody hands on his stained white apron. "You do not speak German?"

"No sir. Just a visitor from the States. But I'd like to buy one of those sandwiches up there," he said, pointing to some freshly made ham and cheese sandwiches on brown bread, "and I'd like to ask you a couple of questions."

"Ya," replied the butcher as he went behind the counter to get Neal's sandwich. "Vat vood you be asking?"

"Have you lived in this area long?"

"All of my lifetime, vich is sixty-nine years."

"Fine. Then perhaps you might have known a family from around here named Prien."

The butcher cleared his throat and said in a firm voice. "Ya, I knew dat family. Dey had a farm just outside town in *Schmiedekamp,* a very pretty farm, too. Until your bombers took it down," he said with a scowl on his face. "Oh vell, vat matter now. Var is over long time and ve build new. Both sides lose really. Ya?"

"Yes, sir, you are sure right there. I was too young to serve, but lost friends and family, too. War is never won by anyone," he answered forlornly, but in agreement. Continuing to pursue his questioning, he asked the butcher if he knew the whereabouts of any family members now.

"Nein, but can tell you how to get to where farm vas. Maybe neighbors help."

He drew a map on a piece of butcher's paper and wished Neal good luck. "Come back and let me know vat you find. Dey vas good people. Tink son vas on U-Boat like uncle. Both sunk. Bad."

"At least I'm in the right place," Neal said to himself as he sat in the car and ate the sandwich. "How come their ham tastes so much better than ours?" he asked himself. He finished the last of a *Coke* and got out to put his trash in a bin on the sidewalk. "Germans never litter," he mused.

Winding his way over one-lane country roads, he came to a broken black fence, long since overgrown with vines and weeds. From the map the butcher had drawn, he knew he should be there. In the distance he could see the remains of what had been a house, crumbled walls in various degrees of height were visible through the overgrowth. A break in the fence revealed the semblance of a drive. "Don't think I'll risk taking the car in there," he said to himself as he got out and started walking toward the ruins. He stumbled over stumps and briars, cautiously watching for holes in the ground. "Doesn't look like anyone has been on this land for years." Looking up he saw a flock of birds fly out from behind a cluster of trees that were beside the remains of a chimney. Bricks and stones were scattered randomly about the ground and broken pieces of slate were imbedded in the dirt. "There are a lot of slate roofs in this area," he remembered. A large crater in the earth nearby gave him assurance that the site did indeed take a big strike. What was a pond, long since dried up, was to the north of the house site. "Wonder where the barns might have been?" he asked himself, looking around for any evidence of farm life. "Over fifty years doesn't leave much." A rusted and twisted wheel that might have been on a small cart was half-hidden by weeds and a large accumulation of fallen leaves. He pulled at the weeds and jumped back as his eyes stared at a shoe, the laces still tied. "S'pose this was on someone's foot when the bomb struck'?" A chill went up his spine as he continued to search beneath the growth. He went back to the shoe, lifted it out, and starting to turn away, a reflection of light caught his eye. Reaching down into the ground, he scraped dirt away from the shining metal. Neal gently pulled it out and found himself looking at a very old watch, a man's pocket watch, partially encrusted with dried mud, and stopped at three o'clock. Slowly rubbing the mud off the watch, he felt what he thought was engraving on the back. He turned it to the light of the sun and read the inscription.

To Gerhardt   Love, Mother
1903

213

Neal started counting. "This couldn't have been given to Gerhardt, it must have been his father's. Maybe he was Gerhardt, Jr." He put the watch in his pocket and continued to search the ground around him. "I feel like the first person to be here since the war. This is eerie." A hawk flew overhead, screeching, as if telling him to leave. Finding a large rock on which to sit, Neal sat. Glad he remembered to bring his camera, he took pictures of what he saw from left to right, though it was mostly weeds and vines. A few small trees ringed the area where the pond had been. Just then a car horn broke the silence and he looked toward the road to see a small black car parking next to his red rental. A tall man got out of the car and walked into the weeds toward him. Neal went forward to meet him.

"Hallo," shouted the man. "Vat are you doing here?" he asked in English. He obviously saw the rental license and Neal's name and address on the grey canvas bag on the car seat, thus calling out in English.

"Hello, I'm Neal Park, from the States. I'm trying to find someone in the Prien family and the butcher in Ponitz told me how to get here," he answered. Laughing, he added, "Obviously no one is home."

"Ya, not so funny," the man said, not looking too friendly. "Dey most die in var. Vy you vant to find dem?"

Neal was beginning to be a bit apprehensive and sorry he made a joke. "Sorry, I really am trying to locate someone who can help me." Walking back to the cars, Neal told him his story and the man listened intently.

The man lived down the dirt road on a neighboring farm. He told Neal that no one had farmed the Prien land since the war. It was his understanding that the land was inherited by cousins who lived in Austria and had no interest in the farm. He said offers to buy the farm by local people were always refused, too.

"I vas young boy when var ended and I remember mein pater tell me all Priens die in var. Somehow I remember though dey have one sister who did not die in var. I tink she vas sick in...*Kopfschmerzen...* he pointed to his head. Take her to hospital in Lubeck. Dat be many years ago. She might be gone now." The man gave Neal the name of the hospital in Lubeck.

Neal thanked him and wondered if he should mention the watch. "No," he thought. "If I find a relative, I'll give it to him or her." Retracing his route, he drove back to Eutin and the hotel. True to the directory's description, the hotel was filled with antiques and original paintings by famous and not-so-famous European artists. The hotel manager suggested Neal get a cocktail at the bar and take a tour of the hotel and the grounds before dinner. "By de vay, tonight chef make *Rote Grutze mit Raspberries* for dessert. Vill be very gut. You try."

"I'll do that," Neal answered. "Thanks for the suggestion." He ordered a scotch on the rocks from the rotund bartender and made his way to the side entrance leading down to the lake. Several white benches were under trees beside the lake, many filled with couples enjoying the early evening quiet. He found a vacant one and sat down. Soon a young man carrying a stein in his hand sat next to him. He was English, "studied at Oxford," and in rapid conversation, gave Neal the sports scores for the day. The most popular sport in Germany being soccer, he recited all of the local teams and their standings. Neal shook his head and tried to be interested and informed, when in reality he had never developed a liking for the sport.

The young man asked Neal to join him and his family at their table for dinner. "Mother and Father are probably in the dining room now, if you'd care to go in. You can join them in another cocktail. Father usually has two or three whiskies before dinner. Mother has her sherry, which I find rather boring, don't you? I like to try the brews of the region when I travel."

"Doesn't this kid ever shut up?" Neal asked himself, though he did enjoy the company and was looking forward to meeting his parents.

The Newfields...Margaret and Patrick, were from London. They and Patrick, Jr. lived in *Hampstead Heath* in a building of three row houses converted into one home. Patrick, Sr. was an investment banker and traveled frequently to Germany, doing business with *Deutsch Banks.* The son was following his father in the business, having recently completed graduate school.

Neal told them about Kersey, they had never been there, and suggested a holiday in the area might be enjoyable. He mentioned Sudbury and immediately Margaret Newfield became very animated and entered the conversation. Her ladies reading club had just finished a book about Gainsborough's life and they were planning a trip to his home. "Then surely you must take a few miles detour and visit Kersey at the same time," Neal said, momentarily thinking about Gainsborough's home and Georgette's studio down the street. "If I'm not prying, what brings you to Eutin?"

Patrick, Sr. told him they had a few days free before attending a big conference in Hamburg and a friend had mentioned this hotel and the "lovely area". He added, "My uncle is a doctor at the mental hospital in Lubeck, so we are going to visit him for a day as well."

"Well, that's a coincidence," Neal said. "I'm going there myself to try to find an elderly German lady." This piquing their interest, he felt obliged to share with them the story of his search.

"You Americans are amazing," Patrick, Sr. said with a hearty laugh. "Your curiosity and actual inability or desire to not let that war go are, yes, amazing." He coughed and added, "Now don't get me wrong, old chap, but over here we try to forget."

"That's okay," Neal responded. "I am a curious sort, or I'd have never gone with the Bureau." Until now he had not told them what he had done before his retirement.

Patrick, Sr. apologized. They had a big laugh at differences, and ordered brandies before retiring. Neal thanked them for sharing the evening and told them to look him up if they came to Kersey in the next two months. That was how long he planned to stay in England. But then there was Georgette.

Upon rising the next morning, Neal looked at his watch, counted the hours and decided he would make calls back to the States. "Guess I should check in with Jordan and Lucretia. Haven't talked to them in a week now and they just might wonder where I am if they call Kersey and get no answer."

"Hi, Dad. How's the search going? Find anyone yet?" Jordan asked.

"Nah," Neal said dejectedly. He gave Jordan the details of his trip here in Germany and told him of his plan to visit the Prien sister in Lubeck today. "Hopefully, if she's still there, she won't be too senile to remember some names and places. Jordan, I'm going to stay tomorrow night back in Bad Segeburg, maybe Otto Schmidt will remember more about Guenther Prien and what he may have told him about his nephew, Gerhardt. Have a reservation to fly back to London on Wednesday and I might stay a few days there to visit some of the museums. Just might stop in Harrod's, too," he said, laughing. "Do my grandgirls want anything special?"

"Dad, you spoil them too much already. But at the moment they've gotten into collecting hair trinkets…you know, barrettes, combs, that kind of thing," Jordan suggested. "Those don't take up much space in a suitcase either."

"Okay, Jordan. Better sign off. Give Lucretia and the girls a big kiss for me and I'll call you next week."

"Mmm, think I ought to call Hildegard and Fritz. Make sure everything's okay at my little ranch," he thought to himself. He dialed the Werner's number.

"Hallo," said the strong voice on the other end of the line.

"Fritz," said Neal. "How's everything on Austin Lane, specifically 150?"

"Neal! Everyting is gut. Your house is just fine. Momma just put strudel in de oven and said she wish you vas here to eat some. How you doing in Germany? You like dos krauts?" he laughed.

"Yeh, Fritz. These people are real nice to me and the country is beautiful. The forests are so green and the whole place is so clean. Now I know where Hildegard learned it." They chatted for a few minutes about the towns he had visited so far and the fact that he had not found out much information. "Fritz, it just dawned on me the other day that I never asked where in Germany you and Hildegard were from," he said, hoping for an answer.

"Vell, Neal, it never came up. Ve don tink about de old country too much. Vas bad time den and ve try to forget. But since you ask, I tell you. Momma and me ver born in small town of Ratekau, just nort of Lubeck. You told us you go to Lubeck, but ve no say anyting, cause you might not understand. I vas in German navy, too, but did not like dat man Hitler and I vas never Nazi," he said emphatically. "I vas to be on U-Boat, too, but mein eyes dey no gut, so dey put me at desk for var. Momma and me escape and come here ven communists take over. Bad times, Neal. No like dat vall. I tell you whole story ven you come home. Ven you come home?"

"Gosh, Fritz. I'm not sure. I have a nice cottage in the country and I've met some interesting people in England. I'll probably stay another couple of months. At least until I find my mystery people or until I decide to give up, whichever comes first. Give Hiledegard a hug for me and I'll call you again in a couple of weeks." He hung up and made a note to find Ratekau. "At least I can take some pictures for them." And then he thought, "I think I'll call Georgette." He did not think of calling Andrea.

"Wilkinson Photoart," said a masculine voice.

"Uh, hello," Neal said haltingly. "May I speak with Mrs. Wilkinson, please."

"I'm so sorry, sir, but she had to go to London unexpectedly and won't be back until next week sometime. I'm minding the shop whilst she's gone. Would you care to leave your name?"

"This is one of her customers, Neal Park," he answered. "Do you by chance know where she'll be staying in London? I may need to call her regarding a special order…a confidential order," he added, sounding very businesslike.

"I believe you can reach her at Number Sixteen, a bed and breakfast on Sumner Place. The telephone number there is 589-5232. I'll tell her you might ring her up, Mr. Park."

He could hardly contain his excitement of the moment. "Sumner Place," he shouted, as he looked at his London city map. "That's the next street over from Cranley Place. She'll be just a block away." Laughing to himself, he thought, "There must be some divine intervention in this. It's too much of a coincidence for her to be there the same time as me and to then be staying so close. Too coincidental. But thank you, God."

Neal packed up his things, checked out of the *Hotel Voss Haus,* and drove south through Susel and in to Ratekau. "Fritz was right, it is a small town," Neal thought as he looked left and right at a town of very few streets and only a few businesses…a bank, a post office, a drugstore, and of course, a bakery. He parked the car in front of the bakery and went in. "I'd like a cup of *kaffee and a Torten,* he said, feeling a calling from his sweet tooth as he eyed a sugar-covered torte. The clerk realized he did not speak German and conversed with him in exceptionally good English.

"I studied in England for two years. I don't get much chance to speak with Americans, this is not on many tour routes," she said, laughing as she put Neal's torte on a plate. Sitting at a black iron and marble table, he enjoyed his mid-morning snack as he asked the girl about Ratekau. He told her his neighbors were originally from here, but she had not heard of them.

"Because of the war, with so many people dying and families scattering, there really aren't many of the old residents here. And Werner is a pretty common name...sort of like your Williams or Johnson."

He asked her if she by chance knew the name Prien.

"Yes, I do remember my grandmother speaking of a friend named Ursula Prien who lived on a farm near Ponitz. The lady is very old now and in hospital in Lubeck." Before she could continue, Neal jumped up and ran close to the counter.

"You're kidding," he said breathlessly. "I'm on my way to see her now. Do you know if she's in a good mental state? Does she remember much about the war and the whereabouts of her family?"

"Oh sir, I don't know anything about her except that she is all alone. The rest of the family died from the bomb that struck the farm or they died serving in the military. She's the only immediate survivor."

He thanked her profusely, paid the check, and went out to his car. As he was getting in, the girl ran to the door of the bakery and shouted to him.

"Sir, Fraulein Prien does not speak English. I hope you can find a translator there. If not, come back and I'll go with you."

Again he thanked her.

Neal nervously went over in his mind the details of what he would ask the lady, "If she understands." And he would offer her something from the box...or her father's watch.

****

Approaching the city of Lubeck, *"one of the three pearls of the North"*, he could see tall towers of Lubeck's numerous churches. Many buildings not bombed during the war were of Gothic style, some dating to the 13th century. Neal asked directions to *the Heilig-Geist-Hospital,* also built in the 13th century, and now a home and hospice for the elderly and infirm.

A nurse wearing a heavy black uniform of some religious order and a starched cap in the shape of what looked like a huge flying bird, greeted him as he approached her desk. He let her know he spoke no German and that he was looking for Ursula Prien. Without speaking a word, she nodded and with her hand motioned for him to follow her down the long hallway. Above dark paneled wainscoting hung ornately framed paintings. Neal wondered if these had been some of the treasures Hitler had had his troops hide. The floors were highly polished wood and he tried not to snigger at the sound of the nurse's shoe soles squeaking as she walked. They passed what seemed to be several offices and came to an elevator bank. The elevator doors were brass-expanding of an obviously ancient vintage and he hesitated to enter as they opened. Creaking closed, the metal box rose, slowly taking its two occupants to the next floor. Again the nurse motioned for him to follow. The swish of her garments broke the silence as they walked this time down a carpeted hallway. She turned into a doorway. He followed.

Sitting in a rocking chair and looking out the window was a tiny lady, Fraulein Ursula Prien, possibly his last chance to solve the mystery of the box.

CHAPTER TWENTY-THREE

The black-robed nurse motioned for him to sit and wait. Pointing to a chair behind the tiny figure, she nodded as he sat down. Ursula Prien made no effort to move and did not seem to respond to the sound of their entering the room. She continued to stare out the window.

In a few minutes the nurse returned, a young man at her side. He introduced himself as Hans, an aide, and said he spoke English. Neal introduced himself, too, and told the man briefly why he was here. "Please ask Miss Prien if I may visit with her," Neal instructed him. "Tell her I have some pictures to show her." He carefully took the photographs from the grey canvas bag and walked toward the tiny lady. She looked up at him with vacant eyes, as if she was seeing through him to the other side of the room. He put the pictures in her lap and she looked down. Hans explained to Neal that she had poor eyesight and might not be able to see them.

Ursula Prien leaned down and squinted. She picked up the picture of the German fliers, and in a very quiet voice, almost a whisper, said in German, "Gerhardt. Is he coming home now? Mother will be so happy to see him." Hans interpreted for Neal, who immediately realized the tiny lady was still in another world.

Neal reached into his pocket and took out the watch, then gently took Ursula Prien's hand and laid it there. Her eyes lit up, she gave forth a broad smile and squealed, "Papa's watch. I dropped it in the field and he was very angry with me. Now I can give it back to him and he will forgive me." Trailing off with an inaudible babble, she broke into tears and wept.

Hans asked Neal if he wanted to continue the visit.

"I can see that she isn't really with us," Neal said with disappointment, "but she does recognize Gerhardt, and the watch is obviously whose I thought it was. I have one more picture to show her and it's important to me to know if she recognizes the figure." Carefully, he put the photograph of the girl in the garden in Ursula Prien's lap. Her hands were tightly holding the watch.

She leaned down and again squinted. "That girl, Cynthia. He took Momma's ring for her and I wanted it. I don't like her," she said in a voice reminiscent of little girl jealousy.

Neal was elated to hear the name *Cynthia.* He instructed Hans to ask her where Cynthia was and each of the three times he repeated the question she would only say, "English".

Reaching into the grey canvas bag he found the duplicate ring he had bought at Portobello Market. Its faux stones shone brightly as he slid it onto her finger.

"Oh," she murmured. "Momma's ring. Now it's mine." She put the watch in her lap and rubbed the ring with her fingers, then laid it against her cheek, all the while making the murmuring sounds.

Neal explained to Hans that it was not valuable and he hoped no one would take if from her. "The value is nothing, but the memories it might instill in her will be precious, I'm sure. However, the watch is a different story and I will rely on your help to see that it stays with her."

The young man assured him that the integrity of the hospital was without blemish and he would be honored to abide by Neal's wishes.

"I understand she has no heirs, so if it would be in order, perhaps a document could be drawn to insure that you get the watch when she dies," Neal offered.

"I will speak to the hospital administrator, sir, and see if that can be arranged." He thanked Neal politely.

"Here's my address and telephone number," Neal said as he handed a business card to Hans. "Please call me if she ever offers anymore information on Cynthia, or where Gerhardt met her." They both exited the room. But not before Neal put his hand on Ursula Prien's shoulder and gave her a gentle pat. She did not look up or respond to his touch, but kept rubbing the ring that was on her hand holding the gold watch.

"Well, now I know her name is Cynthia and she's English. There've got to be a million Cynthias in England and the one I'm trying to find just might be dead." Driving toward Bad Segeberg, the countryside rolled by as he reflected on the past hour with Ursula Prien. "At least I know that was Gerhardt in the picture, but heck, his name was on the back. So I really haven't learned anymore about him other than the few facts people here have told me.

The Romantik Wald, 10 km greeted him as he approached Bad Segeberg and the surrounding forest. The gravel crunched beneath the little red car and he brought it to a stop in front of the thatched roof building, giving him a feeling of familiarity and comfort.

Gerda Schmidt was sweeping the front steps and smiled as she saw him getting out of the car. "Guten Tag," she loudly called to him.

"Hello, Mrs. Schmidt," Neal answered as he took his bags from the trunk. "I'm back again. Have a room for me?"

"Ya. Otto said he hope you come back. Ve have lots of rooms. Mit bath, ya," she laughed.

After checking in, Neal came back down to the lobby, ordered a *Weisswein,* white wine, from the bar and found a large overstuffed chair, from where he could see the lake. As he sat staring at swans crossing the dark water, he thought of the last few days and the melancholy feeling that now pervaded his soul. He felt as if he had been an observer of a time gone by, the second World War and it's destruction of families and a way of life. Piecing together the facts he had gathered, he said to himself, "It's decision time, Neal, old boy. Fish or cut bait."

"Hallo, Herr Park," boomed the male voice. Setting the cut crystal glass of wine on Neal's chairside table, Otto Schmidt then offered his hand. "Gut to have you back. Solve your mystery?"

"Hi, Otto. Thanks," he said as he picked up the crystal glass. "No. Well, I can't fully say no. I did get some information and I did visit Gerhardt's sister, Ursula." He told him of his time with her and her reaction to the gifts, but shared his disappointment in not learning more about Cynthia other than her name and the fact that she was English.

"Ya, so you see de old farm, too. Not gut shape, ya?" Otto sat down and was engrossed in Neal's narrative of the past few days. "And how you like Kiel? Big dat place is, ya?"

"Yes, Kiel is big. Must have been a magnificent base. 'Course it's pretty busy now. Say, I met an old man who ran a bookstore in Kiel and he was on U-352...Gerhardt's boat. He knew him, but no personal details. Seems he was one of those rescued and taken to the hospital in Charleston, South Carolina. He knew of the secret mission, but didn't have any details on that either."

Neal told him about the books he bought in Kiel and told Otto he'd bring them when he came for dinner. Otto excused himself to tend to kitchen duties and told Neal to order the *Makrele mit Spargel,* mackerel and asparagus. "Wonder if that mackerel's from the Baltic," Neal thought. He remembered eating a lot of mackerel when Bureau business took him to Florida.

After dinner Gerda and Otto joined Neal in the bar for brandies, and together they looked at the books he bought in Kiel. "I think my searching here is over. I'm flying back to London tomorrow and I'll try to find "Cynthia" there...if she exists...or did exist," he told them as he sipped the deep, gold liquid. "I have a name, I have some pictures. Maybe someone just might remember the girl in the garden."

Bidding him *Guten Abend,* they retired to their apartment in the rear of the inn and he went up to his room overlooking the lake. Moonlight cast sparkle and starry reflections on the dark water as Neal felt an intense emotion of loneliness. He watched shadows of night birds changing among the tree limbs as he sat by the window and realized how much he wanted to again be part of a pair.

****

The *Lufthansa* flight to London was delayed an hour and he found himself walking through the Hamburg terminal shops. Chocolates and liqueurs were featured, along with strong cigarettes and athletic shirts with soccer team logos. Spotting a display of hair ornaments, he thought, "I'll start a collection for Caroline and Annabelle, some from each country." He chose two large barrettes of tortoise shell, set with colored stones. While waiting to pay for the barrettes, he picked up two magazines to read on the plane. One, a British magazine, had a feature on wartime volunteer organizations with pictures from wars during the twentieth century. The other was a German magazine with a format similar to *Time or Newsweek.* "Need to find out what's been happening while I've been out of pocket."

During the flight, Neal had coffee and sweet rolls while he read the news magazine. The other one he put in the grey canvas bag to read "at home in Kersey". He would later find out that it contained a photograph of *Cynthia Stiles and Margaret Overstreet, young volunteers in the Queens Messengers.*

After clearing customs at Gatwick, Neal called The Tramore and Maureen assured him his room would be ready when he arrived.

"'Twill be good to be seein' ya again, Mr. Park."

"Thanks, Maureen. I'll be there in about an hour."

From Victoria Station the taxi wound its way to South Kensington, turning from Old Brompton onto Cranley Place. As they passed Sumner Place, Noel strained his neck trying to see Number Sixteen where Georgette would be staying. "Wonder why she had to come here *unexpectedly?*" he wondered. He paid the driver and carried his bags into reception. Maureen met him with a smile and an extending hand to help. "That's okay, Maureen. They're not heavy," he said, politely refusing her assistance as he started up the stairs to the second floor. Dropping his bags on the floor beside the bed, he took a piece of paper out of his wallet on which he had written the telephone number for Number Sixteen.

"Number Sixteen, May I help you?" asked the man at the other end of the line.

"Yes. Would you please ring the room for Mrs. Georgette Wilkinson?" he asked.

"I'm sorry, sir. Mrs. Wilkinson is out. Would you care to leave a message?"

"Please tell her to call Neal Park at the Tramore Hotel."

"Well, I'm not going to waste the afternoon. Think I'll walk over to the Victoria and Albert Museum." Described in his tour book as a "Museum of Ornamental Art", he especially wanted to see the collection of John Constable paintings, as well as other artistic treasures from Italy, France, the East, and of course, Great Britain. Neal spent three hours walking through the museum, enjoying both the art collections and the people who were viewing them. In close proximity to the V&A was the Natural History Museum, The Geological Museum, and the Science Museum, all of which he promised himself to tour tomorrow. "Want to see Kensington Palace, too," he thought as he crossed Cromwell Road and over to Old Brompton and then Cranley Place. Sumner Place came first, so he decided to make an unannounced call on Mrs. Wilkinson.

Approaching reception, Neal cleared his throat and asked if she was in.

"I'll ring the room, sir," said the tall man behind the desk. "Mrs. Wilkinson, Mr. Park is here to see you. Right. Right, madam, I shall tell him."

"Mrs. Wilkinson asks that you wait here in reception. She will be down in a few minutes."

"Thank you," Neal said as he looked around for a comfortable chair.

Ten minutes later, the dark-haired beauty appeared, her arms outstretched. "Neal, dear," she said as if they were long lost lovers. "How wonderful to see you here. Whatever are you doing in London?" she asked as she drew him to her.

Stunned at the greeting, Neal stammered on his words. "I'm uh, uh, just been to Germany doing some, uh, research and decided to spend a couple of days playing tourist before I go back to Kersey."

"How very nice, indeed," she said, sitting down on a sofa and pulling him in beside her. "If you don't have other plans, perhaps we could dine together." Smoothing her skirt, she proceeded to tell him that she was called here by one of her vendors who was introducing a new framing material at a conference. Georgette invited Neal into the hotel bar. He ordered a scotch on the rocks and she ordered red wine. After discussing London, museums, the misty weather, and Portobello Market, he asked to be excused. "I'll freshen up at the hotel and be back here at seven to pick you up. If you've never been to Boswells, we can go there. It's not far, but if the rain continues we'll hop a cab."

"Hop a cab?" she questioned.

Laughing, he replied. "Sorry. American slang for "take a taxi."

Service was slow at Boswells, giving them time to savor a good vintage red wine recommended by the waiter. "It's an Australian red, Guv'nor. Full bodied and all that," he proudly announced as he served the first glass and then departed for the kitchen.

Georgette invited Neal to accompany her to the next day's conference, but he told her his plans to tour the other museums. "Why don't I *hop a cab* and pick you up at the hotel after your meeting and we can have dinner and perhaps go to the theatre?"

Smiling serenly, she accepted his offer, they settled on six-thirty for dinner, and he promised to get tickets for *Webber's Phantom Of The Opera.* "I understand it's been a big hit here and is heading to the States. Bet my son and his wife will plan a New York weekend to take in this one."

Returning to Number Sixteen, Neal paid the taxi driver and told Georgette he would walk back to his hotel. She asked him to join her in a brandy before he left. The hotel lounge was empty except for the bartender who was draped across the bar, snoring softly. "Excuse me. Could you pour us two brandies, please?" Neal asked as the man jumped in surprise.

"Right. Right. Sorry there, old chap. Must have dozed off." He brought the brandies to their table and left the check beside Neal. Slowly sipping their drinks and not saying much, they looked like two lovers who had sated their verbal communication and just sat staring at each other.

Neal walked Georgette to the elevator bank. As the doors opened, she took his hand and drew him in as they closed. Her hand still in his, she led him down the hall, through her doorway, and into the bedroom.

Feeling a strong magnetism emanating from the flattery of her interest, Neal put his hands on her shoulders and looked into her eyes.

He sensed her increasing passion as he slowly and deliberately gave her entire body a seductive assessment, his eyes searching the details hidden beneath her black silk theatre suit.

In response, Georgette pulled away from him and fled to the next room, blowing him a kiss as she closed the door. Neal drew back the bedspread, quickly threw his clothes into a nearby chair, and looking up, gasped as she walked through the door, the shapely beauty of her naked body taunting him.

Neal lifted her and laid her on the bed. His hands traced the lines of her soft body, his lips were urgent and insistent as she responded with a hunger that belied her outward calm. Blending contours and emotions, their world became one in ecstasy and harmony. With peace and contentment flooding their spirits, the two lovers laid still as the evening breeze came in through the window and fell onto their spent bodies.

"I think it's time I leave," Neal said, stroking her cheek with his hand.

"Yes," she said. Only "yes".

Walking back to his hotel, he felt amazement at how swiftly their relationship went from friend to lover. "S'pose it's just chemistry," he laughed to himself. "She doesn't appear to be a frivolous person and I didn't detect any evidence of anything but a good reputation from what I saw at her business and the few times I've seen her. Just chemistry." He knocked on the front door of the hotel and Maureen opened it for him.

"Sorry, Mr. Park. We be lockin' the doors at midnight," she said as he came in. "Did you have a nice evening?"

"Yes, yes I did," he answered. "Stopped for brandies after dinner. Guess I didn't realize how late it had gotten," he said, silently wondering if she was wondering why he was really this late. It was two in the morning. "By the way. You're always here. Do you live on the property?"

"Right, I do," she answered, gathering her robe sash tighter. "Mr. Wadsworth travels a good deal and he's needin' me to be here."

"Well, goodnight, Maureen. Er, uh, good morning, too," he laughed as he started up the stairs.

Sleep did not come easy to him that night. His unexplainable attraction to this lovely creature, coupled with the unexpected and intense events of this evening, caused his mind to race with confusion and frustration. "What am I doing," he questioned. "Here I just start making a new life for myself at Jekyll, find a promising relationship with Andrea, and now…Georgette. And, I can't find who or where Cynthia is." He rolled over, beat his pillow with his fists, and tried to induce sleep with deep breathing.

The telephone ringing woke him. "Hello, Park here," answering as he did in Bureau days.

"Mr. Park, this is Trevor from Number Sixteen," said the voice at the other end. "I have a message for you from Mrs. Wilkinson."

"Oh, fine," Neal answered, trying to clear his head.

"She is leaving today for Sudbury and asks that you call her when you arrive there. Said she was leaving earlier than planned, but had an emergency at her shop."

"Yes, thank you. Thank you very much." He stumbled into the bathroom and started the water for a hot bath. Calling downstairs he asked Maureen to send a tray of breakfast.

"Mr. Park. Wouldn' you be a wantin' lunch? she asked. "It's two in the afternoon, it is."

He looked at the clock on the nightstand, laughed, and said, "Yeh, guess I didn't realize how long I'd slept. Don't bother, Maureen. I'll walk down the block and grab a sandwich. Thanks anyway."

The hot water felt good. "Wonder what the emergency was?" He dressed in khaki slacks and a golf shirt. Reaching into the closet for his windbreaker jacket, he saw the grey canvas bag. "I think I'll let Cynthia rest today. Today I'm going to do the rest of the museums…oops, maybe one since it's so late." He bought a curried chicken sandwich and a soda at the patisserie and then walked the few blocks to the Natural History Museum. After two hours there, he went to Harrods and bought Annabelle and Caroline more hair ornaments. "So much for today," he thought as he crossed over to Cranley Place.

The other guests at the hotel were dining out tonight. Colin Wadworth asked Neal to join him at his table. They ate a meal of plaice with roasted potatoes and a fruit custard dessert called *Spotted Dick*. Their conversation focused on Neal's search for Cynthia and he shared with Colin his findings in Germany. "I don't know if I'll find her in Suffolk County or not. After all these years, she could have moved to another part of England, to another country, or even be dead. Who knows, this just might be as we say, *a wild goose chase.*"

Colin listened with rapt interest and said he hoped it was not a dead end. "I say, old chap. You have come a long way and you have uncovered a lot of information. Surely you will find someone up there who knows something about this girl…woman. Don't give up," he urged Neal.

"Thanks, Colin. Really appreciate your support. And, I've also enjoyed meeting you and staying here at the Tramore," he said, folding his napkin and starting to stand up. "Say, if you get a few free days why don't you come up to Kersey. I've got a pretty comfortable sofa. I'll take that and let you have the bedroom."

"Great invitation, old chap, but for now let us go into reception and see if I can find the bottle of brandy I hid in the desk last week."

The next day Neal took the mid-morning train from Liverpool station and got into Sudbury after lunch. Finding his little rental car where he had parked it a week before, he quickly drove to Georgette's shop. Rounding the corner on Market Hill, Neal was shocked to see barricades in front of *Wilkinson Photoart*. He jumped out and ran toward the front door. "What's happened here?" he said out loud.

A man walking down the sidewalk stopped and said, "Seems some bloke drove his car right through the glass, he did."

Neal stepped over the barricades, knocked on the door, and looked in through the plastic taped window. A figure was approaching and the door opened.

"Oh, Neal," Georgette cried. "I am ever so glad to see you. Is this not the worst mess you have ever seen?"

Slivered glass, broken picture frames with photos dangling, furniture shoved askew, and the smell of gasoline met his eyes and nose.

"Good grief," he said, his arms around her shoulders as they gingerly walked among the debris. "How did this happen?"

She told him a young man who had been partying at the pub on the corner missed the curve and came into her shop instead. "The police asked me to leave it as it is until my insurance agent arrives to assess the damage." Crying, she described to him the value of the pictures, some which were irreplaceable, and others whose negatives were with someone else. "I don't know how I'll continue. This is just too traumatic. My customers will be so disappointed." Looking toward the back corner, she gasped and screamed. "The jewelry collection! It is gone." The glass tops on the woodframed cases had been broken.

234

Neal called the police, who suggested perhaps it was an intentional accident, the driver having knowledge of the jewelry and her absence. Attempting to calm her, Neal asked her to stay with him that night and he would bring her back the next morning to meet the insurance agent. He helped her pack a bag and they drove in silence to Kersey, only the occasional sniff as Georgette cried broke the quiet.

Neal wondered if Patti and Tom would see him come in with another *guest.* "They might not understand this…or me," he thought.

Showing her to the bedroom where he made room on a shelf for her things, he went back to the big room and put water on for tea. "Take a rest, it might do you good," he suggested after they had their tea.

"Only if you will rest with me," she said, a coy look in her eyes.

Feeling a smoldering fire being stoked, Neal followed her into the bedroom and found himself conscious again of this intense entrancement. He was as eager as she to continue the fulfillment of their sensual magnetism. And continue they did. Georgette tingled with excitement as Neal held her firmly, but tenderly. His hands explored the folds and hollows of her soft skin. He kissed her neck, her ears, and the tip of her nose. Neal lifted a strand of her dark hair, bringing it to his cheek. "It's like silk," he said. She gave responsive embracement, cuddling into the contours of his body as they kissed again and again, his lips inviting the eventual sensation of mutual desire.

Georgette took an hour's nap.

Neal cooked a skillet meal of tinned meat, boiled potatoes, and canned peas, his version of English *Bubble & Squeak.* He gently woke her and invited her to the feast.

"It looks wonderful, Neal. I am sure I will enjoy it almost as much as I have enjoyed the afternoon. Well, almost as much," she laughed.

235

They shared a bottle of wine he had purchased in Germany and talked about many things. When it turned dark he suggested they sit outside and watch the stars. Lights were on in the big house and he again wondered if Patti and Tom had seen them come in. After an hour, they went back inside for a repeat performance of the afternoon and eventually to sleep.

CHAPTER TWENTY-FOUR

Sudbury police apprehended the youth, who in a stolen car, crashed through Georgette's shop, stole the jewelry, and escaped through the backyard gardens of neighboring shops and houses. He was the same young man who had done cleanup work for her prior to the London trip. His parents were assuming responsibility for the damages… considerable to the old building which had been built in 1759. The jewelry was found intact.

Neal spent the following week sorting out his German information and planning his next search activities in Suffolk County. In between he spent time with Georgette, helping her deal with the construction crew who were not totally dependable when it came to timing. Her living quarters were above the shop and had not suffered any damage. Neal stayed over several nights and found the surroundings comfortable. He liked Sudbury. "In fact, I like this whole county. Hmmm."

One morning, while shopping for Georgette's new shutter hardware in Winch and Blatch, he realized the two ladies were not there. "They still be up in Norwich," said the manager. "Miss Stiles' relative is not expected to live and she and Miss Overstreet will be there until everything is settled. They have worked here so long, they have, that I'll be keepin' their jobs for them."

Neal drove to Lavenham again and talked to people in shops, at church, some waiting for busses, and some at market. No one had any recollection of Gerhardt Prien or Cynthia. Even the photographs did not help. Fifty plus years had blurred memories. He mapped out a ten mile radius of Lavenham and stopped in over thirty towns, spending a full day in Bury St. Edmunds, north by about twelve miles. Still no luck. His patience and optimism about depleted, he contemplated the conclusion of his search. "I just don't think this is going to happen," he said to himself as he sat in a small, garden tea shop in Chelsworth, said to be "one of the most entrancing villages in

237

England". On the River Brett, Chelsworth was noted for its cottage gardens and it was in one of these gardens where he sat drinking his tea and eating a scone. Looking up he noticed a lady, wearing a large straw hat, coming toward his table.

"Good afternoon, sir," she said, smiling pleasantly at him. "Have you toured the gardens yet?"

"Why, no," he replied. "I wasn't aware that was possible."

"Oh my, yes," she answered. "All of the gardens in the village are open this week. It is our annual fall foliage tour. Do come round when you've finished your tea." Adjusting her hat brim, she briskly walked back toward the hedges surrounding the white brick house and disappeared.

Neal went into the house, not sure where he would pay for the tour, or if there was any fee. A few feet inside the front door a white haired lady, her hair in a fat bun on top of her head, greeted him and told him donations were accepted. He put four pounds in the basket on her desk, figuring about six dollars would be a decent donation, and she gave him a leaflet describing the gardens. On her brightly flowered dress she wore a nametag...*Cynthia.* "Nah, couldn't be," he thought to himself, his enthusiasm and hope almost gone. "Still, who knows."

He told her of his search and wondered if by some miracle she could be "his" Cynthia. She listened intently to his story, stood up and came from behind the desk.

"Young man," she said. "I am not the Cynthia you seek, but I seem to recall a girl I knew many years ago. Her name was Cynthia and I do believe she had a beau from Germany."

Flattered to be called "young," Neal again felt the adrenaline flow as this elderly lady gave him hope. She told him she could not remember the girl's last name, but said the girl had a friend from whom she was inseparable and she thought they were from Sudbury. "Oh my," she said, putting her hand to her forehead. "It is dreadful to get old and not remember. You do understand, I am sure. It was such a very long time ago and so many things happened to all of us in England. I do wish I could be more exact for you, sir."

"That's great," he said. "You've really helped. Maybe she is right there in Sudbury…right under my nose."

Back in Sudbury, Neal spoke to every shopkeeper, innkeeper, and resident he could corner. For two weeks he walked the streets. questioning it's citizens. No one knew a Cynthia who had had a German beau.

****

"Patti, I'll be leaving next week. It's been wonderful staying here in the cottage, and I hope if I ever come back it'll be available."

She gave him a big hug, told him to have a safe trip and asked that he stay in touch. "Neal, if you know of any other Americans who want a taste of East Anglia, give them my number."

He'd miss the little village of Kersey with its watersplash and the ducks, *The Bell Pub* and Paddy & Rosie, the pottery, and The Street. "Have a feeling I'll return one day," he said as he packed his bags.

****

The unusual relationship that grew over the past month between Georgette and himself was both confusing and frustrating to Neal. The mention of love was never spoken, yet he felt a deep affection for this woman. He knew she felt the same way, the intensity of their lovemaking was evidence. But how he was to continue or abandon the situation became his immediate concern.

"No, Neal," she said, putting her hand over his mouth as he was attempting to discuss the dilemma. "I knew this day would come, and though I am not happy about it, it must be. Let us be grateful for the time we have spent together and have no regrets."

Standing amidst the sawdust and rubble of the shop's renovation, she looked demure and sad as he put his arms on her shoulders and drew her close. His lips met hers and for a long moment the future was not in question. He put his hands on her face, lifting it up, and buried his head against her throat. Reluctantly, they parted a few inches, then she wound her arms around his waist and clung to him. His mere touch sent shivers up her spine and she knew the end of this affair was far different than any of the few she had had in the past. Georgette took his hand and started to lead him up the stairs.

"No," he said, pulling away. "It has to stop now before I find it impossible to leave. We've two different worlds. Yours is here and mine is waiting for me."

The little bell on the newly repaired door tinkled as he left.

****

"Gosh, it's good to be back home," he thought, as he crossed the Jekyll Causeway bridge and looked down at J.D.'s marina. "Know there's nothing in the refrigerator at the house, so think I'll stop in and see what Effie's cooked up today." Neal caught up with all the island news from George and J.D. and ate a "mess 'o crabmeat" that Effie had cooked with potatoes and celery. Feeling sufficiently informed and fed, he drove to Austin Lane and parked his car in the garage. Dropping his bag on the bedroom floor, he took a hot shower and fell into bed, sleeping for ten hours.

The next morning Neal bought groceries and stopped at the post office. "Wow, what a pile of mail," he said to the clerk who sat a white plastic basket in front of him.

"Mr. Park, you can bring this back tomorrow. There's just too much here for you to carry and we don't have any bags."

"Thanks, Joe," Neal said, lifting the basket which was filled with magazines and letters. "Didn't know I had so many friends," he laughed.

At home he found a warm strudel on the doorstep. "Can't imagine who this is from." Smiling, he gently lifted the foil-wrapped package and brought it into the kitchen. "Mmmmm, smells like apricot. That Hildegard is just too much. Better give them a call, come to think of it."

"Neal, you back. Ve missed you," Fritz said in his booming voice. You get Momma's strudel? She don' know if you still sleep."

"Yeh, got the strudel. I'll give her a big hug for that. Say, Fritz, if you're interested I'll bring all my stuff over and show you what I did and where I went. Incidentally, I got some pictures of Ratekau for you," he said. "You going to be home this afternoon?"

"Ya, come on over, Neal. Ve be glad to see you."

Neal unpacked his bags, throwing the magazines he brought back on to the floor beside his bed. "I'll look through those later," he said, gathering a pile of clothes for his next load of laundry. As he made a sandwich for his lunch, he looked over at the basket of mail. "Guess I'll wade through that before I go over to the Werner's. Neatly separated, he had put the mail in stacks on the dining table...letters in one pile, magazines in another, and bulk advertising junk in still another. A large ivory envelope caught his attention, he took it out of the letter pile and looked at the return address...*A. Rogers, The Plaza Hotel, New York, NY.* After inserting the silver opener, he lifted out the letter.

Dear Neal,

I had hoped to tell you this news on the telephone, but knew you were still in England. Trust you were successful in your search and were able to return the box's contents. Please know that I never meant to deceive you, but I have been involved with someone for two years. When you came to New York, it was so nice to see someone from home, and well, things just happened. I loved being with you. You are one of the kindest men I have ever known and someone will be very lucky to share their life with you.

By the time you get this letter I will be married to my boss, Trent Rosen. He's divorced, has two children who live with him part of the year, so I'll finally be a mother. Well, at least a stepmother. They seem to like me and I adore them.

Neal, be happy for me. Forgive me, and know that you gave me some very nice memories. Please call when you come to New York, I want you to meet Trent.

Best ever, Andrea

"Whew," he said out loud. He walked over to his big chair, sat down and stared out the window. "Bloody well serves me right," he said, using his newly learned British slang. "I should have known there was something strange going on. What with her being so aggressive and affectionate, and then pulling back when I wanted her to live here. What a dunce I've been." He reread the letter and angrily threw it on the floor. Neal opened the rest of the mail, putting the bills in yet another pile. He carried the magazines into the bedroom and put them on top of the ones from England. "Get to these tonight."

****

Hildegard hugged him tightly as he came in the door and took his hand, leading him out to the sunroom where she had a big pitcher of iced tea waiting. "Made you some cookies, too, Neal. You need to eat and take some home."

The three friends sat in a circle around a big coffee table as Neal spread out maps, books, and pictures to share. "I'll take you through the whole trip," he said, opening his map of Suffolk. "I found the quaintest cottage in a small village, Kersey. Happens the owner is the rector of the church there and his wife is an American from Cleveland. They have four cute kids who treated me like a curiosity. Don't think they'd ever met an American before, except their mother. Asked me all kinds of questions." He told them about Sudbury, and about Georgette. "She is the most beautiful and charming lady. Talented, too," he said, realizing he was becoming very animated and excited as he described her. He stopped for a moment.

"Neal, vat's wrong. You okay?" asked Fritz.

"Oh, uh, yeh," Neal answered, jerking himself back into reality and away from his silent thoughts of Georgette. He told them of his searching at the airbase, the military museums, his questioning of anyone he thought might have information, and his final despair in not being able to complete his mission. Leaning across the table, he handed Hildegard a photograph envelope. "Here you are, ma'am. Pictures of how your hometown Ratekau now looks."

She took each one out carefully, said not a word, and after looking closely, hand them to Fritz. Tears rolled down her cheeks and she reached into her apron for a handkerchief. Soft sobbing came in between dabbing her eyes. "Is so different," she said. "No more like vas ven we live der. Is many new buildings, guess de old vons ver bombed."

Neal saw tears in Fritz's eyes also, but the old man kept his chin high. "Ya, nutting ever same no more. Ve had gut times der but var change whole world." He handed the envelope to Neal.

"No, these are for you. You probably want to show them to your daughter and her family. Keep them. I did this for you." He felt their sadness of a time now gone, never to be again. After a few minutes and a second glass of iced tea, Fritz looked sternly at Neal and said, "Neal, now I tell you."

Not ready for what was to come next, Neal settled back into the cushioned wicker sofa and put his hands behind his head, ready to listen to Fritz. "Bet he wants to tell me about Ratekau," he thought.

"You remember I tell you I s'pose to go on U-Boat, but mein eyes not gut?" the white-haired German asked. "Vell, dey make me vork at desk. I send letters to families of Germans killed or missing in de var. Ven you call me from Germany and tell me you near Ponitz, it ring bell in mein head. Von of de letters I sent vas to a family near der. Very famous person in family died on U-Boat...his name vas Prien. He sunk many boats in var. And, he had nephew who vas on secret mission later and he also die on U-Boat."

Neal sat upright, leaned forward and said, "My God, Fritz, those are the people I was trying to find." He could hardly catch his breath. "What else do you remember? Was the nephew's name Gerhardt? Do you remember if he had an English sweetheart?" blurting out the questions in rapid succession.

"Slow, Neal. I tell you more." Fritz looked up at the ceiling, trying to recall facts of the past. "I tink I send letter to nephew's Mutter and Vater." Rubbing his head, he continued. "Oh yes, der vas fraulein's name in his file. Dey leave names to be contacted and she vas listed. Vat vas her name? Oh, me. I have to reach to remember."

Neal blurted out, "Could it have been Cynthia?"

"Yaaa, I do tink dat vas her name. Cynthia. She vas from England. Cynthia, Cynthia," he kept repeating her name. "Ya, ya, she vas Cynthia Stiles. I remember because name sound like German vurd for saddle stirrup. Stile in German is Steig, stirrup. Thought dat vas funny name."

Neal asked if he could remember where in England she was from.

"Ya, tink vas town of Sudbury, But ve haf no street address. I send letter, but vas vartime and dey probably, vat you say, censor it? I tink also dis Prien vas same family who sold vegetables to Ostee Resort. Mein Vater took us der many times before var."

"I can't believe this," Neal said. "All this time the answers to my search were right next door. I should have told you about my find before I left." He told them the entire story, from the find to the search, and apologized for not sharing it with them earlier. "S'pose I was afraid you might not want to talk about it because of the war and all, but now I'm sorry."

"Dat's okay, Neal. Ve don talk about old country much. Too many bad memories der." Fritz took Hildegard's hand and held it tight. "Ve happy to be here and happy you our neighbor."

"I'll be back in a minute. I'm gonna get the stuff from the box and show it to you." He bolted out the door and ran to his house.

Neal got the grey canvas bag out of his closet, put it under his arm and headed back out the door, when the telephone rang.

"Hello," he quickly answered.

"Mr. Park?" asked the male voice with a German accent. "This is Hans from the hospital in Lubeck. You remember me?"

"Yes, Hans. How are you?"

"Fine, sir. I think I have information you might want. It is about the girl in the picture you showed to Fraulein Prien."

"Yes, yes," Neal said, anxious to hear his next statement.

"She was talking into the mirror the other day and was having a conversation with her brother. Of course, the brother is dead, but you know she is senile."

"Yes, I understand. What was she saying to him?"

"Well, sir, she seem to be angry mit him and telling him he should not give the ring to Cynthia. That is the name she used. Does this help you?" Hans asked.

"Interestingly, I just found out her name from a German neighbor of mine. Did Miss Prien say a surname?"

"Ya, er, yessir. She said in a loud voice, 'You cannot give Mutter's ring to Fraulein Stiles because I have it now' and she looked down at the ring you gave to her. I do hope this helps."

"Hans, thanks so much. This is a big help. Don't forget, you get to have that watch. Stay in touch and let me know how she gets along. I really appreciate the call." Hanging up he felt an extremely strong sense of relief and peace, much like being on the winning side of an argument. "At last, progress."

Back at the Werner's he gently laid out the contents of the box on top of their dining room table. Hildegard and Fritz looked closely at each item. Turning toward Neal, Fritz said in a low voice, "You have personal treasure here, Neal. Dis special stuff from dat man. Too bad it never get to Cynthia."

"Oh, but it will," Neal said with a big smile on his face. "I'll find her now. I know I will. She can't be dead."

After his evening meal of tuna salad and sliced tomatoes, Neal read the island paper, took a hot shower, and gathering all the magazines from beside his bed, went into the family room to read. "I'll try to wade through some of these," he said. Six magazines, mostly news types, were thrown to the side of his chair as he picked up the British one he had bought at the airport in Hamburg. The lead story, *Brit Volunteers in Wartime*, gave accounts of various British volunteer organizations. His eyes were drawn to a picture of two young girls standing beside a van.

"Queen's Messengers, Cynthia Stiles and Margaret Overstreet, at the door of their caravan while on duty serving the bombed out citizens of Bexleyheath which took 486 German bomb strikes in 1940 and 7,500 in 1941. The Queen's Messengers' courageous efforts helped feed homeless and injured Brits. Misses Stiles and Overstreet, residents of Sudbury, East Anglia, received the King George VI award for bravery and heroism in volunteer services." read the inscription beneath the black and white photograph.

"By golly, that's her. It's got to be," he shouted. "How many Cynthia Stiles could there have been in Sudbury?" He leaped out of the chair and went to his closet for the grey canvas bag. Reaching inside he found the pictures of the girl in the garden…the one from the box and the one he bought at Portobello Market. "It is her. Cynthia, I've found you!"

****

AFTERWORD

Cynthia Stiles and Margaret Overstreet returned from Norwich in time to attend the wedding at St. Mary's Church, uniting Georgette Wilkinson and Neal Park. Father Thomas Nigel Beacham officiated at the small afternoon ceremony, he and Mrs. Beacham hosted the garden reception at their home on Brett Lane. Lucretia, Jordan, Annabelle and Caroline flew over from Charleston. Colin Wadsworth came up from London, Maureen sent a lace handkerchief for Georgette to carry. Hildegard and Fritz Werner flew over from Jekyll Island and stayed with Pricilla and Charles Abbott. The Beacham children provided music as only children can with their tender voices, and their pets saw to it that no spilled punch or cookies were to be found.

The ceremony was brief. The bride wore a long, flowing, ivory silk gown and the groom a navy blue suit. Roses from the cottage garden were the bride's bouquet and on her left hand ring finger she wore an heirloom ring of rubies and pearls...a gift from Cynthia...and Gerhardt.

After a honeymoon in northeast Germany...Bad Segeberg and Ponitz, the happy couple divided their time between two worlds...the quiet village life in Sudbury, East Anglia UK and the quiet island life on Jekyll Island, Georgia USA.

EFFIE'S LOW COUNTRY BOIL

Some Carolinians call this recipe Beaufort Stew or Frogmore Stew.

1 quart water
1/4 cup crab boil seasoning
3 teaspoons cayenne pepper
2 lbs. cooked smoked sausage, cut in 2" chunks
4 cups red potatoes cut in halves
5 ears corn, halved
5 large onions, halved
2 lbs. shrimp in shells, fresh or frozen

Put water, seasoning and pepper in a large heavy stew pot or stock pot. Bring to a boil. Carefully add the sausage, onions, potatoes, and corn. Bring back to a boil, reduce heat, and simmer for 20 minutes. Add shrimp and cook for 5-7 minutes until shrimp are tender, but not overcooked.

Drain all ingredients and serve in a large platter or casserole. Drizzle over the top a sauce of melted butter and fresh herbs...thyme, oregano, basil. Serve with cocktail sauce for dipping shrimp. Makes 8-10 servings.

HILDEGARD'S APFELSTRUDEL

½ cup butter
1 ½ cups plain bread crumbs
4 cups sliced tart apples
½ cup granulated sugar
½ cup brown sugar
¼ cup raisins
¼ cup chopped pecans
¼ teaspoon cinnamon
2 cups flour
Salt to taste

2 tablespoons oil
1 egg
½ cup water
¼ cup melted butter
1 egg beaten
1 tablespoon melted butter

Melt ½ cup butter in skillet. Add bread crumbs and brown lightly. Add sugar, apples, raisins, pecans, and cinnamon; mix well. Set aside. Mix flour and salt in large bowl. Add oil, 1 egg and water; mix to form dough. Roll out <u>thin as possible</u> on floured surface or cloth. Brush with ¼ cup melted butter. Spread apple filling over 2/3 of the dough. Roll from filled side to enclose filling. Lift edge of cloth to assist in rolling. Place on greased baking sheet. Brush with mixture of 1 egg and 1 tablespoon melted butter. Bake 1 hour at 350'. Makes 6-8 servings.

ABOUT THE AUTHOR

Carol Sue Ravenel is a veteran sales and marketing executive in the hospitality industry, and now works part-time as a bookseller. Combining her love of England and her travel experiences, she has woven The Kersey Cottage and Finding Cyn...into cottage stories to enchant the reader. Set in the small southeast Suffolk County village of Kersey, the two novels span the decades from World War II to the present, as the characters share with you their hopes, disappointments and joy. Ms. Ravenel resides in Roswell, Georgia with her husband, but keeps her bags packed to go anywhere, anytime...preferably to England.

Printed in the United States
17458LVS00005B/109-111

9 781410 795915